SCORCHED GRACE

SCORCHED GRACE

A SISTER HOLIDAY MYSTERY

MARGOT DOUAIHY

GILLIAN FLYNN BOOKS

A **zando** IMPRINT

NEW YORK

zando

Gillian Flynn Books is an imprint of Zando
zandoprojects.com

First Edition: February 2023

Text design by Pauline Neuwirth, Neuwirth & Associates
Cover design and illustration by Will Staehle

The publisher does not have control over and is not responsible for author or other third-party websites (or their content).

LCCN: 2022939804

ISBN 978-1-63893-024-2
eISBN 978-1-63893-025-9

10 9 8 7 6 5 4 3 2 1

Manufactured in the United States of America

SCORCHED GRACE

1

THE DEVIL ISN'T IN the details. Evil thrives in blind spots. In absence, negative space, like the haze of a sleight-of-hand trick. The details are God's work. My job is keeping those details in order.

It took me four and a half hours to do the laundry and clean the stained glass, and my whole body felt wrecked. Every tendon strained. Even swallowing hurt. So, when my Sisters glided into the staff lounge for the meeting, folders and papers pressed against their black tunics, I slipped into the alley for some divine reflection—a smoke break. It was Sunday, dusk.

Vice on the Sabbath, I know. Not my finest moment. But carpe diem.

An hour to myself was all I needed. An aura of menace taunted me all day. The air was thick and gritty, like it wanted to bare-knuckle fight. Sticky heat, typical in New Orleans, but worse that day. The sun, the swollen red of a mosquito bite. Slow simmer belying the violence of the boil. I couldn't sit through another reprimand.

Fall term was a week in, and two kids had already filed grievances about me. *She's always on us*—a student scrawled—*I can't feel my fingertips!* Another (anonymous, I might add): *Music class is TORTURE!!!* I worried that Sister Augustine—our principal and Mother Superior, sturdy and sure as a sailor's knot—would interrogate me in front of everyone during Sunday's meeting. Which would inevitably lead to Sister Honor's weaponizing of minor infractions for her crusade against me. That woman's bullshit was so skillfully honed it was almost holy. And sure, my expectations were high. The highest. Saint Sebastian's School was one of the few private Catholic schools left, far from fancy but definitely elite. I made my classes practice for an hour at a time, five days a week. Like they were real ensembles. How else would they learn? Day in, day out, you must commit. I'd be doing the students—and God—a disservice otherwise. To suffer is a privilege.

Pain is evidence of growth.

The ache means we're changing.

And everyone is capable of change. Even me.

But that doesn't mean I always got it right. Whenever I was punished, my task was to clean the massive stained glass windows of the church. I'd climb up on our rickety ladder and shine the glass, pane by intricate pane. Eleven in total. Bold blue, coral, fern green, and my favorite, sanguine, the color of sacred wine, the living red of a singing tongue during vespers. Our stained glass told stories from the Old and New Testaments. Moses, akimbo, parting the cerulean sea. The Evangelists: Matthew as a winged man; Mark as a lion; Luke as a flying ox; and John, an eagle. The slow-motion trauma of the stations of the cross. Adoring angels floating above the manger during the birth of Christ, our Lord, holding luminous harps like jewels in their small hands. So beautiful, it hurt to look sometimes.

Like watching people in church as they kneel and pray. Howl and lose balance. I see people at their absolute lowest. I hear people beg God and Mary and Jesus for second chances. One planet away from their spouses or kids next to them in the pew. Or so alone, they've thinned to ghosts. We're always there, us nuns, to witness, to hold space for miracles in the terror, in the boredom, in the gore of life. To take it in, watch your hands tremble, validate your questions, honor your pain.

You never see us seeing you. Nuns are slippery like that.

With my special cloth, I wiped Jesus's crown of thorns and the doves of peace. The gilded vignettes reminded me of my tattoos, ink I was required to cover, even in the soupy heat of August, with black gloves and a black neckerchief—one of Sister Augustine's contingencies.

Cleaning the windows was supposed to be my penance, and it was bone tiring, but I liked the work. Each panel bewitched me. Better drama than Facebook. Or a bar fight.

Sometimes, Jack Corolla, one of Saint Sebastian's janitors, brought his ladder to help. *Help* was a generous verb. I'd often have to climb down and anchor his ladder, as he was remarkably clumsy and scared of heights. Jack loved the seraphim window the most, besotted with the angel's fine hair, the incandescent gold of lightbulb filament. "It's it's it's the curse of an ancient building like this," is how Jack explained, in his Southern lilt and stutter, every single problem he couldn't fix on campus. Leaky pipes, flickering lights, whatever. Jack was paranoid about lead in the water and mold spores after storms, convinced something bad was always about to happen. He reminded me of my kid brother, Moose. Neither would ever admit to being superstitious but sure as the sun sets in the west, they both knocked on wood in threes. "Double filter your water, Sister!" Jack warned. "Once ain't enough. Double filter!" Concern bordering on harassment. Sweet harassment. Both guys liked to shoot the shit and tag along under the pretense of work. Both fancied themselves handymen while being the least handy men in the room. But we reinvent ourselves, don't we? We keep trying because transformation is survival, like Jesus proved, like Moose taught me. My brother knew better than anyone the cost of living your truth. I wish I had listened to him earlier.

During the first of countless castigations doled out by Sister Augustine, I discovered that if you pressed your face to Mary's face in the Nativity glass, you could peer right through her translucent eye and see New Orleans shimmering below like a moth wing. On the highest rung of the ladder, my eye to Mary's eye, I saw Faubourg Delassize and Livaudais unfold to the left, Tchoupitoulas Street and the hypnotic ribbon of the Mississippi River to the right. The city was electric at every hour, but at dawn, I was astonished by the wattage of color that vibrated in the silken light. Pink-, yellow-, and persimmon-painted shotgun homes stretched out in the Garden District, long and narrow as train tracks. Purple and green Mardi Gras parade beads and gray Spanish moss dripped from the branches of gnarled oak trees. I watched the streetcar roll up and down Saint Charles, passengers slowly climbing on and off as the metal trolley bell pealed through the air. Most fools imagine New Orleans as schlock and caricature—the tyranny of Bourbon Street and green terror of Jell-O shots. Throwing your guts up on the curb or into your crawfish étouffée. And, yeah, I've rolled my eyes at that nonsense in the French Quarter. But the city is more complex and hauntingly subtle than I ever imagined. Mythical and true.

As true as any story can be.

The intoxicating musk of sweet olive and night-blooming jasmine. Cobblestones the size of Bibles. The terrible symmetry of storms—the eyes and rainbands of hurricanes. Sudden downpours chainsawing the air. Floods and rebirth.

Across the city, I stumbled into random treasures, like divine visions, Saint Anne's face in the palm trees. During my first week in the Order, after picking up my uniform from the Guild, I walked into a dusty curiosities shop, painted in the velvet black of a Dutch still-life painting, that sold only bird skulls, scrimshaw, and marbles. I've never been able to find it again. Through Mary's portal, I watched peacocks roam the streets with the technicolor hues of an LSD flashback and envied their freedom. I saw fog hover like a neon white veil over the river and the corner shop on Magazine Street where Sister Therese learned you could buy one bar of soap and one vial of love potion for five bucks. She never brought the potion home, but her eyes sparkled every time she mentioned it.

Sometimes, as the quiet desperation of my breath settled on the stained glass, I wanted to run outside and join the spontaneous porch concerts that erupted at all hours—washboard jazz, bebop, zydeco, funk, punk, classical, swing. I wanted to pull a guitar out of a musician's hands and play. To leave this earthly realm for a moment and let my fingers think for me. Sweat dripping from my chin.

But the Order challenged me to stay, to soften the barbs of my mortal coil.

Earth can be a heaven or a hell, depending on perspective. Control your thoughts, choose where to focus, and you can shift your reality.

Looking through Mary's eye, I could see the four distinct buildings of Saint Sebastian's campus. Our convent, church, and rectory were three standalone buildings closely grouped on the north side of Prytania Street. Our school, with its three wings—east, central, and west, arranged like a squared-off horseshoe—was across the street, due south. A grassy courtyard injected color and life into the center of the school's *U*, between the east and west wings. Students lay flat as shadows in the grass under old palm trees, or they sat on the long granite benches, gossiping, swooning, doing anything but homework. A riot of flowers strobed in the courtyard all year. Even at night, their blossoms and orbs danced with their own fire.

Not that I was outside much carousing after dark. Without cars, the Sisters had to walk everywhere. In the lacerating rain, we walked. In the harsh sun, we walked. Through the punishing winds, we walked.

We had no computers in the convent. No cameras. No phones, except one corded green wall-mounted rotary relic in the kitchen. No money of our own. Our radio was a vintage model with a working dial, gifted by Father Reese. We bartered for goods like books, chicory coffee, red licorice, and Doritos (blame Sister Therese). We grew seventeen varieties of fruits, vegetables, and herbs in the garden, between the church and convent. No students were allowed in our garden, but once or twice I noticed Ryan Brown munching on figs and satsumas that looked rather familiar. Our eggs were from our own hens: Hennifer Peck and Frankie. When we had special Masses or post-storm fundraisers, we went house to house in our faubourg. That's how I met a few neighbors, wondering and worrying what they made of a nun like me. Not that *I* knew what to make of a nun like me—gold tooth from a bar fight, black scarf and gloves concealing my tattoos, my black roots pushing through badly bleached hair.

God never judged me as harshly as I judged myself.

If you talked to anyone else the way you talk to yourself, Moose said, *it'd be abuse.*

Fortunately, there wasn't much time to let my mind wander. When I wasn't in Mass, teaching guitar, grading lackluster homework, or practicing with the choir, I cleaned, mopping the rich wood floor of our convent, carrying Murphy Oil Soap and warm water in a tin bucket, trying not to splash bubbles over the sides. I wore my white apron when I scrubbed, as Sister Augustine instructed. That way, we'd have a record of the dirt and grime, our toil, how hard we worked. We had to keep our facilities clean. Insidious *wet* penetrated every edifice, gnawing beloved structures from the inside out, like lies. All our buildings were drowning in mold. You'd bleach one corner, then notice mold blooming on a new wall the next day. Tarmac-black rashes.

Every Wednesday before dawn, I tiptoed around the convent in my slippers, with the telescoping duster, to remove the gothic cobwebs from our tallest corners. We never killed any kind of creature, appreciating the sacred energy of every living being, even faceless hell-things. Using a cup and newspaper, I carried centipedes, roaches, spiders, and giant moths outside to the garden and placed them gently under the orange blossom tree, the wasps hissing and thwacking against the side of the cup. Some spiders were big enough that I noticed their dozen eyes, glistening like iridescent black holes.

Freeing insects, saving souls—we did it all. Service meant action. Talk was cheap. Even the students were expected to pitch in. That Sunday, during my sweaty marathon of cleaning, I heard the heavy chime of the altar bell. It was Jamie LaRose and Lamont Fournet exiting the sacristy, their arms full of metal objects that caught slices of color from the windows' prisms.

"Hello, Sister Holiday!" Lamont's voice was as enveloping as a bear hug as he yelled from below. They were stowing liturgical gifts from Mass. "So sorry to bother you!"

I wondered about people who apologized for no reason, like they were currying favor for a future infraction. But Lamont and Jamie, both seventeen years old, seniors at Saint Sebastian's, were the most reliable of our altar servers. Never late for choir practice. Never dropped the incense boat or backtalked Father Reese. Lamont was nearly six feet tall, and waxed loudly about his Creole family, crowned deities on the Krewe du Vieux float. Jamie was the quieter of the two, and stout, built like a bank vault. Always looking down and shuffling his feet. A definite heaviness about Jamie, smiled only with his teeth, never his eyes, like the kid kept his soul locked deep inside. He was from a Cajun line, French Canadians that migrated to the Gulf in whatever century. The boys' surefire earnestness, their tucked-in shirts and desire to tell me everything about their young lives, was refreshing—unnerving, even—in the sea of teenage sarcasm and squalor.

After Jamie and Lamont left the church that Sunday, I finished cleaning in the sludgy heat and locked up. Made sure the courtyard and street were empty, avoided the procession to the imminent shitshow of a meeting, then I snuck into my alley. I called it mine because I was the only sucker who braved the clamor of the theater and the rotten stench of the dumpster. It was my secret.

Everybody's got secrets, especially nuns.

Like a good mystery, the alley was both hidden and obvious. You could walk right by it and never see it. A gap by design. My secret smoking lounge. And, that day, my front-row seat to the crime that would change everything, the first rip of the unraveling.

I had no money for cigarettes, of course, but smoking what I confiscated from my students was fair game. Students aren't allowed to smoke at Saint Sebastian's—it was my duty to step in. And Sister Honor says waste is a sin. So, there I was on my stoop in the alley on Sunday night, minding my own business, roasting in the delirious heat that never ceased, not even at dusk. Django Reinhardt guitar spilled from a car somewhere on Prytania. Music was the connective tissue of New Orleans—there when you needed it, like prayer. Both prayer and music were holy, and they saved my sorry ass more times than I could count.

A true believer, me, despite the optics.

That's why Sister Augustine positively welcomed me to Saint Sebastian's School last year. She saw my potential. She was the only one who gave me a chance when no one else would, not even the daycare where they employed security guards too rough for correctional facilities, or the auto repair shops where everyone was on meth, or the insurance agencies in Bensonhurst. I was willing to work nights and weekends, for fuck's sake, and I had the makings of a damn good investigator: equal parts methodical focus and capriciousness with the patience of a hunter and an appetite for femme fatales. They still said no. But not Sister Augustine. She invited me to New Orleans, into the Order, with a few provisions.

There were only four of us: Sister Augustine (our devoted Mother Superior), Sister Therese (a former hippie with a resting beatific face who fed stray cats), Sister Honor (an interminable killjoy who detested me), and me, Sister Holiday, serving the impossible truth of queer piety. We were as different from one another as the book of Leviticus to the Song of Songs to the Book of Judith. As an Order, though, as the Sisters of the Sublime Blood, we made it work. For God's love—the only real love—and for the sake of the kids and our city. Our motto, *To share the light in a dark world*, is carved into the plaque on our convent door.

We were a progressive Order, but Catholic Sisters all the same, with rules to follow or, in my case, to test. We were focused, working diligently at the school, the church, the prison, and our convent. Our bedrooms were modest. Our convent bathroom was spartan and cavernous with a musty, sepulchral air. No mirrors anywhere. No blow-dryers. The shower stalls sported cheap plastic curtains. When I spaced out in the shower, never for too long (Sister Therese timed me to preserve water), I'd watch droplets form little stalactites on the ceiling. The convent's common areas were as austerely appointed as holy tombs, and as cold, a blessing in the sweltering, insistent heat.

Even my shady alley was blazing hot. I had my goddamned gloves and scarf on that Sunday, as Sister Augustine demanded, and it felt like they had melted into my skin. It was still a glorious moment alone, before the staff meeting adjourned, before I stepped into the convent for supper, with two cigarettes collected on Friday afternoon, nabbed from behind Ryan Brown's pointy ears. "Aw, Sister, again?" Ryan Brown, a sophomore at Saint Sebastian's, the king of self-owns, whined after I took his smokes. "C'mon." He threw his hands in the air like a toddler. Of all my students, he had absolutely no street smarts. My contraband supply flowed through this curious kid. Most students fled the instant I walked into a room, whereas Ryan Brown lingered. His flagrant violations of our tobacco rules made it seem like he was trying to get caught. Or he was bad at being bad. Not like me.

I held up the cigarettes. "Showing off your smokes makes you a tough guy?"

"But I—"

"Learn how to fight for what you want," I cut Ryan off. No time for excuses. "Or learn how to hide it better. Otherwise, you'll lose everything."

My wisdom held a kind of grace, I'll admit.

I offered my students the only thing that mattered in life— honesty—and I served it the way I meted out revenge, ice cold. I was a fuckup about most things, but when it came to commitment, I was all in, like a python eating a goat, sinew and toenails and skeleton and all. Like my Sisters, I did everything I could to lift each student, to help them carry the light in their own hands, not hold it for them. Sometimes that meant calling out their sloth and turpitude. And I knew how to clock BS because I lived it. To break a horse or a human, you must first understand wildness.

All weekend I had waited for the perfect moment to savor the cigarettes, and it had finally arrived that Sunday. I was sweating through every layer of my uniform, but I needed more time outside. Without a minute to myself, I'd snap at Sister Honor. My fuse was still dangerously short, and Sister Honor knew how to wind me up.

I pulled out one of the stolen cigs that I kept hidden in my guitar case. Ran it under my nose, sniffed it, and lit it with the last match in the book. A cloud of gnats dispersed as quickly as it formed, not like the sunset, which remained, the battered gold of a pocket watch that seemed to slow time itself. Twilight was the hinge between day and night. Gauzy tides of heat pushed and pulled me. My skin pruned under my gloves. They say if you can make it in New York, you can make it anywhere. But New Orleans is the crucible. The home of miracles and curses—neither life nor death but both. In such a liminal space, like standing in a doorway, you could be in or out, doomed or redeemed.

Sweat rained down my back. I was surprised it was so quiet out there, in the moth-thick alley, no live show or rehearsal in the old theater. PUTTING THE DEVIL BACK IN VAUDEVILLE, the poster promised. Like the devil would let anyone tell them where to go. The theater, like so many grand spaces in the city, was devastated by the storms that grew stronger every year. Paint on the front door peeled off in big mahogany rolls. On route to ruin, still delicious. More opulent than Buckingham friggin' Palace.

With all the matches gone, I had to chain-smoke my contraband, lighting one with the other. Such luxurious tobacco—probably an import. Our wealthiest students were fuckers—I'm sorry, Lord, it's true—but their smokes were superior to the garbage I choked on back in Brooklyn, back in my old life where my fingers bled for rent money, for tips, for my next whiskey.

A crescent moon floated like a talon. Frogs croaked in the privacy of their night disguise. A creaky chorus, the nocturne. Ever more haunting in the tropical steam and amber smoke of the streetlights. Meaty magnolia blossoms held glinting veins of pink, little hearts pumping inside each petal. I took another drag, let it sink in.

Suddenly, the back of my throat soured. My eyes watered as a wave of extra heat slapped me.

Then, a smear of red and orange. The night sky exploded. It took a beat to understand what I was seeing.

Fire.

The school. My school on fire. The east wing of Saint Sebastian's was burning.

Livid flames stabbed through an open window.

In a few seconds, the horror erupted. That's how it feels—the fastest slowest moment. Anything so unexpected warps time, with wretched clarity and blurriness. Like a car accident. Like your first kiss. The tiniest details at once magnified and obscured.

A flaming body dropped from the second floor of the burning east wing and pounded the ground like a vicious fist.

"Dear God." I dropped my cigarette and tore from the alley across First Street, to the person in the grass. "Help!" I screamed, but nobody was around. Breathless, voice clipped.

Jack. It was my cleaning confidante, dead.

"Jack!" I knelt by his side. "Oh my God."

He didn't blink or flinch, just smoldered. A thin line of blood trickled from his right nostril, so delicate, like it was painted with care by a rare brush.

Jack charring in the grass, his limbs splayed—the devastating choreography of a stomped roach. His burnt flesh smelled acrid and terribly sweet.

Did he fall through an open window, trying to escape the smoke?

Was he pushed?

Lord, hold Jack close.

The doors were always locked after the staff meeting, which ended more than an hour ago, the meeting I skipped.

Help.

I thought I heard a cry from inside. I had to be certain the building was empty. The door handle was not yet hot, so I placed my short scarf over my mouth like a bandit and unlocked the door. Smoke blasted into me.

"Hey!" I sprinted down the hallway screaming, coughing. A peculiar strength led me forward. "Anybody here?"

Plumes of smoke crab-crawled sideways across the ceiling. Ashen tendrils dripped through seams in walls, silent as breath.

The fire alarm was stiff. Old red paint flaked off as I tugged at the lever. I cursed at it, as if that would help. It finally budged and clicked down, sounding a shrill alarm that would shake the dead. But no sprinklers activated.

"Anybody here?" My throat was raw.

"Help!" someone yelled in the distance. It felt simultaneously far away and right in front of my face, but I could barely see. "We need help!" It was a familiar voice, but I was so panicked I couldn't place it, like a song in fast-forward.

The smoke smelled like hot garbage as it spun me. Like in Brooklyn, the night of ignition. The night my old life ended.

Nothing was in its right place. No one should have been inside. "Keep talking! I'll find you."

The air was cement-thick, but I saw movement—someone at the end of the hallway.

"Hey!" I choked as I ran toward them, sliding over a sharp puddle of broken glass. "Hey."

The shadow elongated then vanished in an instant with the clean, continuous lines of a fish in motion. A blessed spirit. Been waiting my whole life to see the Holy Ghost, and it had to be here? If bad timing was a religion, I'd be the pope.

The cries amplified behind me. I snapped around, tried to follow the voices. The door to the old religion classroom was open and inside the room, squashed on the floor, were Jamie and Lamont. Why were they there? What did they see? What did they do?

I ran to them.

"He's cut!" Lamont pointed to Jamie's leg where blood flowed from his thigh. "My ankle broke or something."

Both boys were sitting side by side under the chalkboard. They looked like kindergartners preparing for story time, save for the furnace of fire and smoke, and the blood pouring out of Jamie's leg. A wedge of broken glass, the size of an open hand, stuck out of Jamie's thigh. The shattered transom I skated through in the hallway. He squirmed as he held the outsides of his left leg. His blue eyes raged as he howled.

"I'm carrying you out." I knelt. "Lamont, throw your arm around me. Jamie, next. Did you see Jack up here?"

Neither boy answered, frozen with shock. Or was it guilt?

I tried to carry them both but could barely lift an inch before all three of us slumped back down with a horrid thud.

Jamie roared. The glass in his thigh must have lodged deeper.

If I tried to carry them again, it could get even worse.

The workings of the body were as mysterious to me as the mind, but even I knew I had to stabilize Jamie's leg. "One, two," I said, and on "three," using my glove for traction, I pulled the blood-slimed glass out of his thigh. Bits of him remained on the glass, on my gloves. He screamed like he was getting carved alive by a butcher.

Lamont sat helpless, trying to comfort a gnashing Jamie as blood spilled down both sides of his pulpy thigh.

Hail Mary.

Nothing prepares you for the cruel wet red of an open wound. A second mouth. Demonic.

I prayed, tried to channel Moose.

Praying is schizophrenic, Moose'd say to piss me and Mom off. *You're talking to nobody.* I pleaded with him not to join the army, the way he begged me not to join the Order. Like it did any good. Reverse psychology was a family practice. I joined the convent and Moose signed up for combat medic training on the very same day. We traded old lives for new lives like it was a simple or silly thing, easier than making a quarter disappear. Stagecraft. Who'd ever think the queer-ass Walsh kids would become a nun and a soldier. *Ta fucking da.*

I ripped off my scarf—the thin cloth Sister Augustine made me wear—and tied it tightly around Jamie's thigh. A quick tourniquet. "I wish I could carry you both, but I'm taking Jamie out first—he's lost so much blood."

"Don't leave me!" Lamont cried; his brown eyes were bloodshot, leaking fear.

I tightened Jamie's tourniquet, placed his left arm around my shoulders, and lifted him from his waist. "Up!" Like a drunk couple on a cheap jazz honeymoon, we hobbled as one being. Jamie was taller than me, solid muscle, but I lifted him enough to walk.

"I'm coming back, Lamont. Swear to God."

Adrenaline thundered through my veins, like the uppers I used to snort, like the divine surge of Godly strength in the parables I came to love.

Hail Mary, Mother of mercy, our life, our sweetness, our hope. My third eye.

I kept us limping into the hallway. Lamont whimpered on the ground, dragged himself like a seal after us, crying out for me, for God. Blood powered out of Jamie, making quick work of my shitty attempt at a tourniquet. It would have been aces if the Holy Ghost delivered a miracle right then and there, but we couldn't wait for divine intervention.

A flaming ember shot into my left eye—"Fuck"—like a bayonet landing in my cornea. The awful precision of what cannot be controlled.

We staggered to the stairwell. Momentary lee from the smoke, a small prayer answered. That's where I saw Jack's ladder and toolbox. The janitors did most of their cleaning and tinkering at night, but on a Sunday?

Did Jack *start* the fire? The boys? None of this made sense.

But it never does. Twice now I've stared Death in the eye. I know it's gunning for me. For all of us. If I can keep outrunning it, I will.

Jamie's eyes were open, but his gaze was blank, the resigned look of someone who's given up. I slapped him hard across the face. "Focus," I said, even though my mind was running in ten directions. I thought *we're fucked!* and *we'll make it!* at the same time, and I needed to know what the boys knew. I drilled my tongue into my gold tooth, hard enough to draw blood. It was a nervous tick, but it grounded me, a secret covenant, invisible to everyone but me and God; it helped point me ahead.

As we reached the ground floor, a different alarm began to shriek. The tall, heavy emergency fire doors of Saint Sebastian's east wing started to swing slowly.

The automatic doors were locking us in.

"We're getting out of here." I surprised myself with the jolt of energy the word *we* imparted.

I kicked my foot into the main door, one breath before the magnetized fire doors sealed the east wing shut.

Holy Ghost, don't leave us.

I grunted as we staggered outside, where school papers and ash rained. Jack Corolla's body lay perfectly stiff near the east wing's entrance. A now-empty shell that had once held everything that made Jack *Jack*—the talking-with-his-mouth-full, the walrus laugh, the nervous energy. Jack's spirit vanished.

Jamie, barely conscious, murmured, "Is that . . . a body?"

The wail of police sirens, ambulances, and fire engines shook me. A fire truck slowed then stopped in front of us as we wobbled. Firefighters leapt off, unraveled their orange hoses, and ran to the blazing school.

Jamie collapsed on the ground, his eyes closed, mouth hung open as if in a deep, sloppy sleep. Paramedics rushed. Seeing that mangled, bloody kid in their capable hands was such a relief, almost unbearable. *Thank you, Lord.*

"There's another student inside!" I yelled with my sandpaper tongue. "Lamont. He's hurt."

"Where?" asked a medic.

"Second floor, street-side. Jack fell through the window." I turned around and pointed to Jack's body in the grass. My hand, as I lifted it, felt like carved marble.

A woman with a badge appeared and helped steady me as I started to fall. For a lightning-quick moment, we fell together. But she posted her legs, straightened her back, and flexed her arms to keep us both upright.

"Chill Sunday night, eh," the woman said with a smile that lifted higher in one corner, like a capsizing ship.

"I have to"—I choked—"inside." I couldn't string words together.

She tightened an iron grip around my bicep. "Nah. We'll take it from here. You'll be less dead outside with me."

The woman's ID was clipped to the left chest pocket of her wrinkled blouse—Fire Investigator Magnolia Riveaux, New Orleans Fire Department. "Keep breathing. I'm Maggie." In the ambulance headlights, her face glowed with sweat. "You hurt?" she asked, knowing the answer.

"Cinder in this eye."

"We'll get that flushed out." She walked me toward an idling ambulance that had parked in the courtyard. The EMTs were creating a staging area.

"You saw the fall?" she asked. "I hear that right?"

"Jack Corolla." I coughed, and when my lips smacked, I realized they were chapped from the heat. "Don't know if he jumped or was escorted out or what. Jack's our custodian."

She swiftly lifted her two-way radio, pressed her lips against the perforated surface of the mic. "217 to Dispatch."

"Go ahead, 217," said the voice in the radio.

"Got a witness"—Investigator Riveaux locked her eyes on me—"what's your name?"

I opened my mouth to talk but no more words came. How enraging to be silenced by my own body.

"Lungs might be scarred here," she told the invisible radio person.

The night air was thrilling and sickening, like a gulp of swamp water. That was the marshy taste on my tongue as I passed out. My body turned to goo, and I slipped through her grip.

■

When I woke, I was surprised to feel the elevation of a gurney. The plastic cup of an apparatus covered my mouth. The oxygen was smooth and glorious, did the breathing for me.

How long had I been out? Where were Jamie and Lamont? Each second held complex layers—imbricated as gills. Screams, cries, relief, prayer, fear. My black polyester trousers, my uniform, seared into my skin. Gloves long gone.

Somehow, my gold necklace hadn't broken, my cross still pressing its weight against my chest. My blouse, torn and loose on my shoulder, slipped, revealing my ink. Tattoos extended around my neck, above my jawline, to the base of my skull. Buttons must have popped off as I carried Jamie. Riveaux's eyes narrowed as she studied my exposed skin, tracked my tattoos. LOST and SOUL were inked on my knuckles. On my throat was Eve holding her apple. The palindrome DEIFIED was drawn in glittering green and gold cursive, ominous opulence, like the snake in the garden of Eden, across my chest. It was my most painful tattoo. A reminder of the price of selfishness, of what's at stake when you think only of yourself, no matter how good it tastes. It was also a favorite because I could sort of read it in the mirror. Not that we had mirrors in the convent. Riveaux mouthed the word *deified—* she was reading me or trying to.

I covered myself with the stiff blue blanket the medic had given me.

"Nice grille." She pointed at my gold-capped tooth with her bony finger.

I bared my teeth like a dog. Lifting my lips was exhausting.

"217 to Dispatch." The investigator pressed the receiver to her mouth again. She said, "Arson. No doubt."

Arson. How could she know so quickly? What was the tell?

Riveaux looked into my good eye. "Name again?"

"Holiday Walsh. I mean, Sister Holiday."

"*Sister*?" She was stunned. "I thought you were the school's death-metal lunch lady."

"I do feel dead. The boys okay?"

"Badly injured," Riveaux said, "but they'll be all right. Once they're stable at the hospital, I'll give them the third degree." Her puns were stellar only in their consistent miss rate, yet she seemed pleased with herself. Riveaux's eyes gleamed with purple and wood, the moody light of a sun storm.

Searing hot, I needed to feel cold ground underneath me. When Riveaux got pulled away by the fire captain, I slipped out of my mask, rolled off the gurney, and crawled onto a patch of crabgrass. In front of me were scattered worksheets and test papers and a small wooden cross on the grass. One section of the cross was scorched, burnt down to the stub. It looked as if it could be carried easily, like a gun. I wanted to hold it close. I reached for it, but an EMT scooped me up, his strong hands under my wet armpits.

Back to the stretcher.

Riveaux and a medic watched me as I lay down in the ambulance. The oxygen mask was placed back over my nose and mouth. They were monitoring me closely. I choked trying to catch my breath, drowning in my own body.

With the adrenaline burned off, I felt it, the battle—angels, devils. I saw Death and survived the flames twice now. No need to read the Bible to learn how the elements torment and sustain us. Fire, anger, water, redemption. What plot twist sparked it, the arson? I'd figure it out, eventually, or die trying. Sleuthing and stubbornness were my gifts from God, tools They knew I could use. Yes, my God is a They, too powerful for one person or one gender or any category mere mortals could ever understand. That day, God and the Holy Ghost opened the door, and I ran into the flames to help the boys. We were in the fire, inside its red-purple grip, the rhythmic walls of a beating organ. But it was equally obvious, lying there on that gurney, half blind, half alive, that no person nor saint nor psalm would save me. I'd have to do it myself.

2

DUSK SHIFTED INTO NIGHT as I waited in the back of the open ambulance. After scolding me for removing the glass from Jamie's leg—"never, ever do that!"—the medic repeated "calm down" as he took my vitals, but I kept sitting up on the bleached white sheet of the stretcher to watch the flames.

The fire's refusal. Its ease. How closely our world is nailed and joined together, how quickly it can all ignite.

Firefighters blasted the east wing with serpentine hoses. Water made the flames bite back. I blinked, scanning the dark courtyard for the Holy Ghost, but I could hardly see. My eye itched, like it had been stung by fire ants.

After picking their way through the crowd from our convent across the street, my Sisters formed a half-moon at the ledge of the ambulance.

In their veils, Sisters Honor, Augustine, and Therese could have been figures in a daguerreotype from the last century. They were the only nuns in New Orleans who wore the traditional habits, long black tunics like tents. Gold crosses. A full mood.

Sister Augustine raised her arms to the choking sky. "Lord, have mercy." Phrases people say every day with irony or humor, but to us, the words are as real as blood. No different than a witch's spell. Our principal's voice was grounded, and though her blue eyes were clear, she had to readjust her habit, regain composure. Wipe beads of sweat.

Even a saint could fall apart, not that Sister Augustine was a saint, but she was so restrained, I sometimes forgot she was mortal.

"O Holy, Holy, Holy Lord," recited Sister T in her musical voice, "guide us." She had the olive skin and respectable face of my Aunt Joanie, a face you trust because it's plain. Her back hunched, a signpost that the woman was inching toward eighty years old. But she was tougher than she looked. Sister T could move great stones in the garden and pick up a barrel of rainwater by herself.

As unremarkable as announcing the time, I said, "Jack's dead."

Sister T stacked her small hands over her heart and looked at me with the worried eyes of a mother cat. "You saved Jamie, Sister. And brother Jack's soul has an eternal home."

Yes. Jack is gone, but he's safe. He's free.

As long as he didn't start the damn fire. If he did, his forever home will blaze eternally.

Sister Honor had been covering her mouth with her puddy hands, then she spoke: "How could you leave Lamont *inside*?" She shook her block of a head and sucked her teeth.

"Hush now," Sister T pleaded. "How could she possibly carry two boys at once?" She blessed herself.

A swell of guilt made my flaming chest and face even hotter.

My heart seemed to stop beating for a second. *Moose, I'm having a heart attack.*

No, you're not, I imagined Moose correcting me. I could hear and see my brother schooling me, a queen when he wanted to be, but always with the kind eyes of a husky puppy, appreciating each syllable as he uttered it. *What you are experiencing is a panic attack.*

Riveaux and a medic shoehorned their way through the tight arc of my Sisters. The medic had mercifully cold hands and a dimple the size of a jelly bean. He irrigated my eyes and placed a patch over the burnt one.

"Liking that eye patch. Shiver me timbers," said Riveaux. She was a married-to-her-job type, judging by her unironic mom jeans, split ends, and shapeless blouse with all the je ne sais quoi of an airport bar. Sopping sweat marks drenched her armpits. Her metal-framed glasses were two sizes too big for her narrow face. She shone a flashlight for a better look at me.

Who was this woman? Her bad jokes. Her bad jeans. Why wasn't she leaving me alone?

Neighbors, students, and news reporters huddled in the street between the church and school. One reporter zipped up on a motorcycle and started filming before she removed her helmet. Clumps of red rhododendron nodded with the crowd's percussion. I spied the noodge Ryan Brown taking photos with his phone, close to the staging area in the courtyard, until he was shooed away by cops. The Sisters broke their ambulance formation, moving in a wave of black, an unkindness of ravens, swooping in and leading Ryan Brown across the street to pray.

In the ambulance, Riveaux's radio hissed with voices. Cryptic codes, cross talk.

A half hour had passed since I brought Jamie out. The entire second floor of the east wing was engulfed. The epileptic strobe of emergency lights hurt my unpatched eye.

The dimpled medic prodded me on the gurney. I was too weak to swat him away. "Pulse oximetry, okay." The medic took my blood pressure, listened to my heart. "Blood pressure, 90/60. She's pushing it, but at the edge of normal."

The courtyard buzzed with the hustle of a field hospital. Another police car parked near a shabby red pickup truck, which I'd later learn belonged to Riveaux. The bumper was falling off.

I sucked the soft air of the respirator, ripping the mask off every thirty seconds to cough. I needed to spit—soot coated my teeth—but my mouth was too dry, my tongue like gravel. It was a well-worn feeling, the trauma of filling my body with poison, pushing every inch of myself to its absolute limit. Moose used to say people like us start smoking so we can have excuses to take deep breaths. He was right about that too.

"Punch me in the stomach," Moose said years ago, after his attack. "Punch me as hard as you can."

"I'm not going to hit my baby brother."

"Do it." He took my right hand and balled it into a fist. I wasn't used to callouses on his normally fine hands. His fingers were usually more elegant than my scarred digits.

"No."

"I need to get stronger. Punch me."

"No."

"Punch me." Moose closed his eyes. "Do it."

So I did. My brother asked me to punch him—to hurt him—to help him heal, so I drove my tight right fist into his belly and felt his soft flesh separate. He groaned as I made contact. The strange elixir of hurting someone, being good at making something hurt.

Riveaux's voice pierced my internal smog. "Any staff, yourself included, or students have a history of arrests or arson?"

I had been nearly arrested in Brooklyn, more than once. But thanks to my old man, a longtime copper, I was never charged. I omitted those factoids.

Sister Honor rematerialized and chimed in. "Prince Dempsey!" She pointed to Riveaux. "Write down *P-R-I-N-C-E D-E—*"

"Mm-hmm," said Riveaux, terminating the spelling lesson. "What's Prince Dempsey's story?"

"A troubled student," I said. "Talks a good game but he's just a petty vandal."

"This we do not know, Sister Holiday!" The plush fury, the theatricality of her words, everything out of Sister Honor's mouth was scripture or Shakespearean sonnet.

She was right, though. Prince Dempsey was a wild card. "I don't know," I said, which was honest. "Prince rescues dogs," I added, "but he's terrible with people."

Sister Honor shimmied her shoulders and fussed with her veil as sweat slalomed down the creases of forehead. "Well, Prince Dempsey started two fires last year, right here on campus." She had the staccato rhythm of someone trying to keep it together, to quell tears before they started again.

"Firebug. Interesting." Riveaux scribbled in her steno, squinted at my tattoos again, then turned away from me to talk into her radio. More codes, fire words. Terminology I didn't understand.

What I did understand was body language, and the way Riveaux and Sister Honor were both looking at me, almost as if they suspected I had some role in the fire. Or Jack's brutal fall.

I'd have to solve this puzzle myself, if only to prove everyone wrong.

Riveaux moved between the ambulance and the edge of the burning wing. Each time she returned to the vehicle, she seemed more convinced. Of what I didn't know.

All three of my Sisters were well into their golden years, but now back from their prayer circle, none of them asked for a chair or to make room on the ambulance ledge to sit.

Sister Honor's cheeks sagged as she looked at the burning wing. "Look upon our sorrows, O powerful Lord." Cavernous wrinkles surrounded her eyes. I watched tears carve her face. "Sister Holiday," she barked, "what in the good name of our Lord are you staring at? Stop making a mockery of my grief!"

What, I thought, *makes you despise me so much?* I felt my disdain for Sister Honor—or was it fear?—on a physical level as it cascaded through my chest and head.

Forgive me, Lord. I am trying to be better.

With me on the stretcher and my Sisters below on the ground, it was like I was on stage. Sister Augustine smiled. Being near her was a somatic comfort, the pendulum that sets the rhythm. She took a long breath. "The Lord is our Shepherd. We will be okay."

"No one is okay! Jack is dead," Sister Honor cried, "lying on the ground like trash! And in the chaos, Sister Holiday is reveling." She blessed herself with messy arcs instead of the tight longitude and latitude of the cross.

Sister Augustine raised her hands into prayer position and locked into my working eye. "Forgive Sister Honor, she is very upset. We all are."

"I tried to help."

"*Help*?" Sister Honor huffed and turned to Sister T. "The only person Sister Holiday helps is *herself*."

"What could she do?" Sister T dismissed Sister Honor. "Give her a break."

"All Sister Holiday gets is breaks!" Sister Honor's voice hardened. "She shouldn't even be here. I see through her. I see *everything*."

Sister Honor was as unforgiving and unappealing as a hurricane during Jazz Fest, but she didn't pick on everyone. Only me. I used to try to win her over by doing extra chores: carrying palmetto bugs out of her room, gagging every time; washing her underwear, praying it wasn't as nasty as I feared and adding an extra tablespoon of bleach; dishing out compliments about her singing, even when it was pitchy. Charming a surly character was once a fun challenge for me. An addiction. I didn't bring that skill to New Orleans. Sister Honor shot me down at every turn.

She spun on her heels, her center of gravity as low as a penguin. She held Sister Augustine's hands and again they prayed.

I wanted to rip off that mask and run. Disappearing never fixed anything, though. That much I knew for sure.

Riveaux, sweaty from jogging back and forth to the smoky wing, sat next to me in the ambulance, the front pleat of her bad jeans bulging like a codpiece. "Hang on. We're leaving."

"Huh?" Why would the fire investigator leave the scene of an active fire?

"To the hospital," Riveaux replied. "I'm questioning the boys and you're getting X-rayed and checked out."

"Check me yourself. Give me drugs. I want to go home."

"Nah." She crossed her legs at the ankles. "Not up to you. Can't take any chances." As she looked at the flaming wing, she nodded. "Fierce. Fierce." Her fixed stares, the way she talked to herself. Riveaux's presence was intense but calming as heavy rain. She was petite, five feet four inches at most, but her confidence—her fuck-it attitude—made her seem taller. She rested her chin on her knuckles as she stared at me. "Nuns live in the convent?"

I nodded, which made me dizzy. It was as close to being drunk as I had been in a year. Part of me held myself there inside the toxin, the sinister spin, reliving the familiar escape. Riding the mechanical bull until you're thrown to the floor.

"Were you inside the school when the fire started?" The way she tilted her head made me think she was listening deeply.

"No," I answered.

"Where were you?"

I lifted my chin to indicate the theater alleyway. "In that alley, smoking."

"A nun smoking? Well, well, well. See anyone else from the alley?" she pressed.

Besides a flaming body falling from the sky, you dumbass, I thought but didn't say. I was out of breath, so I shook my head no. Just as well, because I wanted her to leave. Her hovering was starting to suffocate me.

"No." I felt the word leave my mouth, but I couldn't hear myself. Like my ears had unplugged from my brain. I silently recited: *Hail Mary, full of grace. Please get this woman away from me.*

"What do you do at the school?"

"Teach."

"What do you teach?" Riveaux dabbed her brow with a shredding tissue, leaving flecks of white on her forehead. She tightened her ponytail.

"Guitar."

"You sing too? Sister Mary Clarence style. Classic." She smiled at her corny comedy. "You fly too? *The Flying Nun*? Or with that gold grille, you might prefer *The Fly Nun*?" She chuckled.

I saw pink light trails whenever Riveaux moved her head. I wiggled my toes to make sure my feet were still attached. My nostril hairs felt burnt. I removed my breathing mask and useless eye patch. "Jack's dead"—I coughed—"and you're joking?"

"I know, I know." She cracked her neck.

Why was she still in the ambulance with me? She wasn't a medic.

"When you see what I see every day, you gotta laugh. Know what I mean?"

Unlike the insufferable singsong upspeak of my students, Riveaux's sentences hammered down at the end, making her questions land like declarations. She scraped her hands down the thighs of her jeans to wipe sweat from her palms.

The ambulance jerked. Emergency break released. The sooner they checked me at the hospital, the sooner I could get home, get to work. Get out of this damn oxygen mask. I was used to masks. I've worn them my whole life. But I couldn't get air in fast enough or deep enough, as if I had been punctured inside, and the hole was expanding.

"The school was indeed locked, question mark." Riveaux spoke the words *question mark* out loud, which morphed her question into a bizarre statement.

"Yeah. I unlocked it with my key."

Riveaux patted her chest, right side then left side, but besides her ID and badge, her shirt pockets were empty. She moved to her jeans, oversized for her slender frame, legs like broom handles. She patted each pocket until she found her pack of cigarettes. "Students hang out here on weekends, question mark."

I inhaled, baffled by her delivery. "Not usually. They cherish every second they don't have to be here."

The paramedic next to Riveaux responded to the name of Mickey. He faced me. It was the dimpled-chin dude again. Eyes like sapphire torrents. SEMPER FI was inked on his forearm. A marine.

Last I knew, my brother had two tours as a medic in Afghanistan. Maybe three.

Moose and I were so similar yet astoundingly different. We both had "the Walsh look"—heavy-lidded blue eyes that inspired friends and strangers to ask us if we were stoned. And we probably were. Whereas he had the soft, dewy look of a deer, I was more of a wild fox. The absurd ways we both tried to prove our mettle—me and Moose. Showing the world we could take it. Resurrection? Bring it. On stage, when the magician cuts a person in two, it's an impressive trick, and the crowd goes crazy, but what's the cost? Can you ever truly fit the people back together?

The smoke cleared for a moment, revealing a wink of the skull-white moon through the ambulance window.

We slowly exited the courtyard but stopped again on Prytania Street.

My life was apparently no longer in danger, evinced by our slow pace.

The east wing burned. Jack Corolla was dead. *Why?*

More important, *who?*

SCORCHED GRACE ■ 33

Riveaux thought it was arson. Someone started the fire.

I wasn't as well educated as the other nuns (college is a Ponzi scheme and following orders wasn't exactly my forte), but I used to read detective stories to escape life, so I know a thing or two about puzzlers. The old ones were my favorites. Classic PI books are sappy, ridiculous, and completely intoxicating, just like "killer" karaoke songs. *Trouble is my business,* said Philip Marlowe, the best of the private eyes. His obsessions despite the doom, his taste for annihilation made him feel the most real to me. Funny how tall tales let us see ourselves, like the startling recognition of my reflection in the stained glass. And I wasn't naïve. As a queer woman and a Sister of the Sublime Blood, I looked beyond the immediately obvious. Occam was a friar—points for that—but Occam's razor was a joke. Answers nested in contradictions. First impressions were usually wrong.

Dead wrong.

Every town, every campus, needed a sleuth. I was it, for worse or for better. I had solved a slate of low-profile mysteries during my first year in the convent: The Case of the Missing Rosary (it was in the refrigerator) and The Case of the Purloined Spectacles (Sister T's reading glasses, snatched by Voodoo the garden cat and hidden in her nap site under the bench). The Case of the Missing Faith was a bigger affair.

The ambulance barely moved. Riveaux dropped her notebook and muttered to herself as she fetched it from somewhere on the floor. Her forehead was slick, her glasses kept sliding down her strong nose. "How did kids get inside the locked school?" she asked.

Terrifying images of the boys—Jamie's blood bath, Lamont crying, begging me to stay—made me wince. But I put my queer sleuthing skills to work. Two teenage boys alone. Both athletes.

Both attractive. Lamont's hand on Jamie's shoulder. Both altar servers from seriously observant religious families, pray-the-gay-away types of nutjobs. After hours. Too young to hang out at a bar.

I pulled off my respirator. "Kids always find a way with the right motivation. They could have been studying, but hooking up is the more likely scenario."

Riveaux removed her glasses, wiped sweat from the corners of her eyes. "Young love," she said. "Hanging in *school* of all places, though."

"Maybe there was nowhere else they knew they'd be alone."

She side-eyed me. "Think Jamie and Lamont set the fire?"

I shrugged. Until I was sure I could trust Riveaux, I kept my cards close, filed the details in my mind. Jack's flaming body sliced air like Icarus, then he barbecued on the grass. I found Jamie and Lamont in the second-floor classroom. If Jack discovered Jamie and Lamont in flagrante delicto, they could have pushed him through the window so their folks wouldn't find out. Highly unlikely, but I couldn't rule anything out.

"Someone called 911 and reported the fire," Riveaux said, pushing past my silence. "The Good Samaritan didn't leave a name. Was it you?"

"No. Nuns don't have cell phones."

She popped her knuckles in a way that seemed to comfort her as much as it hurt, as habits do, tics that become so familiar we no longer question them. "Mm-hmm."

"Don't believe me?"

"I just met you." Riveaux fished a smoke from the hard pack and eased it into her mouth. We were in a closed ambulance, so resting an unlit cigarette between her dry lips seemed to be part of her act. Not unlike Ryan Brown or Prince Dempsey.

Or me.

"Fire is a very specific science, a distinct, artful science," she said with the cigarette still in her mouth and something like wonder crackling in her voice. "A chain of *reactions*." Jazz hands.

"Sent by the devil."

"You're lucky, Sister."

I blinked my watery eyes. "I don't feel lucky."

"Don't worry. You're in good hands." She tapped her fire department badge. "I'm the first Black female fire investigator in New Orleans, so you know I'm fifty-five times better than those white guys."

"I'm the first punk nun."

One of Riveaux's violet eyes closed as she stifled her amusement.

She said it would take several more hours to ensure there was no live ember ready to spark the inferno back to life. It would be 3 a.m. by then.

Driving south to the hospital, my insides burning, my muscles aching, I imagined my Sisters were leaving the chaotic street, shuffling tearily into the quiet convent. Through the small rectangle of the ambulance window, I watched a police drone hovering gently, like a robotic angel. Must be out for an aerial view of the damage. What would it be like to float high enough above the havoc to see but not feel the heat?

The fire, how easily it devoured wood, with the raw hunger of a tide. Fire is immense and immeasurable; it will keep expanding, reproducing, until water or air stop it. If the Lord cherishes us, why are we so fragile and fire so grand? Pointless debate. We are the fire, and the fire is us. We were born with electricity in our hearts, the divine flame. When we die, we return to the elements. Ashes to fucking ashes.

3

I RECALLED MY UNEVENTFUL discharge from the hospital, but I don't remember who walked me home. My next clear memory is at 4 a.m., taking an ice-cold shower in the convent bathroom. The light fixtures were bare bulbs, but the wattage was incarnadine and low, giving our monastic bathroom the quiet illumination of a walk-in freezer. There was no art on the walls. I stepped out, shivering but still sweating. Too weak to towel-dry my hair.

For an hour I sat in my spartan bedroom, naked on my narrow bed, lungs rattling. Though every ounce of energy had been drained from my limbs, I couldn't sleep. The smallest sounds drummed my ears. My left eye still throbbed with a scalpel-sharp pain.

I needed to hear music, but I couldn't wake anyone up with my guitar. Couldn't even hold the damn instrument. I'd trade just about anything for my stereo and my mixtape, shreds of my old life I had brought back with me from Brooklyn. Sister Augustine had confiscated the tape and my vintage boom box, though, on my first night in the convent, a year ago. "Too loud." Sister Augustine rushed to my door, her frail hands clamped over both ears. *"SISTER AXE,"* she read aloud the chicken scratch title of the mixtape, written with black Sharpie. "Is 'SISTER AXE' what you might consider 'irony'?" she inquired. I nodded. It was a mix of Bikini Kill, mostly, and eight of our band's early cuts. Nina had left it on top of my mailbox the day I left. For good. Never said thank you and listened to it only once, but it haunted me.

I thrashed in my stiff bed until 6 a.m., when it started pouring. Over and over, I saw the image of Jack's body, and I heard it hit the ground with its astounding crack. Water punched the roof. Noah's Ark rain. Like the invisible magic that governs this wild city, the rain ties heaven to Hades. And vice versa.

As quickly as the gully washer came, the rain receded. Our cranky old bantam, Big Red, freaked out. Damn rooster made himself hoarse. Our garden cat, Voodoo, mewled. Voodoo and Big Red weren't friends, but they didn't try to kill each other. Better than most people.

My pillow burned the back of my head. My sheets felt hard and pokey as straw, the kind we stuffed into the Nativity scene every Christmas. I needed coffee. I could smell that Sister T had made a pot of her chicory root blend. The first time I tasted it, it was a revelation, the earthy depth of toasted hazelnuts. But I was afraid of anything hot. Smelled like Sister T made fresh bread too—was probably buttering some for me at that moment—but I had no appetite for breakfast.

When I counted all my garments, as I did each morning—the ritual soothed my mind, like touching every rosary bead—I noticed something unusual. One of my black blouses was missing. Every Sister had five black blouses from the Guild. I counted two blouses in my closet. The jacked-up one from last night and the one I had laid out for the day made four. I searched everywhere in my modest room, under the bed, in the hamper, in the dresser drawers. Nothing.

On Sunday, who knows when, or how, one of my blouses had disappeared.

Someone *took* it from my room.

Sherlock said, *the game is afoot*. But a mystery's more like jumping from a moving car. No going back once you decide you're in. No do-over until it's solved. And I was just getting started.

■

At seven in the morning, it was hot, but the sky was strikingly clear. In New Orleans, the mornings were deceptive. They unfolded calmly, slowly, as heat gathered its tremendous wet strength. Palm trees nodded toward each other. Bright green canaries traded bird words on oak branches. I let my working eye search the exterior of the burnt wing, then observe the flowers and trees that survived the ambush of fire trucks and traffic and rain overnight. The sweet olive shrubs, bee balm, and interludes of blue phlox that Bernard Pham, our other janitor, tended. Jack and Bernard were always fixing a plumbing problem or shoddy hallway light together, but landscaping was Bernard's true gift. He had a green thumb and an eye for details. Spent endless hours under Sister T's mentorship cultivating the school's flowers, herbs, and fruit trees in our garden.

Two women biked past as I stood on the church steps. They were riding against traffic, their billowy hair dancing sideways in the wild wind. One woman pedaled hard as the other sat in the cradle of handlebars. Any buckle in the road would have sent Handlebar Mary flying, face first, into oncoming cars. They whooped as the rider pedaled faster, as if she were unraveling time itself, pushing forward as the passenger raised her hands above their heads, shields against the raging sun. More often than not, women demand this of each other, sustaining impossible positions to balance, finding equilibrium in the contortion. My whole body shuddered as I breathed, like my lungs were burnt. A hawk moth zipped by.

The Sisters of the Sublime Blood attended Mass every morning. Monday was no different, except for the fact that Jack was dead, our east wing had almost burned down, two students were severely hurt, my left eye was swollen shut, one of my uniform blouses was missing, and my chest felt caved in. We sat together in the pew closest to the altar. Sister T rocked in prayer, her body possessed with Worship. Sister Augustine hummed softly, rubbing my shoulders and upper back as I coughed.

Our priest, Father Reese, gave a dreadfully uninspired homily "honoring" Jack Corolla and extolling the graces of repentance. Somehow, he turned Jack's death into another reason to hate ourselves. What about mercy? Comfort? If punishment is straight, forgiveness is queer, if only because we are addicted to apologizing.

Sister Honor quietly harrumphed and whispered across me, to Sister Augustine. "Just what we need right now, half-hearted words from Father Reese. How shameful of me to say, but to not praise the Lord fully feels inappropriate and in fact dangerous, as we have already been infiltrated by *Evil*."

"Amen," Sister Augustine replied, still rubbing my back.

Father Reese's homily was pathetic. Like Sister Honor, I grieved for the congregation who hungered for inspiration in the wake of Jack's fiery death. The reassurance of the Word was what all of us wanted in church. Defibrillate us. Shock our hearts. Tell us that pain is okay. That life is fucked but still worth it. Tell us that pain is a crucial part of everyone's story—every birth and rebirth. Tell us we don't need to answer every question. The divine mystery sparked my conversion. If it worked on me, it could lift anyone. Perhaps Father Reese was exhausted. We all were. But come on. So often I wished it could be me or any of my Sisters up at that pulpit, sharing that passion that we felt every day. Even thorny Sister Honor could stir us into feeling the Lord, or at least scare us. Feeling something was better than being numb.

"Is it not our calling, Lord, to hear your call, the call of Thee?" Father Reese blathered.

I sighed loudly, prompting Sister Augustine to nudge me.

A slip of a man in the grand pulpit, Father Reese had returned from the Houston leg of a tour for his most recent book. He authored a dozen tomes on the evolutionary spirit of the Second Vatican Council—twenty years of his sermons glued together as an elliptical memoir—which were bloated odes to his own intellectual triumphs. After the news of the fire had spread last night, a congregation member drove through the long night to bring him back to New Orleans, practically carrying him to the door of the church, like a feckless prince rescued from the forest. I watched Father's mouth move, but all I could hear was the ghostly whirring of the fire alarm. Frankincense burned the side of the bronze boat anchored on the altar, without Jamie or Lamont to hold it.

Usually, I loved singing in church, our old rituals, candle smoke, dripping wax. The paraphernalia that had been touched by hundreds of hands before mine. So much of contemporary life is about the newest app, the latest trend, the most recent way to control your image. It's a moving target, an ever-shifting goalpost. In church, power is in the old. The oldest. Fire, water. A baby's cry or an animal groaning in pain. Song and prayer activate the same frequency. The hum of Worship. But I couldn't stand upright, let alone sing. The open air of the church felt overwhelming.

Bernard Pham sat behind us and wept throughout the entire Mass service. "Jack!" He raised his fists in the air, like he was pounding an invisible ceiling. Bernard, like me and Jack, was a musician. Unlike me, Bernard went to college. A fancy college called Bard, which seemed to be made up because his name was Bernard. He postponed graduate school indefinitely to play bass in Discord, a local art punk band consisting primarily of Vietnamese American kids. The kin of the fishermen, doctors, bakers, and professors who migrated from Vietnam to Louisiana during or after the war. Bernard's mom ran Phamtastic, the most popular king cake bakery in Metairie.

After the Eucharist, the Communion wafer unable to dissolve on my dry tongue, I looked with my good eye at the faces of the saints. The stained glass, my trick mirror, both see-through and opaque. Panes, pain. Mother Mary holding Baby Jesus then cradling Jesus's wounded body. The textured glass refracted the morning light.

Then the healing glow was snuffed out by *them*. The Diocese.

"They're here," said Sister Honor and Sister T simultaneously, breathlessly.

"They're here," echoed Sister Augustine, with defiance and humility in her voice.

The bishop and his two vicars—his two cronies—strode into the church. I called the bishop the Don. Vicar One was the Ghoul, because of his sinkhole cheeks and tombstone teeth.

Vicar Two was the Beard due to his gross facial hair, like a cloud of bees nibbling on his dead skin.

We referred to this unholy trinity as the Diocese though it usually indicated a district. A region of intolerance. They had complete control over Saint Sebastian's budget, the menus for our school lunches, the kind of coffee we brewed in the convent and faculty lounge, the color we painted the hallways.

Now the Diocese would micromanage our catastrophe.

Sister Honor recited a Hail Mary as the entire front row emptied out to give the trio the best seats in the house. My Sisters always gave our congregants the space closest to the altar. The Diocese took everything that was most holy for themselves.

■

Classes were canceled, but half of the student body showed up anyway, in track pants and PJs instead of their school uniforms, but with book bags slung on their backs. Sometimes routines comforted. Sometimes routines replaced thinking.

Small puddles of rain had formed in the early morning storm. They glimmered in the light breeze until the heat of the day dried them. The stench of the east wing—charred linoleum, singed wires, and burnt computers and desks—almost made me retch. But I needed to review the scene, inch by ashy inch.

A news van and the full force of the NOPD was out too. Women and men in blue and black, their shirts pulled taut over body armor. Each officer was as tightly wound as the gun chambers in their holsters.

Saint Sebastian's other staff, Rosemary Flynn, our science teacher, and John Vander Kitt, our bespectacled history teacher, had arrived on campus. John was a highly caffeinated

know-it-all but a genuinely kind dude. Hardcore D&D cogno-
scente. Dour Rosemary Flynn grimaced at the sight of the
police, firefighters on ladders, news crews. She could have won
awards for her virtuosity. Holier than thou, even among actual
nuns. Rosemary's arms were tightly folded. A lace-trimmed
handkerchief was clasped tightly in her left hand. She carried
herself more modestly than the Sisters. Ironic, because by her
own account she was an atheist. Rosemary never cursed nor
gossiped in the teachers' lounge nor spoke out of turn. Never
wore accessories or ornamentation, except her lipstick, the
gasping red of a gored animal, and a single strand of pearls.
Her strawberry-blond bangs were severe, like everything else
about her, and cut straight across her eyebrows. The rest of
her hair was pulled agonizingly tight on the top of her head
in a knot. Rosemary's vintage aesthetic intrigued and confused
me, but I understood extreme behavior. I was drawn to it. She
too wore a uniform, like Bernard and Jack's coveralls, like the
Sisters' generic black. Creatures of display, all of us. Curating.
Acting out our roles in the play, the story, the theater of life.

Rosemary, John, and Sisters Therese, Augustine, and Honor
were huddled with me, by the wasp-yellow tape.

"Oh dear oh dear oh dear," said John. His eyes looked beady
through the thick lenses of his glasses.

Investigator Riveaux was also back, wearing the same gray
blouse and regrettable pair of jeans, and looking exhausted.
She cracked her neck as she turned her head left and right
to take in the growing crowd. "Every citizen of New Orleans
here?"

John said proudly, "I teach here. I'm John Vander Kitt." He
extended his right hand quickly, with force, but Riveaux didn't
shake it. With his left hand he gripped his coffee thermos.

Riveaux cast her eyes on each of us, pausing on Rosemary Flynn, who recoiled and looked away. "Everyone give their statements?" Riveaux asked the group.

"To the police, yes," said Sister T.

"I didn't see anything," said Rosemary Flynn. "There is nothing to report."

A wooden rosary was wrapped loosely around Sister Augustine's right hand and wrist. "We're all still in shock," she said.

John wobbled, perhaps because of the chemical fumes.

The canopy of mossy trees on Prytania Street still seemed to hold smoke, though none remained. Fire leaves its ghosts—smoke, ash, soot, cinder. A quiet exterior with a combustible heart inside.

Investigator Riveaux sidled next to the semicircle of teachers and Sisters. "Who was at the meeting last night?"

"We were all there." John Vander Kitt spoke in loud bursts.

"Except Sister Holiday," said Sister Honor.

"Ignore her." Bernard Pham appeared to my left, put his arm around me. He tried to wink at me stealthily, reassuringly, but Bernard couldn't control his facial motor skills, so his covert wink turned into an eye spasm. I was grateful for Bernard's clumsy affection. *Dear Lord, let me be as warm as Bernard.*

The first time I met Bernard, he hugged me like an old friend he hadn't seen in years. He was gregarious, sometimes bored at work but always happy to see me. With his tattoos, goatee, and beat-up Converse, Bernard looked like a sound tech back in Brooklyn.

Like Rosemary Flynn, Bernard wore his long hair tied in a bun at the top of his head. Whereas Rosemary's hair was red, Bernard's was ink black.

Sister Augustine readjusted her veil. "Our committee meets from 6 p.m. to 7 p.m., every last Sunday of the month."

"Mm-hmm."

More people had arrived at Saint Sebastian's, gathering in the street, behind the police tape. Some students cried. Their parents cried too.

A man and woman in plain clothes with NOPD badges clipped to their jackets slowly walked over to me and Riveaux. They looked me up and down, eyeing my bad dye job, my generic black clothing, neckerchief, and gloves. They nodded hellos.

"Riveaux, staying cool?" the woman asked. No handshakes. "Sergeant Ruby Decker." She flashed her badge to me. "This good ol' boy right here is Detective Reginald Grogan."

He smiled an easy grin and waved floating dandelion fluff away from his face. "Call me Reggie." Detective Grogan took a breath. "We're Homicide."

"Finest homicide squad in the state of Louisiana right here," said Riveaux.

Homicide? Jack Corolla's potential homicide. It wasn't sinking in. Jack was gone. We were just getting to really know each other. At first, he exasperated me, making clichéd jokes about Jesus's sexual prowess due to his "second coming." I punched him in the arm once. But Jack cracked wise to get attention, any kind of attention. Bernard would flail without him. They were pals, cast as screwballs by an uncaring, cookie-cutter world. The guys seemed to understand each other. And I understood them.

"When did you first see the deceased?" Sergeant Decker asked.

I hesitated. "The deceased?"

"The body of Jack Corolla." Decker was irritated. "Want to tell us exactly what you saw?" She smelled strongly of soap. Squeaky clean. Too clean. Like she was trying to scrub something off herself.

Detective Grogan stepped in front of Decker. "The Sisters of the Sublime Blood is a faithful Order," Detective Grogan said to his partner, "and a bit, uh, creative." He tapped the lapels of his sport coat as his gun-metal dark eyes locked on the damaged school. "I was a student here, back in the day." He turned to me, "Smart thinking on that tourniquet for Jamie. The doctors told us. We have lots of questions for you, if you are up to answering them this morning."

Sister Honor must have been eavesdropping because she tut-tutted at the tourniquet compliment. Her cheeks drooped, face frozen in a perma-scowl, like a cheap carnival mask.

"What's the latest on the boys?" I asked the Homicide Squad.

"A few more minutes of smoke would have knocked them both out," Sergeant Decker added. "Lamont will be fine. Jamie needed surgery and a skin graft."

Detective Grogan put his hands on mine. "They will both pull through, God willing, thanks to you." His thick blond hair and low, slow Louisiana drawl gave him a curious familiarity, like a great-great uncle who spends all day watching baseball on a grainy TV from a rocking chair.

I heard a voice laughing behind me. It was Prince Dempsey talking to himself, flicking his Zippo lighter on and off. Blond and blue-eyed and smaller than most boys in his grade, Prince was one of the few students at Saint Sebastian's with tattoos, a collection of guns and hearts on his forearms, an unusual tat combo for a bully like Prince. He had walked over from a crowd forming behind the police tape. Next to him was his white pit bull, BonTon, on a red leash. Prince was a student in my Music class, and I worked hard not to hate him.

"Heard someone lit it and quit it last night," Prince said, then he wordlessly signaled for BonTon to sit. BonTon's right eye had its lid sewn shut. There was either no eye there to begin with or it had to be removed. Both options seemed horrendous.

"This is no time for your irreverence, Mr. Dempsey," I said, though Prince's dark humor often struck a chord with me.

Sister Honor's voice rang out. "Prince has a lighter!"

"Sister Honor, please," I said calmly, an octave lower than usual.

But Prince did have a lighter. Prince always played with that damn lighter.

Ryan Brown took pictures—of the police, of the crying parents and neighbors, of me—with his phone.

"Mr. Brown," said Sister Augustine, "enough nonsense. You students"—she looked at Prince and Ryan—"are God's promise, so show your gratitude. Have faith."

"Janitor Jack fell to earth," Prince said with a vexing smile as he signed the cross backward, BonTon's leash in his hand, "like an angel God was done with."

I began to cough again, and Sister Augustine approached me. "Do you need to visit the hospital again, Sister Holiday? Did the X-ray reveal serious damage?"

You have no idea of how damaged I am, I thought, but refrained from sharing.

"I'm fine." I pushed a cough down my throat.

I leaned in the direction of Prince, eliciting a growl from one-eyed BonTon.

"Where were you at eight o'clock last night?" I asked Prince.

"Cute. Sister Holiday wants my alibi. Eight on a Sunday. I was walking my girl, escaping my bitch-ass mother."

"Who can corroborate it? Anyone see you?"

Prince wiped his nose. "How should I know?"

Sister Augustine turned and faced the ravaged wing, her thin arms raised high in prayer. "Let us rise from the rubble on the strength of your wings, Lord. Sisters, join me."

Sisters T and Honor moved closer and then chanted in unison. "Strengthen us in the power of Your might, O God. Dress us in Your armor so that we can stand firm against the schemes of the devil."

Ephesians 6:10–12. I said it every morning.

"Amen," said Sister T, her voice small and bright as a daisy.

"Amen," wept Sister Honor.

"Why's everybody so wrecked?" Prince asked. "Don't we all want to go out in a blaze of glory?" Prince gave BonTon's leash a tug and spat a glob of green phlegm onto the sidewalk. "Accidents can happen when you play with fire. Right, Sis?"

I said nothing, wasn't going to let Prince reel me in. Instead, I pierced my tongue into my gold tooth, hoping to taste blood. I watched the dog who watched Prince who stared at me, a triangle of suspicion and loyalty.

Prince's recalcitrance was like looking into a mirror—a mirror I wanted to smash.

4

IN A NORMAL WEEK, I'd be demonstrating a Mixolydian scale to my third-period Guitar Ensemble 1 class. But that day, the kids were lighting candles and laying flowers on the sidewalk. People had left rosaries, incense, notes, and prayer candles—a makeshift sidewalk shrine—for Jack. A picture of him looking pissed off, wearing a white flat-brimmed cap that read SLAY ALL DAY, lay with a flower bouquet and the candles on the pavement. Being out in the heat had already made the carnations shrivel. Poor Jack. My stained glass comrade. Parents and students cried while others took selfies near the yellow police tape. All tears and nerves and detached teen malaise.

Most of our students were wealthy, the progeny of New Orleans old money, magnates, and, undoubtedly, some KKK members. White supremacy is like wet rot—hiding deep inside, insatiable, and utterly destructive, disguised very well until it falls in on itself.

We taught students on the other side of the financial coin too, like Prince Dempsey. Our scholarship students, at least a dozen, were the at-risk youth of Louisiana, failed by the system or by their families. They attended our private school for free, thanks to the kids who paid full tuition. But our scholarships were in danger of getting cut. The Diocese kept threatening that we'd have to "graduate the program," meaning no new scholarships. But Sister Augustine would never let that happen. The hard-knock kids had the most to gain from Saint Sebastian's education, but they were most prone to dropping out early and falling off track, without the net of a trust fund to catch them. We were cut from the same cloth, so I knew the allure of the abyss. Unstable grace is wobbly, but it's still a miracle. Every blessing is worth fighting for.

"Did Jack, like, jump?" one student asked another, their voices too low to ascertain who was speaking. "Isn't suicide, like, the worst sin or whatever?"

"I hate this school," said another student. "Wish the whole thing burned down. I'll pray for that."

"We need security cameras," a parent declared to the crowd.

"The staff needs to be fingerprinted," said a mother in a trench coat and hat, though it was so hot my face dripped with sweat.

"That's illegal!" another parent replied.

Detective Grogan and Sergeant Decker kept casing the wounded east wing. Near them was Investigator Riveaux, who carried nothing except a travel mug. A phone in her back pocket. Her radio was clipped to her belt. She lingered like a shadow in a cypress swamp. A cigarette was tucked behind her left ear, violet eyes softly gazing. Where was her urgency?

We had to rule Jack out as the source of the fire, piece together Jamie and Lamont's movements.

I instinctively scanned the ground again, looking for anything unusual. So often the crucial details hide in plain sight. If you stop looking, if you get soft for even one second, you'll miss what's right in front of you. That's when I saw it in the middle of the street, approximately where the ambulance sat idling the night prior. I held my weak arms up high, signaling for traffic to pause and walked to the middle of the road. There, I saw, flattened like roadkill, a single brown glove. ULINE, it read. It looked like a gardening glove but much thicker. Where was the other one? With my own gloved hands, I peeled the Uline from the pavement and returned to the huddle with the other teachers and students.

"Was this deliberate?" a parent asked an NOPD officer.

A shrieking voice shouted from the middle of the crowd: "Tell us what you're doing to protect our children!"

"This is the moment for unity," Sister Augustine said into her megaphone as crowds pressed closer. "Our collective faith is being challenged, but we stand steadfast, bolstered by divine love. Let us pray together." She made the sign of the cross and I echoed her movements. Hand up to my forehead, to my heart, then left to right. The cross was like sleuthing, too. The horizontal line represents *action*. The vertical line, *faith*.

From my invisible perch among the Sisters, I clutched the Uline glove. It was definitely a clue. Someone dropped it in the middle of the road. I needed to tell Riveaux, but she was at the other side of the cluster. Inside the east wing—I had to figure out a way to move through the cop line—I could search for other clues, perhaps the other glove.

"In these times of catastrophe," Sister Augustine told the crowd, looking each person in the eyes, blessing them with her hands in the air, "the Lord gives us the clear path forward. From this fire we will all be reborn."

"Amen," someone shouted. I turned and saw it was Bernard, with his hands in prayer position, palm to palm over his heart. Bernard, like Rosemary, wasn't a believer, but sought the comfort of faith all the same.

A dragonfly hovered near Jack Corolla's picture. Its bright wings trapped the sun. It was easy to forget that something beautiful was also a predator. Every dragonfly has four wings, like it's two in one. A doppelgänger of itself.

"We place our trust in the police and investigators." Sister Augustine pointed to Grogan, Decker, and Riveaux, who waved to the crowd. "But most importantly, our faith in Jesus Christ will inspire forgiveness. This is the test."

Half the parents prayed with Sister Augustine. The other half hollered about surveillance and locker searches.

The triumvirate of Riveaux, Grogan, and Decker moved closer to me in the crowd. "Riveaux!" I called, holding up the Uline glove, but she was deep in conversation and didn't answer. With my thumb over the letter *N*, it read U LIE.

"Take statements from every person at Saint Sebastian's—teachers, staff, students, the works," Detective Grogan told Decker.

"Let's look into this Prince Dempsey kid ASAP," Riveaux said. "Started two fires on the premises, according to"—she flipped through her steno—"Sister Honor."

"Roger that. Wrangling all 260 students will take a day or two, as you well know," Decker said with a pinch of condescension in her voice.

"Riveaux," I said, "I need to talk to you."

"Sure. In a minute, Sister," she said, her tone dismissive.

Grogan chomped on a toothpick and when he slid it out of his mouth, I could see a tiny tear, like a snake's forked tongue. "Pity. Saint Sebastian's is a rock of the community," he said. "This is a real church. Not that PC crackerjack idiocy. Though

Sister Holiday looks like she is in bad shape," he said to Riveaux and Decker, as if I were not standing right in front of them.

"Want to join me as I get her statement?" Decker asked Riveaux.

"I questioned her at the scene last night," Riveaux replied.

"Full statement," replied Grogan, "but don't tire her out."

"Ain't you sweet," Decker mocked.

"Sweet as a sledgehammer." Riveaux laughed.

"Ladies, there's plenty to go round." He patted his broad chest and smiled lightly. His nose in profile was as pointed as a spear blade.

"Decker, won't your wife get jealous?" Riveaux teased.

"Y'all aren't 'gay divorced' yet?" Grogan asked Decker. "Can I say that? Can't keep up with what the gays and the transgenders want us to say or not say these days. We straight white men are becoming an endangered species." He bent his wet toothpick. Even though it was soggy, it still had enough dry wood to snap.

"Not fast enough." Riveaux offered a smug smile.

They talked so freely in front of me, they must have thought I was praying. And I let them think that. I made the sign of the cross again. People view nuns as nameless clones, a collective noun rather than individuals. That was ironic, because, denuded of so-called luxuries like cell phones and social media, leading lives of service and prayer, nuns cultivated rich inner worlds. Real inner dialogue. Most female mystics were nuns. Beatrice of Nazareth. Consolata Betrone. Sister Helen Prejean is more of a badass than most self-proclaimed radicals moaning about the ethical failings of single-use plastic straws. Nuns forge genuine connections, soul to eternal soul. What choice do we have but to be achingly present?

Not that anyone asked me.

"Investigator Riveaux," I repeated.

She turned toward me. "What's up, Sister Goldsmobile?" She tapped her canine.

My gold tooth, quite literally a choice made in desperation, seemed to amuse her. It was most likely a sign that her life was boring.

"Long night? You're wearing the same clothes," I said.

"Aren't you observant."

"More than you apparently. I found this clue." I held up the brown Uline glove from the street. "Since no one seems to be actively working this scene, I thought I'd give you a hand."

"That is a flame-retardant glove, Sister." She grabbed a plastic evidence bag from a nearby kit and dropped the glove into it with a pen. "Excellent find. Where was it?"

"Just there." I pointed to the middle of the street that separated the church and convent from the school.

"Yo," said Bernard, who had walked over from the makeshift shrine. "Why is my glove in your bag?"

"It was in the road," I said.

"Huh. It's one of my work gloves."

"When's the last time you saw it?" I asked.

"Let me ask the questions, Sister." Riveaux squinted. "When did you last see the glove?"

"Friday. I had them on to haul the trash and pull a dead tarantula from a student locker. We got a tip there was an exotic arachnid in the building."

I blessed myself. "Poor thing."

Riveaux stepped back and took a long look at Bernard. "Why do you have fireproof gloves? Burning trash or something?"

"I didn't know they were fire gloves. There are, like, six different pairs of gloves in the utility shed." He pointed to the shed, barely big enough to fit the riding lawnmower.

Riveaux turned quickly and fiddled with her radio. She pressed the wrong button twice, before delivering cryptic instructions.

"This city is cursed," said Bernard, who wore a Cure T-shirt underneath his custodian uniform. He looked like he hadn't slept in a week, his charcoal eyes on stalks. He hugged me, and his long arms practically wrapped around me twice. Rosemary tilted her head at the sight of his embrace.

"Sister Holiday," Bernard whispered, his mouth close to my ear, "you're our school sleuth. Tell us what's going on."

Bernard's body heat was too much. I tried to wriggle out of his sweaty hug, but he wouldn't let go. He smelled of freshly cut grass and gin.

"I can't breathe," I said.

"Sorry." He loosened his arms and ran to light one of the shrine candles that had been extinguished in a gust of wind. "I'm nobody without Jackie. The Jack of All Trades. The Jack Attack."

I knelt to light two candles and send two prayers into the ether. "I've lost people," I told Bernard. "People I've loved. It's an unbearable weight. It's gutting and it never goes away. But we find ways to survive. I am praying for you and Jack. For all of us."

Just then, Bernard was peeled from me.

A police officer was behind him, turning his body to face the street, handling Bernard like a mannequin.

"That your glove?" asked the cop with a comically threatening head, the shape of a cannon ball. He nodded in the direction of the evidence bag in Riveaux's hands.

"It is." Bernard set his glassy stare onto Riveaux. "I already told her."

"Come with us."

"Why?"

Before the officer could answer, in front of the gathering students and parents, he pushed Bernard toward a police car, nudging my friend into the back seat.

"Hey! Don't hurt him," I yelled, to no avail.

Riveaux dashed to hand the cops the evidence bag, then returned to the huddle. The door slammed with a hard crack.

Total douchebag move—taking Bernard to the station for questioning, with everyone watching. Let the rumor mill start grinding.

"Can't believe they took Bernard in by force," I said. "He willingly admitted the glove was his."

But sometimes the best criminals play this hand, I thought. They plan and plan, move each pawn until the king is cornered.

"They will question everyone at the school," said Sister Honor, "not only your 'posse.' They will speak with me, every staff member, and every teacher."

Rosemary Flynn caught my eye again. She wasn't praying. Not surprising, since I had never seen her pray. She looked instead at the impromptu memorial for Jack and shook her head disapprovingly. She rearranged the candles into a tight row, shortest to tallest, and then deadheaded a carnation.

The sun was atomic, with a metallic heat. The air woody and harsh.

I stood behind Rosemary and said hello. My voice must have frightened her because she jerked back.

Rosemary turned around and blinked. "You look frightful."

"You always say the right thing."

"Get some rest before you fall over dead."

"They took Bernard to the police station," I said.

"I saw," Rosemary replied quizzically. "I—" She paused, either not knowing what to say next or not knowing how to say it.

Mourning doves cooed somewhere on a tall branch. I noticed police officers photographing the area of the street where I found the glove.

Detective Grogan and Sergeant Decker stepped closer to me after exchanging words with the officer who ferried Bernard downtown. "We have more questions for you," said Decker. "Need a full statement on record."

"You feelin' all right?" Grogan put his large right hand on my shoulder. "Got hit in the eye, huh, Sister?"

I nodded. "I'm fine. They gave me eye drops at the hospital."

Grogan's clothes were impeccable. Crisply starched white shirt, matte black tie, trouser legs starched, black shoes polished into mirrors.

He was a model of tidiness. The only exterior messiness about Grogan was the chewing tobacco that had appeared in his mouth. His cheek bulged like he was stifling a laugh. He spit soot-brown liquid into a paper cup.

"Again, with that garbage?" asked Decker, annoyed. "Thought you gave up dipping."

"No way," replied Grogan, "it keeps me focused."

"Quit the dip before I quit you," Decker said. "That stuff will turn your gums into acid."

Grogan chuckled. "Well, well, Sergeant. You care about my well-being."

"That shit is the devil's spit," murmured Decker. She turned her frustration toward me. "Where *exactly* did you first see

Jack's body?" Her large sports sunglasses showed me my phantom image. Bags under my eyes like I was wearing goth makeup.

"In front of the school. I saw him fall as I was running from the alley."

"Which alley?" Grogan asked, then loosed more liquid into his repurposed coffee cup.

"By the vaudeville theater."

"You didn't see anyone in those windows up there, someone that might have pushed him?" Decker's skin was unbroken. No wrinkles that I could see. Maybe she didn't laugh very often.

"No."

"Did you see anyone else inside the wing at the time? Other students, like this Prince Dempsey that Sister Honor mentioned?"

"Other than Lamont and Jamie, I didn't see any students. I fainted outside, so I might have missed something."

I had tried to follow that strange shadow in the burning wing, but I didn't tell the Homicide Squad that. How could I explain it? It looked—felt—like the Holy Ghost. Like it was meant to be there. To guide me. To deliver us.

Another NOPD officer approached and said something into Grogan's sunburned ear. "We have to attend to a quick matter. More questions are coming. Stay hydrated."

"Don't go anywhere." Sergeant Decker pounced.

Rosemary sighed. She had been listening in on my interaction with the Homicide Squad. *Back off,* I thought. I was the only one allowed to eavesdrop.

"Need something?" I asked Rosemary, after Decker and Grogan walked away.

She motioned to my neckerchief, which had come slightly loose. "You're *exposed.*"

I tightened the knot.

Rosemary ran hot and cold with me, as if she didn't like me, or she thought I was a wreck, which I was. The science teacher versus the music teacher cliché at play. Rosemary Flynn was impossible to read—vitally present for a moment, backseat-driving and anxiously meddling, then vanishing quickly, like a bright drop of blood dissolving in water.

Sister Augustine joined me and Rosemary. Besides Rosemary's red lipstick, the women looked alike, could even be mother and daughter. Both tall and pale, both convinced that the "old ways" were superior, from long division to cursive writing. Where they diverged was in their life callings: Rosemary into science, Sister Augustine into the church.

"Sister Augustine," whispered Rosemary, "will the Diocese shut us down? Force us to cancel class?" Her gray eyes were buttoned tight and high on her head, her closed mouth made a heart shape.

"We will persevere. We will never give up on our mission or students. God never gives us more than we can handle, and He works in mysterious ways," Sister Augustine bulldogged. The gravitas of our principal, our Mother Superior, softened Rosemary's usually brittle body.

Sister Augustine gave Rosemary a hug and with a gentle pat on the arm directed her to comfort some of the students' parents. Sister Augustine then met my gaze with her clear green eyes. "We must be strong, Sister Holiday, for the community, for ourselves, and for the Lord. As the Holy Rule says, 'In order to be good teachers, the Sisters will strive to remain calm, often recalling the presence of God.'"

Sister Honor flailed her wide arms. She had appeared again after praying with worried parents across the street, though

I can't imagine they felt soothed by her. She directed her red eyes, like two angry lasers, at me. "Look at them." Sister Honor indicated the throngs of neighbors, students, and parents who paced near the police tape, taking pictures and crying. "Scavengers. We never see them at Sunday Mass. They never support our bake sales. Then a fire breaks out, Jack perishes, and we can't keep them away from the cameras." She glowered. "Some people live for attention."

Sister Augustine extended her hands to Sister Honor. "I know you're shaken, but our community will have questions. It will be *you* and me and our Sisters and the life-giving love of Jesus Christ our Lord that will comfort them."

Sister Honor's eyes brightened. "Bringing our neighbors— our city—back to the Word."

"It's not what you look at that matters, it's what you see." Sister Augustine gazed at the charred school. "I see survival. I see renewal."

"Thank you for keeping our spirits high," Sister T intoned in her gentle way, like a sunbeam peeking through a knot of maroon-bellied clouds. "You even smell reborn, Sister Augustine, like new trees, new leaves, and calendula," Sister T said.

Sister Augustine smiled and hugged Sister T tightly. "All of your work in our garden and in the prison has given you wisdom. You set an example for us."

■

Bernard chuffed as he returned to the school. I was still outside, a ball of sweat after walking to the hardware store and two nearby pharmacies to see if any accelerant had been purchased, or any security cameras smashed. No dice.

"The police friggin' questioned *me* about the fire and my alibi!" Bernard was livid. "They asked me a hundred questions. Jack was my homeboy! I'd have put myself on the tracks for that dude-brother."

"Those chumps will have to get statements from all of us." I spit. Remnants of soot remained even though I brushed my teeth twice. "What did they say when they let you go?"

"My alibi was solid."

"Good. But someone targeted us. This feels all wrong. I'm getting to the bottom of this."

Bernard looked at me and dropped his voice. "Bet you fifty bucks it's Prince Dempsey," he side-mouthed. "He loves looking tough, doesn't he? Prince, with his pit bull and his fake gold chains."

"He is always lurking around, showing everybody he's in charge," I said, "but we need to keep eyes on *everyone*. By the way, what is your alibi?" I knelt to examine a piece of green paper on the ground, but quickly realized it was a wilted leaf from one of the shrine bouquets. "What did you tell them?"

"I told them the *truth*," said Bernard. "I was at my garage last night, rehearsing with my band. Jasper, Chuck, and Dee can all vouch for me." He was taken aback by my questions, covered his chest and curled slightly, as if he were bracing against a crosswind.

"We're true blue, me and you," I said, making a mental note to ask him about his alibi later, to see if his story had changed. No one could be truly trusted. Not even myself. "We need more evidence. Hard evidence. Fires leave clues. They don't start themselves."

"I started a few fires in my day," Bernard said while tilting his head to look at me. His feet pointed toward the school. "Not to hurt anybody, though. To see how it works. No two fires move the same way, no matter how you try to control them."

A spiraled cloud blocked out the sun. The Diocese were back on campus, standing at the shrine, all puffed up like they owned the sidewalk, the campus, the city. They oozed the putrid odor of old-school authority. The bishop and his minions didn't give a shit about us nuns. They couldn't care less about our school, our students—how hard we all worked for the kids, to nurture deeper connections to themselves and to God. The Don's thick neck bulged as he prayed some mumbo jumbo about His Grace. When the Beard smirked, my blood ran cold. His casket-black eyes, his mouth spilling with tiny opossum teeth. Their days were numbered, God willing. The patriarchy and all the "good" it's done the world. Change couldn't come fast enough.

When Sister Augustine left to greet the men and guide them inside for a meeting, like a nanny tending to obnoxious children, Bernard left too.

Sisters T and Honor turned toward one another.

"It was so much *easier* when she was in charge," Sister Honor offered with the zeal and conviction of teenage gossip. "Remember when *we* made the decisions, and Sister Augustine didn't need clearance on every little thing? We had so much more latitude then."

Sister T blessed herself twice. "Amen, Sister. Oh, indeed. I remember. It was only five years ago, the change, but feels like a lifetime." Then she added with flair or despair, "Men insist on holding the power, don't they?"

5

MONDAY NIGHT ARRIVED CHAOTICALLY. A storm stirred over the Mississippi but never landed. I couldn't sit in my bedroom and do nothing. My eyes stung and my chest was still sore, but I needed to search for clues, and make sense of the ones I had already found.

All of Saint Sebastian's faculty and Sisters—plus Bernard, Jack, Jamie, and Lamont—clearly had access to the building. Prince could worm his way into anything. His Timmy-and-Lassie alibi was as weak as watered-down Communion wine. But his motive, as far as I could tell, was to annoy me. Lamont and Jamie might have set the fire to safeguard their relationship. They could have even pushed Jack to his awful death. People will do anything when cornered.

I walked slowly around the school, church, and convent. The Diocese were gone, the ghastly trio back in their gaudy rectory downtown. It was humiliating to watch my Sisters scamper after them. *Yes, Bishop. Yes, Vicar.* Fuck that. It's especially disgusting that Sister Augustine had to play their tired games.

My eyes moved like rovers over the pavement. I scrutinized every inch of the ground. But the street was littered with detritus from the fire. Scarred, like everything else in this storm-chewed city. It all looked suspicious.

The tropical texture of New Orleans surprised me when I first moved. The palm trees, their big personalities. The ever-green trees here held an order, or an appearance of order, while the deciduous trees back home in Prospect Park were gnarled, moody affairs that spent half the year in an orgy of color and foliage, and the other half naked. The palms of the Gulf stood tall and rarely shed, unless storms shook or uprooted them. Ever-present disciples.

Three police cars idled outside of the east wing. Each car held two officers, and their bodies were so still they seemed to be sleeping. Suddenly a black hat turned toward me. It was Sergeant Decker. I kept walking. Every step I took felt echoed, like I was being trailed and mirrored on screens somewhere out of sight. Two, three, four of me.

The sky swirled. Wavy navy clouds hung low, threatened a downpour. I watched a car of rubberneckers slow in front of the east wing. It had been less than twenty-four hours since the fire had finally been extinguished. Its miasma remained repulsive. In the grass was wet wood, plaster, and burnt paper. Jack's makeshift shrine had gathered more candles. Some tall and multicolored, some short and white. Their flames spat in the sudden wind. There was so much to smell, to see, but I needed method. Order in the searching.

With surveillance on the east wing, I walked to the school's west wing to examine classrooms, the gym, and the cafeteria.

"ID?" asked the police officer standing in front of the west wing's main door.

I flashed my Saint Sebastian's faculty card, which I wore on a lanyard over my gold cross. The police officer cocked his head as he read my name, then scanned my face, my necker-chief, and my gloves. "'Sister Holiday, Music.' Huh! Yer a nun?"

I stared blankly and nodded.

"'Sister Christian' is my go-to karaoke song. You don't know that song, because nuns don't listen to stuff like that, right? Besides, you look way too young to be a nun. What are you, like, twenty?"

"Thirty-three, the age of our Lord when he sacrificed himself for your sins."

"I got no sins." He laughed. "I'm as pure as can be. What you need inside? We have to keep the school empty."

"Urgent exams to collect and grade for my students," I lied.

"Two minutes."

"God bless you," I said to him but also to myself to keep from punching him in the teeth.

I walked through the west wing's first floor, poking my head into every classroom. Nothing looked out of the ordinary, but the air felt uncertain.

Upstairs, in the doorway of my music room, I took in the spaciousness. It was the ideal hub for my clumsy, budding musicians and their huge backpacks, guitar cases, and music stands. We often rearranged our chairs into a large circle or smaller groups. One corner of the music room was devoted to my desk where I also did my investigative work. Every hard-boiled sleuth, even Mike Hammer, that dick, had an office. But I draped a poster—the Circle of Fifths—over my evidence board, so no one was the wiser.

Within a minute of being in the room, I noticed my trash bin had been moved. I often made a theatrical display of ripping plagiarized music theory assignments and throwing them away in front of students, so I knew where the trash usually lived. I moved it closer to my desk and dug my gloved hands inside. Among the papers, used tissues—nauseating—and gum wrappers, I found it.

A black blouse with a burnt right sleeve. More than burnt, it seemed to have melted. Cheap polyester, exactly like the one I was wearing at that moment. It was a Sisters of the Sublime Blood garment. We all wore identical black blouses, standard issues from the Catholic Guild downtown. Each Sister had five blouses, enough to keep clean and in rotation, but under the threshold of excess.

It has to be my missing black blouse. Why was it in my trash? Who would want to frame me? Sister Honor and Rosemary Flynn had no problem making their indignation toward me, at my unlikely arrival on their campus, plain for all to see. But would either of them go this far?

I had to tell Investigator Riveaux and Detective Grogan about the shirt immediately.

The church bell chimed six times. Six p.m. Mass would be starting soon. I exited the school and made my way to the steps of the church with the burnt blouse under my arm.

My forehead was slick with sweat. I noticed Bernard across the street, walking out of the utility shed. It was still bright outside, the buttery light of early September on the Gulf Coast. Why was Bernard working late? To heal the campus after the disruption of emergency vehicles? Or maybe he was trying to find the other Uline glove.

Bernard looked up and noticed me. "Hey!" His voice carried across Prytania Street. "Sister! What's up?"

Too weak to yell, I signaled to Bernard to join me.

He ran across the street and skipped up the church steps, two at a time. "Heya."

"Why are you still working?"

His eyes darted around as three people walked into church behind us. "The police station freaked me the fuck out. Gotta stay busy or I'll go nuts."

"Same. And I need to talk to you about—" I lifted the blouse in my hands, but Mass was starting and I couldn't miss it. "After Worship?"

"Sure. I'm not going anywhere." He nodded and walked across the street, checking right and left, over his shoulders, and returned to the shed. Bernard was never still, always in motion.

■

Evening Mass calmed me, especially when my mind raced or if I was at a low ebb. Our services were usually lightly attended, with most of the pews empty. Catholic churches across the country shed parishioners by the day, and Saint Sebastian's was no exception. When I was a kid, everyone I knew went to church. In my one novitiate year, it was odd to see more than two or three congregants at service. But, that night, dozens of people attended and prayed, joining me, my three Sisters, and Father Reese, who had, despite his Paleolithic age, a voice like a radio DJ. If only he said something inspiring with that voice. My weak reflection in the stained glass, the first station of the cross, shadowed me as I gripped the back of each wooden pew on the walk to Communion.

Afterward, near the church exit, as I dipped my hands in cold holy water, I tripped on my own feet. Almost cracked my head against the marble basin. My legs felt hard to operate, like my body was not my own.

"You're all right," said Sister Augustine as she helped me up. Her voice was gentle, but by the way she looked at me, it was clear she was worried. "Should we see if Nurse Connors can pay us a visit?"

"No. I'm fine, just tired."

She smiled. "Well, we're going to need a trim before Jack's funeral." She put her warm hand on the back of my head. Sister Augustine had a steady hand with scissors, and she cut my hair in Saint Sebastian's garden as Voodoo wrapped her black tail around my ankle. I was surprised by how quickly my hair grew, stubborn black roots reaching through my bleached white hair. Sister Augustine allowed me to dye it with the convent's jumbo bottle of peroxide.

I persisted until she relented. One small scrap of vanity I couldn't relinquish.

I lifted the shirt I had found in my trash earlier. "Sister, I found something in my classroom."

"Do not worry about laundry tonight, Sister. Please do not exhaust yourself."

"But, Sister."

"Sister Augustine!" A group of worried congregants ambushed her. She walked outside with them calmly, out of earshot.

Bernard was standing at the church door. "Tell me some news."

"I found a black blouse with a melted sleeve in my trash can."

"What?"

"The Sisters all have five identical black blouses, and one of mine is missing."

"And the shirt was in your trash?"

"Someone is trying to frame me," I said.

"It's not me!" Bernard's mouth fell open.

"I'm not accusing you. But someone is trying to set me up, and put a burnt shirt in my classroom trash."

"We did see Prince today." Bernard pinched his goatee. "Maybe it's him. He was swaggering outside the west wing. What if he got in somehow, past the cops?"

"Prince is an obvious suspect, but we can't focus only on him. We'll miss something. I'll check his alibi."

I ambled into the street to find Sister Augustine again, to finish telling her about the burnt blouse, but she was nowhere to be found. I was worn out, and I made my way to the convent. A searing wind blasted side to side, then up and down.

In my bedroom, I counted two blouses in my closet again. I'd have to tell Sister Augustine first thing in the morning. And Riveaux. The cops too.

The brass already thought I had something to do with the fire, and now someone was setting me up to take the fall. Whoever it was made a critical error. By underestimating me, they showed their hand. They were arrogant. Almost as arrogant as me. I was a disaster, sure, but no one should ever have doubted my commitment. When I locked onto something—a plan, idea, or person—forget it. I was a dog with a bone. And I'd sooner choke on it than let it go.

6

TUESDAY MORNING WAS ROUGH. I'd barely slept as my mind spun with the horrifying image of Jack's fall, Jamie's savaged body, Lamont crawling. I prayed in my stiff bed, named the books of the Bible, and counted backward from one hundred, but nothing calmed me.

At dawn, Sister Augustine was at the sidewalk shrine. Praying, eyes closed. I joined her for a moment. *Hail Mary, full of grace.*

A police car drove past us slowly.

Sister Augustine opened her eyes, as if she were emerging from a trance.

"You'll never guess what I found yesterday." I held up the burnt blouse. "This was in the garbage, in my music room. One sleeve is burnt. It has to be connected to the arson."

"My child, this is a shocking discovery," said Sister Augustine, with prosody in her voice. She had the gift of calm, staying rooted in high winds.

"I know, I—"

"Did you," she tilted her head and, without losing equanimity, "have something to do with the fire, Sister? If you need to confess—"

"Fuck no. I mean . . . Sorry." Sweat collected under my eyebrows. I clenched my fists until I carved half-moons into my palms. I hated slipping up in front of Sister Augustine.

"Did you tell the police about the blouse?"

"Not yet. I didn't want them to think I had anything to do with this. They already suspect me—I can feel it. You saw how they handled Bernard."

"We must tell the authorities now. No time to waste. Let's find Investigator Riveaux."

We were practically arm in arm looking for Riveaux. It was exquisite, walking with such determination, such purpose next to Sister Augustine. As the wind circled us, I sensed the pulse of the larger world, and how I too was a piece of that world. Growing up queer, "tolerated" by my parents, forever worried about Moose falling apart, scared of Pop's temper and Mom's martyr melodrama, getting tossed out of our apartment—it all made me crave a different kind of family, a community of my own design. I appreciated being a Sister, belonging to our Order. It was a pain in the ass, at first. The deluge of snide remarks during my first days of teaching. Biting my tongue with Sister Honor. But the weeks rolled on. With my black gloves and scarf—my generic black uniform—I eventually became just another nun.

We lapped the campus but didn't see Riveaux.

"I need one moment," said Sister Augustine. She made a break for her office to phone the police, her black veil like a protection spell behind her.

The sky was a mottle of blue and white, threaded with the inflections of birdsong. Parrots, robins, and silver mourning doves incanted their secret codes.

Our east and west wings were far enough apart, separated by the central wing, for the police and fire department to give the safety clearance for classes to resume that day, but in the west wing only. My eye was still bloodveined, my body still tender, but, like Bernard, I couldn't just sit around. It would have done my head in. If I had access to the scene and every report and forensic photo, I could crack this case wide open. The cops were useless. I hated hating them, but the clock was ticking. There were clues to find, corners to search, people to poke.

Sister Augustine reappeared outside—"Praise the Lord, Sister Holiday, I called the investigators, and they are on their way"—and walked with me across the street to school. The fire doors had kept the smoke mostly contained, but inside the west wing, the foul fumes of burnt computers and melted plastic ripped the back of my throat.

Without the use of one whole side of our U-shaped school, Saint Sebastian's teachers doubled up in the west wing. We combined our students in shared classrooms. Despite my protest, Sister Honor, head of the Classroom Committee for Christian Values and responsible for upholding decorum, declared that Rosemary and I had to share my room. Rosemary Flynn's science room was destroyed in the fire. Apparently, every window had blown. The music room was the largest space left and the easiest to reconfigure because of the movable chairs and tables. Only my desk, at the front of the music room, was immovable. The heavy wood monstrosity. That corner was my PI office, housing my notes on the fire, my list of suspects (everyone), and a list of clues. Just two so far: the burnt blouse and the Uline glove from the road.

I stuffed the burnt shirt in my desk and settled in for class as students meandered into the room. Rosemary and her students filled out the other half of the space. I grumbled and tried to ignore them, but every sound from the other side of the classroom irritated me.

Hail Mary, please give me strength.

Cops watched my movements as they walked past the open door of the classroom. I hugged my guitar and felt eyes on me everywhere I turned. Or was it the fuzzy heat of the blaze that I couldn't shed? Phantom fires tickled my earlobes. My guitar pick, a lucky charm, smoldered in my back pocket.

When my lesson began, my students took turns practicing solos. At the other end of the classroom, underneath a giant crucifix on the wall, stood Rosemary Flynn. She over-enunciated every *t* in her monotonous lecture on fluid friction.

"I heard Sister Holiday cut Jamie's leg off," one of the science students said excitedly, loud enough for the whole class to hear.

"Bernard Pham was charged with arson!" another student offered. The rumor factory in full effect. "It took six officers to restrain Bernard, he was so high on the drugs!"

"Enough!" Rosemary and I said in unison. The first—and probably last—time we'd agree on anything.

"Bernard Pham was not charged, nor will he be charged, with any crime," I said to the mass of wide-eyed students, realizing one kid was recording me with her phone.

Before I could scold students for using phones during class time—a pursuit as fruitless as telling birds not to sing—Sister Augustine's strong voice piped in through the PA system.

"Dear students, welcome back to school after an unspeakable tragedy," she said. "Your loyal classmates, Jamie and Lamont, are healing—*praise God*. They will be out of school for an unknown amount of time as they recover. We will pray for our custodian, Jack Corolla, Lord rest his soul, who perished in the fire. We will pray for resilience. We will pray." Sister Augustine concluded her announcement and powered off the PA with an electric spark of microphone feedback.

Prince Dempsey raised his hand. I ignored him. He set it down, clearing his throat. He flipped open his Zippo lighter and ignited some of his arm hair and a piece of scab that he had ripped from his elbow.

"Put that lighter away." I played an E major chord, letting the vibration ring out. "Fleur, the E5. Ryan, you too." Fleur inhaled and Ryan Brown bit his lip as the students readjusted their left hands on the strings.

My Guitar Ensemble 1 was an intro course but definitely not basic. We refined finger independence, triads, barre chords, pentatonic scales. We tackled strumming, proper timing, and tone. Improv techniques were the key to keeping it fun so the students wouldn't completely hate class, and me, and not practice. At least most of them. Kids left my class with confidence. I started them with the Ramones and we worked our way to Vivaldi. Some Beatles to cut their teeth. Jimi Hendrix for the yummy funk. Django Reinhardt for the fingerpicking.

It was a small class. Without Jamie and Lamont, it was just six students. Sam, a competitive swimmer who fumigated our room with chlorine. Fleur, who was fifteen going on fifty, with hair so carefully styled and a manner so appropriate, I could imagine her being a good cook. Tall Rebecca, a wholesome sophomore who seemed to genuinely love Christ. Her giveaway was how she shut her eyes so tightly during the Lord's prayer. Ryan Brown, the noodge, intent on being cool and yet still wore a tam with a pom-pom in the winter and never removed the *#1 SON* pin his helicopter mom fixed to the lapel of his uniform blazer. Drama queen Skye, captain of the Speech & Debate Team, who always sang with perfect pitch, though her ADD restlessness made sustained practice a challenge. And Prince Dempsey, juvenile delinquent. The complaints against me could have been from kids in other classes, but I wondered if Prince Dempsey had just deployed two different handwriting styles. It's something I absolutely would have done to mess with a teacher I loathed. Revenge is a stupid way to feel in control. Like all drugs, it doesn't last, but it sure is fun in the moment.

"What's the most painful way to die?" Prince asked with a smile. BonTon sat curled up next to his desk. Her collar was a large-gauge hardware store chain that Prince had probably stolen. Prince's one-eyed bruiser followed him everywhere. BonTon was sanctioned as a service animal for Prince's PTSD and Type 1 diabetes. The dog was trained to detect low or high blood sugar by smelling her human's saliva.

I stopped playing and blinked slowly. The students looked at me, waiting for me to say something. "Carry on, everyone. Ignore Mr. Dempsey."

Prince smiled again. "Hey, I asked you 'what's the most painful way to die?' Burning alive, falling to your death, or getting stabbed?" Prince's eyes, the blue of a propane flame, were fixed on me.

"What's the *most* painful way to die?" I repeated Prince's question. "Being your music teacher."

Students laughed. BonTon lifted her bubblegum-pink nose toward Prince, yawned, then returned to forming a white spiral on the floor.

I hugged my guitar again. I missed my electric. The crackle of it. But my Yamaha acoustic was the more huggable, moodier instrument. I wished it could hug me back.

Rosemary stood tall on her side of the classroom. She was statuesque—as certain as a commandment. She was either so deeply engaged with her lecture that she didn't hear the kerfuffle in my corner, or she was pretending not to notice.

I slid my guitar pick out from the pocket of my black trousers.

Prince Dempsey whistled at me. His dirty blond hair, his scarred face and ever-present smirk. A loudmouth who never did his homework, who regularly harassed the school's small LGBTQ Club, now cauterized more of his skin, and flung a fleck of elbow scab into the middle of the circle.

When Prince was transferred into my third-period music class last term, I understood that God was testing me.

"What we feel inside is what we give to the world," Sister T told me before term began.

Sister T was right. I knew Prince's strongman show. Armor instead of pain. But I couldn't let that derail me. Sister Honor and Bernard were convinced Prince was behind the fires. I needed to study him closer.

The students practiced their finger independence exercises and G scale. My fingers needed to move, so I leaned over my guitar and played an arrangement of the circle of fifths. Music was another vessel for prayer. With the guitar tucked into my body, my fingers became my brain. I have dreadful dexterity, except when it comes to sex, fighting, or playing the guitar. I'm single-minded that way. Can't dance for shit or hold a yoga pose, but helping others learn how to play an instrument was one of the gifts I could offer.

"Okay, everyone," I instructed and readjusted my guitar, so the neck was practically touching my chin. "E major, A major. Four-four time. Good." Rebecca, Fleur, Sam, and Skye jumped in nicely, in sync, landing the chord changes and strums just right. Ryan Brown fumbled. Prince didn't even have his guitar—one of the banged-up school rentals—out of the case.

Skye sang along operatically to "I Wanna Be Sedated." Sam and Ryan Brown hummed timidly, shy, still, to share their voices.

Sister Honor choked when she heard the lyrics, but she didn't remark as she waddled into the room. Even wet-blanket Sister Honor could not deny my instructional powers. Barely two weeks into the start of the year, and my kids were already playing a full song. An easy tune with a steady beat, but still. When it came to teaching, I was as serious as a heart attack, and the faculty knew it. Sister Honor delivered a stack of papers for Rosemary Flynn. As I played, I felt their penetrating stares, both looking at that moment like they'd happily frame me for arson and murder.

I observed the students' faces, tapping the Ramones timing, and correcting Rebecca and Fleur on some sloppy, muted chords. I watched the clock, needing what it could not deliver, time to myself, to assemble the clues and see how anything fit together.

The difference between me and other sleuths isn't that I'm a nun. It's not about me at all. It's about maintaining the balance—fighting for the greater good.

And what good is greater than God?

7

ROSEMARY FLYNN ABRUPTLY DECIDED to take her class on a field trip to the New Orleans Planetarium later that afternoon. I was beyond relieved. I needed my room back. The fire must have spiked Rosemary's anxiety. Her shoulders were tense, hugging her ears. She was so superior, so controlling—all that chaotic energy beneath her cool exterior—that it was hard to relax in her presence.

Dismissal was less than an hour away and the police had been pulling students, one by one, out into the hall and into Sister Augustine's office for interviews. I imagined the burnt shirt turning to ash inside my desk. When I glanced out the window, I noticed parents parked outside the school, worried.

BonTon barked suddenly.

"Shh, Bonnie." Prince calmed her. "It's okay, baby."

I saw Sergeant Decker in the doorway. Detective Grogan stood behind her.

"Have a minute?" Sergeant Decker flipped her spiral-bound notebook open.

"Sure. I'm hanging out in the green room with all my adoring fans. No, I don't have a minute."

"You look busy," Decker ragged, "with all your toys." She picked up a capo and twirled it around her finger.

"I'm teaching a class, as you can clearly see."

Detective Grogan ran his hand through his mop of honey hair. Sergeant Decker cracked her gum. She was short and strong. One-note except for her long braids held together at the base of her skull with beads of purple, gold, and green—the colors of Carnival. "Augustine said you had something to tell us. We need a few more details about the east wing."

"Now? Here?"

"Now," answered Decker. "Unless you'd prefer to come downtown?"

"Oooooh," chanted theatrical Skye.

"Sister Holiday's in trouble," sang Ryan Brown.

"Zip it, Mr. Brown," I said, which inspired a reflexive wink from Rebecca. "Five minutes, folks. Try not to burn down the rest of the school. Rebecca and Fleur, you're in charge. If anyone pulls out a phone, tell me."

The girls nodded.

Rebecca and Fleur were my top girls, the only reliable students in Jamie and Lamont's absence. Sam was not offensive but not all that promising either. Obsessed with swimming and nothing else. Ryan was hard to predict but too soft to be a real threat. Most boys couldn't be trusted. *Testosterone poisoning*, Moose was fond of saying about guys and their bluster. I imagined the cartoon poison flowing through boy veins whenever my brother said that.

My scarf was astoundingly wet with sweat. I pulled my gloves on tight. I stepped out into the hallway with the Homicide Squad. "Okay, what?"

"When you carried Jamie down the steps, did you hear anything?"

"The fire alarm. Lamont crying his head off. Besides that, nothing."

"You didn't see anything outside the school's main entrance before you fainted?"

"No."

"How long were you out?" Grogan asked.

"How should I know? I was"—I leaned forward—"unconscious."

"Cool your jets, Sister," Sergeant Decker said with a smirk, like it was a hilarious and original statement she had invented herself.

I collected myself. "You're the detectives," I said. "Look at the crime scene photos. Or better yet, show me the photos."

"Cool your jets," Sergeant Decker repeated. "Work with us, Sister. Did you see anything near Jack Corolla's body outside? A phone? Wallet?"

"No, I—"

"Did you see the other custodian," Decker's eyes blinked in agitation, "er, Bernard Pham?"

"No. Didn't see Bernard. The school was empty besides Lamont and Jamie. What I wanted to tell you earlier was that Jack Corolla said something bad was about to go down before he died. Maybe this was premeditated, and the fire was about shutting Jack up. He was always obsessed with his premonitions."

I kept the blouse to myself.

And the Holy Ghost.

Cops didn't trust me and I sure as hell didn't trust them. I'd already handed over the glove, and I'd give the blouse to Riveaux first, to see what she made of it.

"Uh-huh." Grogan surveyed me head to toe. "Premonitions." Decker laughed.

Even in my scarf and gloves, I still felt naked.

"So, Jamie and Lamont. They're already POIs," said Decker. "That means 'persons of interest.' That means potential suspects."

"I know what the hell it means!" I was irked by Decker's attitude. "Casting a wide net of suspicion makes sense," I batted it off, "but those boys are sweet. Wouldn't hurt anybody."

Should I have shared my suspicions about Jamie and Lamont and their possible queer Romeo and Juliet saga? Perhaps. But not until I was given assurances that the cops wouldn't ambush my kids. I had to protect them. Racist, homophobic brutes like Grogan probably daydream about brassknuckling gay Black kids like Lamont. Bashing Jamie would have been a bonus.

"Um, okay," Decker remarked. "Now onto Prince Dempsey. The student has quite the rap sheet. And he's set two fires already. So, we're thinking—"

"What's the motive?" I interrupted.

Prince Dempsey was a clear suspect, of course, but my queer paranoia had trained me to search unexpected places.

"We're looking into that," said Grogan.

"Did you check Prince's dog-walking alibi?"

"His dog ain't talking," Grogan quipped.

"We did," said Decker, "and no one in the neighborhood noticed him. Also, he knows this building well, and can move about easily."

"So do I." I crossed my arms.

"Oh, we are aware." Sergeant Decker smiled at Grogan.

"And besides, that's not a motive," I said, lifting onto the balls of my feet.

"Okay, Sister," said Decker. "Let us know when you nail the perp. But remember New Orleans ain't Cabot Cove."

I'll solve the case faster than you two, I thought as I made the sign of the cross. The flex and dance of my muscles soothed me. It was a ritual that was both fluid and grounding. *In the name of the Father, the Son, the Holy Ghost.* Was it wrong to feel myself present inside each name, one in the same? Aren't we all sacred flares in the mystifying fire of life?

Grogan stepped in front of Decker, placed his hand on my shoulder again. My old man was a cop, and he never touched a civilian unless he had his knee in their back during an unruly arrest. For such a big guy, Grogan's hand was refined. "Thank you, Sister, for caring and for sharing your ideas. Don't worry. We're working on this from every angle."

Decker looked at her notebook again. I read a list of names upside down: Bernard Pham, John Vander Kitt, Rosemary Flynn, Father Reese, Sister Augustine, Sister Honor, Sister Therese, Sister Holiday (underlined twice, to my chagrin), Jamie LaRose, Lamont Fournet, and Prince Dempsey (circled).

Decker pinched her nose and closed her book. "Want to make a move?" she asked Grogan.

"All right, let's roll," Grogan said as he scratched his crotch grotesquely, out of reflex or maybe to signal his role as the apex ape. The duo turned and walked down the hall.

"Rebecca, tempo," I said after I returned to class. I was flustered, but with the guitar in my hand I regained focus. "Closer to the fret."

I demonstrated how to arc their wrists and strum using their thumbs like paintbrushes. I wanted to shut my brain off and let my hands move. My body was its happiest when playing. I didn't hide behind my instrument, but I was my truest self when holding it. Even with energy vampires like Prince Dempsey in the mix, it never felt like a waste of time to teach music. My students needed to learn techniques well enough that they could start to cultivate their own musical sensibilities. To let their bodies take over during a performance. Muscle memory. Playing guitar—whether it was nailing a lick or just messing around in practice—was the best way to get out of your head and blow off steam. But instead of mirroring my movements, the students stared at my hands, Sam narrowing his big, chlorine-green eyes. My knuckle tattoos were hard to read as my fingers moved, but the kids already knew what they spelled. LOST (right hand). SOUL (left hand). They still stared.

I'd long since grown used to my tattoos, but one felt so alive it was impossible to forget. It was the matching tat I shared with my brother. Growing up in Brooklyn, everyone mistook us for fraternal twins. I called him Moose and he called me Goose. We read the same books (Nancy Drew, Sherlock Holmes), worked on the same puzzles, played the same detective board game (Clue). We had our own language. Our eighteen-month age difference didn't present an obstacle. I was in my own head (too id, according to Moose, not enough super-ego) a lot of the time. There was standard rivalry. We looked alike even though my hair was coal black—a bitch to dye blond—and his was chestnut. Our eyes were our one completely identical feature.

My brother needed me. He was constantly bullied after coming out in his freshman year of high school. When I was sixteen and he was fifteen, Moose was savagely attacked in the locker room by three members of the varsity football team. He needed four stitches in his head, and more in other places. He was on the track team, but he shared the same locker room as those football Neanderthals. After they punched him and kicked him in the head and stomach, they blocked the doors, and three of them raped him. I had never heard of such a thing. I didn't think boys could be raped.

How naïve I was back then. After, I pledged to never take men's insatiable appetite for control for granted. Nothing would slip by me again.

Mom and I were in the hospital with Moose for two days after the attack. Dad came in the mornings before his shift.

I remember the feeling of Moose's soft hair as I petted his head. "Tell me who did it."

"Let it go, Holly," said Mom. "He doesn't want to press charges. Let him rest."

Moose's eyes closed, his long eyelashes casting shadows on his sunken, scarred face. Fifteen years old and already ruined.

"They will pay for this," I said, ignoring Mom.

The wheels of his bed squeaked as Moose turned away from me.

"There are fifteen dudes on that team. Just say 'yes' or 'no' as I list them."

"Holiday, drop it!" Dad walked into the room so quietly I didn't know he was there. "Gabriel is not going to press charges."

"The school won't act unless Moose names names. He's terrified. We have to help him!"

"Listen to your father." Mom couldn't look at me.

"*Mom*. Moose's jaw is shattered. Those bastards are going to pay."

"Only God can judge the sinful."

"God needs my help getting these animals to trial."

"Drop it, Goose." Moose cried into his pillow.

Mom shook her head. "Only God can decide their fate. Forgive them, Holiday. Only the broken can break others." Words echoed by Sister Augustine years later. "Only the damaged can damage," Mom said. "Focus on your brother. Don't make this about you. Not everything is about *you*." As she leaned over to touch Moose's shoulder, tears rolled down her face, dripping from the hook of her long nose.

I carried out my own investigation anyway.

At school, I asked if anyone knew anything. Everyone had heard some piece of the story, of course, but no one would talk. I signed up for track and field trials, learned sports schedules, and shadowed all fifteen team members. I played dumb. I played straight. I ingratiated myself. I did whatever it took to cozy up to them. Over the course of three weeks, I made out with four of the team members to try to coax out information. The losers didn't put two and two together that I was Moose's sister, but my plan wasn't working. I sucked one guy off in the locker room after a game. I had numbed my gums and lips with coke, but the hardest part was disguising my disgust. At a house party in Greenpoint, I spiked the drinks of four others with grain alcohol to get them drunk. Booze isn't a truth serum, but I wanted to lower their inhibitions. Finally, it worked. Todd McGregor, so wasted he couldn't open his eyes, confessed. "Sooo whatttt? I did it." He slurred into my phone recorder. "Faggots—they all want it. They all wanna get drilled. I did 'em a favor." He licked his lips like they were covered in frosting. Slim lines of drool leaked from the corners of his mouth. "Was bound to happen sooner or later. At least we're all hung. He prolly loved it. Cuz I got the good dick. I could be an underwear model. Wanna see?" He named two other boys and started to unzip his fly before he passed out. I spray-painted RAPISTS on the lockers of the three attackers. And Todd McGregor? I left him at the house party, hog-tied with his belt and tie, lying facedown in his own sick.

Sounds harsh? Believe me, I was practicing restraint. I wanted to go full Judith on his Holofernes ass. Trailing the team was easy. Tricking them was fun. Punishing them was delicious. That's when it all started. When I first knew sleuthing was another gift I could offer to God. Delivering justice in a broken world. If even for a fleeting moment.

I emailed the recording of Todd McGregor's drunk confession to my father, but he deleted it without listening. Said a coerced confession would never be admissible in court.

"For the last time, Holly, think of the *family*." He shook his head. "Sounds like your brother made the first move. An unwanted advance? You know how boys are. Real men . . ." Dad stopped mid-thought, perhaps aware of the magnitude of it all, for the first time. The bigness of the attack and his reaction to it, a tornado that would rip us all apart and reshape the landscape of our family forever. But he dug in his heels. "Gabriel should have known better."

"You're not saying Moose deserved this?"

"Move on. I'm too close to it. Police can't make one wrong move these days. You know that. I'm very sorry, Holl. We will help Gabriel back on his feet as a family. Boys can be cruel but—"

"*Cruel?* Are you not looking at what they did to Moose? *Look* at him. They ra—"

"Stop." He put his hand over my mouth before I could finish the word. "Stop it. Trust me. I will make this right. We will make this right." Dad hugged me, his cheek soft against my forehead. Brooklyn cops were harder than the steaks my Mom regularly cremated, and Dad had a reputation to uphold.

Moose was too afraid to return to school after his assault. We started skipping classes together, then he dropped out and got his GED at a night school. Lost his light. Couldn't sleep a night without Ambien or weed. Even sitting still triggered him. Before the assault, we'd make each other laugh so hard at our inside jokes that we'd choke. Clowning around at mini golf. Moose and Goose. Throwing snowballs, aiming for each other's heads. But quickly we taught each other how to need nothing, how to separate, sublimate. Memories were like IEDs—we learned where to step. He thought I saw him only as Moose, the broken boy, when he was supposed to be Gabriel, the protector. He wasn't wrong. I couldn't help but want to hold him, reverse the hourglass.

I thought it would cheer him up to get a tattoo together. We decided on the Tree of Life. A reminder of our roots, how he and I would always be connected. Knotted together by what we could see and could not see. My tree covered most of my back. I wanted it to be big and brazen—loud enough to block out the sun, casting its own light in this scary world. Moose's tree was smaller. He said he wanted to leave room for it to grow. He waited in the lobby as I lay on my stomach on the tattoo artist's table. My bones vibrated with the hum of Aimee's ink gun. She sang during the four-hour tattoo process. I liked the way her breath settled on my neck as she worked. Her strong grasp on my shoulder kept my body perfectly still as her needle etched roots, branches, and impossibly subtle veins of bark. Trees were one of God's many miracles. Meridians of energy, life, shade, protection. But these days, my Tree of Life would stay concealed. One self buried below another.

Prince's laughter startled me from my daydream. He had picked off more of his scab and was staring out the window.

"Mr. Dempsey, there are no answers to life's pressing mysteries through the window. Eyes on the music, if you can manage it."

"Stop being a bitch, if you can manage it." He scratched the nape of his neck. Though a foot away, I could smell his bad breath, like sulfur and cheap cigarettes.

Prince examined the classroom, tracking to see what kind of rise he got from the other students. It was all about attention for him. Maybe igniting the school generated the infamy he craved. I wanted to knock Prince out of his chair and grab him by the scruff of the neck. Instead, I used my foot to slide his guitar case behind his chair, outside the circle of students. Then, I dropped a complex exercise—an arpeggio, a broken chord in which the kids had to strike notes one by one, rather than simultaneously—so they would have to stare at their six guitar strings.

With the students' eyes off me, even for a minute, I could open Prince's case, undetected. Behind Prince, with BonTon still snoozing, I searched his case to find proof—anything that could show Prince was innocent or guilty. I ran my hands along the satin pockets of the case. Nothing. I searched for a false bottom. For a moment I worried a student would turn around and ask what I was doing. But, as usual, they were so self-absorbed it could have rained grasshoppers and they wouldn't have noticed. All I found was a plastic bag of beautiful blue-gray marijuana buds tucked in a side compartment. I pocketed it for me and Bernard.

Bernard would appreciate it. His punk mischief and big, chaotic heart were anchors for me, and I was glad to offer him a moment of liftoff, one small note of rhapsody. He had lived a life parallel to my own in some ways—his decent, hardworking parents misunderstood him, seemingly from birth, and had tried to convince him he didn't know himself. His father, a Gulf fisherman, was convinced that art was a self-indulgent pursuit. Not quite a sin but oceans away from salvation.

Prince rested his boots on his guitar case, which I had placed back in front of him without him or anyone else noticing. Invisible again. A nun and a sleuth have much in common. Both camouflage out in the open. And, go ahead and try, but you cannot wear us out. We're as patient and stubborn as blood.

Ryan Brown yelped as he dropped his phone. He must have been trying to text covertly. Or recording the class. Snooping. He was also snapping photos the night of the fire.

"Phone, please." I extended my hand, and Ryan Brown placed his smartphone on my palm. "Thank you. I will return it after class." I put it in the back pocket of my black trousers, then played three chords, floating my left hand up and down the neck of the guitar. "And Mr. Brown, don't backtalk me."

"I didn't say anything!"

"You wanted to, though, right?" I nodded slowly, and Ryan nodded along. "Pardon me," I said a few decibels louder for the whole class to hear, "I see Detective Grogan again."

Except, I didn't see Grogan. I slipped into the empty hallway with the smartphone. How light and bright it was. I missed having a phone—the cure for boredom. I searched for his photo app. There were images of blunts and kids playing video games, some pictures of me from Sunday night in the ambulance (looking absolutely wretched), and a few shots of the burning school. Nothing I hadn't seen. The sound of the students' chaos leaked into the hall. I turned off Ryan Brown's phone and ducked inside.

BonTon stood and stretched her muscled body. Rebecca was crying. Her lanky body crumpled like an old scarecrow.

"What now?"

"Prince pulled out some of my hair," she said, her voice cracking.

The room smelled of singed hair.

"Mr. Dempsey." I closed my eyes, "Did you actually pull hair from Rebecca's head and set it on fire?"

"Crazy bitch," he said. "She's making it up."

"He does it all the time, ever since he lit the bathroom on fire," said Ryan, somberly.

"Where's the proof?" Prince smiled, held his hands up high. His Zippo was on the desk.

"Rebecca, please accept my apology for this abuse." I turned to face Prince. "Watch it." I reached to grab his lighter, but he moved his hand too quickly.

"Give Prince room to learn and make mistakes, to *grow*," Sister Augustine told me after he set the bathroom fires, eight months ago. "Prince and his mother spent twenty-four hours trapped on the roof of their apartment after Katrina."

"As did many other people." I readjusted my neckerchief.

Sister Augustine perked up. "Being tough is easy. Compassion is hard." Our principal always evangelized with a smile.

"Be patient. Think of the bigger picture. Every Sister has a vital role to play in delivering the Word. You might have the most important contribution of all, Sister Holiday."

"Stop being such a faggot, Ryan." Prince's voice wrenched me back into the moment.

"Prince Dempsey, shut your white trash mouth before I shut it for you."

Prince's face flushed red as he shrunk in his chair.

I went too far but couldn't undo it.

The dismissal bell rang, but Prince sat motionless, BonTon by his feet.

Lord, forgive me. Grant me the strength to understand. I squeezed the wingtips of my shoulders together. Prince was a kid—despite his temper and bluster—a wounded, lost kid, mad that life was unfair. Angry that the world took more than it gave.

8

AFTER DISMISSAL, I had to trek downtown with my guitar to join Sister T for a shift at the Prison Birth Center. It was my community devotion, five hours of service every week.

Before I left, I noticed Prince and BonTon strolling in front of the school. The two police cars that had been parked there all day were nowhere in sight.

Heat emanated from the purple crepe myrtle. A black butterfly fluttered through the steam. Prince and BonTon circled Jack's candle shrine. Prince had his back to me and must have thought he was alone, or he didn't care, as he stood directly over a prayer candle. With one hand, Prince held BonTon's leash. His other hand was in front of him. Something splashed. Two candles went out.

The kid was pissing on the memorial shrine. Maybe irreverence and fury were motive enough.

A police car returned, and Prince and BonTon padded away.

Rage swelled inside but I said nothing. Didn't stop him. On the street, I memorized the details of the scene.

Nuns couldn't buy a pack of gum let alone a high-res camera. My memory served as one of my most useful assets. Some people encode memories by saying names, details, and time-stamps out loud, like an incantation. I recited details silently, for the ear of my mind. An hour or two could be eaten up recounting the intricate tributaries of cracks in the bathroom mirror of a dive bar I had visited only once.

Everyone clocked it as obsessive. Except Nina.

But Nina clocked me.

"The Holiday Tax," Nina called it, the price she had to pay to get close to me.

Nina Elliott. We played in the same band. Also, she took my virginity, if you could call it that, but really, I gave it freely. Eagerly.

Not that any sex ed class I ever took discussed the mechanics of lesbian sex or what "queer" meant, so, at the time, I wasn't sure. Nina was the daughter of a stock-market maverick and virtuoso in the world of cool jazz, which was far from cool and as jazzy as a car alarm. She had that smoky 1970s *Playboy* look with bronze skin, and cinema flair, replete with tight-fitting striped tops, and infernos in each of her different colored eyes. One green eye. The other, the sepia brown of an old photo.

"Typical bisexual," I said, "even your eyes can't make up their minds."

"You're just jealous," Nina replied, and double blinked.

Of course, I was jealous.

We started messing around when we were seventeen. She was the smartest and hottest person I had ever met, with a body that drove me crazy. Her ass was so tight you could bounce a dime off it. Her brain turned me on too. Listening to her wax poetic about library science. We were still messing around fifteen years later, when I left the mess *I* made, for New Orleans.

If either Nina or I had too much to drink and sent a text, we'd end up in bed together, even after she married Nicholas.

Nina and Nicholas: The Perfect Match read the inscription on the save-the-date mailer that I burned in my sink.

Their marriage destroyed me, and though I never admitted it to Nina, she knew. I didn't respond to the wedding RSVP. Skipped the rehearsal dinner. Showed up at their nuptials, some wedding factory in Long Island City, wearing a devastating blue dress and stratospherically wasted. After watching them dance to "I Swear," I pounded three bourbons, neat. Bless the open bar. Then I took it upon myself to kick down their wedding arbor, sending snapdragons and allium flying. How good it felt to stop them for a moment. Crush their roses. I stomped on the *N + N* grandeur until I impaled my foot on a rusty nail and a bald guy called Uncle Kevin carried me out. Spent the rest of the night at Mount Sinai waiting to get a tetanus shot. What was love but an infection. Like poison milked from the fang of a rattlesnake, a little can heal you. A deep bite will stop your heart.

Nicholas Nieman Jordan had a name like a serial kidnapper and the narcissism to match. Nina met him while studying abroad in the rarefied air of Paris. He was her painting professor that semester, an art scholar who seemed to actually hate art, the way he ridiculed it. Nina seemed to like his bravado. The antidote to her wishy-washy parents. The American in Paris cachet. Everything was sport for Nicholas Kidnapper Jordan—academics, polite conversation, marriage. I saw right through his charm, but he anchored Nina more than I could. She even gave up her last name and took his when they married.

During all those long years of entanglements, when Nina and I said we'd keep each other at a safe distance, we were set up to fail. She loved me and I loved her, but we didn't trust ourselves. Didn't think we'd ever be enough for an "us." The sexism and homophobia we metabolized, how deep it drilled, into the marrow. What did I expect, showing up at Nina's wedding? That she'd change her mind on the spot and say *I choose Holiday,* drop to one knee and hand me the ring, like in the dumb airplane movies that made me cry? (I'd blame my tears on being drunk and dehydrated.) I was appalled by the path Nina chose. But look at me now, Sister Holiday, a Bride of Christ, with no last name at all.

Nina and I had three things in common: music, fucking, and leaving. That feeling of a door swinging shut behind us. Maybe it was true love—giving our bodies to each other, reveling in each other, being so in sync we didn't have to talk or fuss or label our relationship. Leaving it balled up on the floor until we were ready to put it on again.

I felt so alive when I was with her, it was almost frantic, so raging with life my blood tried to tear through my skin. Desire like tinnitus of the heart—wing-thin buzz underneath every other sound. I was angry that Nina would never be mine. Angry we never gave us a real shot. Her mismatched eyes. Her skin, warm to the touch, always smooth and firm, like a stone baking in the sun. I hated myself for wanting to possess her. Hated myself for learning to love the pain. Is there any torture more elegant than chasing what you'll never catch? A love kept pure by denying it, trapping it in glass. Forever a wish, a haunting. Maybe it was God's test, the matrices of truths I had to discover about myself.

That Tuesday was another test. I trudged to the prison with my guitar during the hottest part of the afternoon, drowning in sweat as I trailed behind a Second Line. Women with trumpets and white dresses played and sang as they marched. No need for a special holiday. Every day brought a parade. Waking up was a reason to celebrate debaucherously. Even the puppets seemed drunk in New Orleans, raunchy and burlesqued. My mind swirled with the gruesome and miraculous discoveries I had made in my year as a Sister, as I cleaned or ministered: a bag of money glowing inside a false wall of the church (handed it over to Father Reese). A mummified cat in the convent crawl space (buried it in the garden). A bag of marbles and an empty bottle of absinthe in a school vent (gave the marbles to Ryan Brown, advising him: *try not to lose your marbles*). People of all ages danced in the Second Line, carrying a large portrait of an elder, honoring the life of their father, cousin, neighbor, friend, boss, fellow human being. All the sinners and healers together, drunk on warm beer, donning ivory funeral attire, praying for redemption, crying for rebirth. Like me. At least I had a plan. Actually, it was God with the plan. But I was one hell of a wingwoman.

A holy instrument, me. God's mercenary in a scalding town where the air was as thick as the vice grip of a whiskey hangover. Not that I've been hungover recently. But some fevers the body doesn't want to forget, no matter how hard you try. No matter how much you sweat. When Saint Augustine stared into the inferno, he cried not for water, but flames: *Give me the fire.*

After walking three miles, cooking in the heavy heat, my arm numb from lugging my guitar, I was grateful to see Sister T at the entrance to the prison. She smiled when she saw me. Her massive overbite imbued her with a cartoonish quality, like a grandmother rabbit, a surreal sight under the spools of barbed wire lining the prison roof. Always thinking ahead, she brought me a glass of ice water, condensation streaming down the side. Without saying thank you, I grabbed the glass, tipped my head back and drank it down quickly, half of the water missing my mouth, splashing down from my cheeks and chin, into my soggy scarf. I cracked ice cubes with my teeth like an otter in an aquarium. Sweat pooled at the small of my back, the roots of my Tree of Life.

We walked through the metal detectors, signed our names on the ledger, and followed the prison guard, CO Janelle, to a space no bigger than my music room at Saint Sebastian's that housed the Prison Birth Center. It provided pre-delivery lodging and care for pregnant inmates, with a lactation room for nursing moms who visited intermittently, pumping breast milk three or four times per day. Sister T and I stored the milk in the refrigerator—names, dates written in black marker on the bottles—until it was time to bless it and send it off with the guards. Precious cargo.

I was proud of our work at the Center, created by Sisters Augustine and Therese after Katrina in 2005, blessed by the Diocese, before the bishop and vicars tightened our leash, making Sister Augustine justify every new program request, schedule change, and, according to Sister T, roll of toilet paper. But the factors necessitating the Center were heartbreaking. These women, many survivors of abuse, entered prison pregnant. Sentences ranged from eight to sixteen months. Drug and theft charges. Damn sure my transgressions were worse. These ladies needed help, not incarceration, not further violence by the system. Correctional officers tended to do more harm than healing.

Hurt people hurt people, Mom told me and Moose. *And healed people heal people.*

The lack of contact between the new mothers and their newborns was appalling. Incarcerated mothers could hold their children for only twenty-four hours after delivering at the hospital. Some vaginal births, but most were C-sections. Quicker, easier to schedule. After twenty-four hours of "bonding," the mothers were forced back to prison, their babies taken away, sent to stay with relatives or foster parents. Or brought to special care homes. Families ripped apart, right from the beginning.

Linda confided in me and Sister T that she dreaded giving birth. She entered prison carrying her daughter and was terrified to lose her. In the womb, she could feel her, feed her, learn her quirks and habits. Once her daughter was outside of her body, Linda would remain on the inside, locked up. The absence so cruel, a second sentence.

The women found small comforts in the Center—with one another, and with me and Sister T. We read scripture and horoscopes. We sang, prayed, and cried. Some days, the ladies wanted me to listen to them. Think death metal is intense? Try hearing the primal screams and hard sobs of women who pined to nurse their babies, to hold them close, breathe them in. The Center was a space in which women could grieve and rejoice, under the watchful eye of CO Janelle and two security cameras. How often I wanted to climb up and shatter the camera lenses. But I tried to maintain some level of respectability. Hard to do in such a dehumanizing place.

Mom would have been proud.

Sometimes I handed over my guitar to the women, hanging back as they tried to strum.

"Do I look cool?" Yasmine asked.

"Smokin'," said Linda.

"It really does suit you," said Sister T, smiling like a broken zipper.

For me, playing music was like being in the womb. Fully absorptive. I wanted the pregnant and nursing women to have that opportunity, if they also wanted it.

Being a parent crossed my mind once or twice. Nina and I even discussed it. How could we not? It's the ultimate magic trick. We're the first 3-D printers, women. Additive manufacturing. One body—or two, in the case of Renee's twins—pulled from another.

That Tuesday afternoon, Renee was pumping milk for her sons. Yasmine, Peggy, Linda, and Mel, all at varying stages sat around, talking, gossiping, trading stories. Sometimes, it felt like the old days, in Brooklyn, with my band. Minus the drama and drugs.

Beauties, these women. The scars and stories. All the masks they wear.

Though we cannot hide from God.

There were no windows in the Center. No light show from grand stained glass. No calming plants or blue teddy bears. No fluffy pillows. But the women said it was the only quiet spot in that sardine can of a prison.

That day, Mel and Linda snoozed on their sides in their white uniforms, carving half-moons into the thin tan mattresses, the color of old paper. Yasmine sat on her narrow bed, rubbing her growing stomach. As Peggy read, I could see her orange wristband, tagged with her inmate number. Drab walls, the hum of the breast pump, and breeze-less air thickened the torpor of the Center.

"Aren't they just perfect?" Sister T pointed to the picture of Renee's premature twin boys sharing one incubator.

I nodded, adding, "Little toughies, those two. Double trouble."

But the picture of the twins scared me.

They were too small. Wires tangled over their impossible bodies in a NICU incubator.

My eyes darted around the concrete walls. Renee was pumping in a gray rocking chair in the corner. What it must have been like to see her fragile sons, born so early, but not hold them.

"Miracles are everywhere." Sister T seemed awed by her own words. "God has showered us with blessings," she said to Renee, and perhaps to me, too. "It may be hard to see right now, but God's divine hand is at work." She carried a stack of baby books for the mothers to inscribe. We would send them with the next shipment of breast milk.

CO Janelle shadowed us as we moved about the room.

"Jack Corolla was welcomed into God's Kingdom," Sister T paused and made the sign of the cross, "the same night two new lives emerged from Renee." Her smile and kind eyes warmed the musty space. "Life is an infinite circle," she said. 'The sun rises and the sun sets; And hastening to its place, it rises there again.' Ecclesiastes 1:5."

I thought of Jack's life force splitting in two, imparting extra fight into those tiny twins.

"Can you bless the milk?" Renee asked me. She had an elegant oval face and the gentlest eyes.

I took off my gloves and rested my hand on Renee's shoulder. She stopped rocking in the chair and inhaled sharply at my touch. We prayed to God to keep her and her children healthy.

After we blessed the milk, I retrieved my guitar from its case near CO Janelle.

Mel, serving a one-year sentence, called out from her bed. "Sister Holiday, could you play 'You Are My Sunshine'? It's my Jenny's favorite."

With a kid on the outside, and her second on the way, Mel kept a picture of her bright-eyed sprite, Jenny, on her beige pillow.

Sister T sang in her warbled voice as I played. Mel hummed along with her eyes closed, and I wondered if she was praying, channeling Jenny, or just transporting somewhere outside of those walls.

I cycled through the Center's greatest hits—"Somewhere over the Rainbow," "On Eagle's Wings," "Turn! Turn! Turn!"— then needed to change the mood. "How about my favorite hymn of sorts, 'Ring of Fire'?"

Renee and Mel laughed.

Mel sat up. "Love Johnny Cash. That song makes me want to be naughty. Can I say that?"

CO Janelle lifted her shoulders, straightened her posture in her dented folding chair.

"You can say that," I said, and started strumming. "Speaking of fire," I asked, "anyone know anything about arson?"

If they had even the faintest insight, it would help me to see the east wing blaze from another angle. But asking such a question felt vile.

The room was quiet until Yasmine spoke. "Years ago, back in Texarkana, fuckin' pit, my ex did time for arson." Her green eyeshadow was flawlessly applied. She was obviously careful with details. "My first husband," she continued. "Eric. He lit up his barbecue joint for insurance money. Then he sat outside of the scene the next week, right in front of the cops. Pyros do that, you know."

"Do what?"

"Return to the scene of the crime," said Yasmine. "They love checking out their handiwork. They get off on it. Cameras caught Eric unloading two refrigerators and a smoker the day before it all went up. Fucking idiot. Husbands are good for one thing, and even that thing they don't always deliver, if you know what I mean. Oh, sorry, Sister! I—"

I winked. "I know what you mean."

The ladies seemed to appreciate my unconventional nature. Commenting on my bleach-blond hair and my knuckle ink when I played "Let It Be." I was the youngest nun in the Order by forty years. In my old life, one of my gay superpowers was making straight women feel relaxed enough to share their darkest secrets. Deep listening was a skill of the unholy and the holy alike, from Svengali puppeteers to the pope. But I'd never betray them.

Sister T, intuitive at her core, always quietly watching, caught me drifting. "Sister Holiday, ladies, let's pray." She finished drying a small bottle with a threadbare towel, placed it on the counter, whistling as she dried her hands. Sister T always whistled. Music and silence were both ways to share and absorb the Word of God.

The Word has always mesmerized me, but nearly every priest bored me. That's why I started going directly to the Bible, even when I didn't understand the text. Growing up, Father Graff gave the same droning homily on forgiveness so often, Moose and I held staring contests to keep from falling asleep. Mom rejected grand, marble churches, instead demanding our parish be Saint Peter's, the smallest and oldest Catholic Church in Bay Ridge. It was cold in our dilapidated church, with a relentless wet wind. With the Eucharist melting on my tongue, I let

myself listen for God with my face in my hands. I used to mute
Father Graff and tune into myself. Even Sister Regina com-
mented on my piousness.

I recall Moose trying so hard to stifle his laughter.

"You're even competitive about praying." He elbowed me.

I removed my gloves a second time and took Linda's warm
hands in mine. With my eyes closed, I said, "'Take pleasure in
infirmities, in weaknesses, in insults, in hardships, in persecu-
tions, in difficulties,' said Paul in 2 Corinthians 12:10, 'for when
I am weak then I am strong.'"

"Hell yeah," said Linda.

9

I WAS THIRSTY AND FAINT with hunger as Sister T and I walked home from the prison. We passed Josie's, a dive bar with neon signs in the window and a mosaic-tiled façade. I imagined my old self there, drinking cheap whiskey with an ice-cold Abita chaser.

Three blocks from the convent, we stopped for a moment. I rested my guitar on the ground and shook out my arm as we listened to an impromptu brass band in green and gold suits. Their instruments quaked dramatically as they convulsed with sound, pumping the horns, music practically incinerating the red honeysuckle along the sidewalk. Sister T bopped to the beat. Even the bougainvillea seemed to kneel, enchanted with their music. Jazz is everything in New Orleans. Not the buttoned-up kind where folks sit politely or stand behind podiums. New Orleans jazz curves and swerves. A map so twisty it can only be real. Strumming banjos, slapping washboards, banging piano keys, thrashing trumpets and trombones and who the fuck knows what else. It all melts together and people cannot get enough.

We arrived at the convent, exhausted and drenched with sweat, but instead of continuing into the kitchen for dinner, into the cacophony of clanging plates and the iron maiden of Sister Honor's judgmental eyes, I said farewell to Sister T and wandered around the campus.

Yasmine said, *Arsonists return to the scene of the crime. They get off on it.* Maybe I could catch the fucker—or fuckers—in the act. There were more clues to find.

A dove rattled her throat. I felt a presence closing in, as if I was being tracked. A bullfrog called from the east. Another answered from the west. I said a prayer of thanks for the small beings I'd never see that let me know I was not alone.

In the courtyard, pinwheels of jasmine dripped into the breeze. A centipede scuttled its fur of legs in front of my feet, then disappeared into a crack in the slate sidewalk. The wooden bench had started to splinter from the insistent humidity. The air a demanding hot, a hot demand. I swatted a mosquito that landed on my black pants. New Orleans mosquitoes could eat through metal.

I studied the curbs and storm water drains and rummaged through the bushes where I saw candy wrappers, an empty M&M's bag, and a Carnival mask. Looked under the stone benches. Nothing. A trash bin on the corner of Prytania and First was overflowing. I made sure no one was in eyeshot, then I walked over to the steaming mess. There was a bottle full of piss. A Zapp's crawdad-flavor chip bag. Congealed pizza. Cigarette packs, empty. Nothing seemed strange in my survey, but I knew better. First instincts were suspect.

Night birds trilled. Voodoo hooked her sleek black tail around my calf. She looked at me with mischief in her eyes.

A city hawk swam in the changing light before it plunged into the tall grass, eyes locked onto a kill. I caught Nina looking at me that way once, like a predator watching flesh as movement before tearing it apart. It stirred my blood to remember.

There is a sublime wholeness in holding one another, fitting into other bodies. We eat the body of Christ. We drink the blood. So many years later, Nina's taste still laced my mouth—champagne, sweat, graphite licked off a thumb. "Nicholas is my husband," Nina said once, "but I love you."

Suddenly, a pack of students tumbled toward the main doors of the school's central wing, donning masks and crowns. A half dozen kids, transformed in their makeup and extravagant costumes. In the melee of that awful week, I had forgotten about the student ball, the late-summer dance for Catholic school students in our region. Mini Mardi Gras minus the booze.

Sister Augustine promised to keep the ball on schedule, despite the fire and police on campus, student and staff interviews, and parental protests. Despite Jack's death. The Diocese, who had been circling like vultures since Monday, begrudgingly acquiesced, wasting time and energy in the process. The Don and his blimp of a head made most of the decisions regarding our school's curriculum, admission, and closures, with the Ghoul and the Beard egging him on. The ball must go on because the students needed the *creative expression*, Sister Augustine pleaded.

The ball would be held in the auditorium, with John Vander Kitt and five parents chaperoning. Kids rarely showed up on time for class, but when it came to revelry, they were early. Riotous laughter erupted from an approaching crew. Boys and girls alike wore curly wigs and long green beads.

But no Prince Dempsey. Saint Sebastian's tough guy, notably absent.

One student wore a velvet dress and fishnet stockings. Chiffon. Silk. Satin. Another wore a bird mask, corset, and ruby-red slippers. And another was dressed like an aristocrat from a Versailles court—flowing pink wig and powder-white foundation.

From afar I watched my students horsing around in their ball costumes, soaring with the narcotic-like high of being someone else for a night. More students gathered in the court-yard where two days earlier I lay on the stretcher, fielding questions from Investigator Riveaux. I couldn't tell who the masked kids were, but Ryan Brown was easy to clock, wearing green tights and a long jacket with tails. On his head was an enormous pair of white papier-mâché stag antlers.

Ryan left the tangle and wandered to me and Voodoo, who was now napping behind a bench. "Sister Holiday, it's the ball tonight!"

"Indeed."

"Why aren't you wearing a costume?" he asked.

"I am."

"If you say so."

I couldn't imagine how he could dance in that getup, but he didn't seem to care. No one cared about much in this town, besides living well. In the infrequent letters I wrote to Moose, who rarely responded with more than a *take care*, and my father, who never responded at all, I tried to describe the quirks of my new city. Ancient trees always in bloom. Certain neigh-borhoods in danger of catastrophic flooding. New Orleans was ornate in every way, especially in its punishment. Like wispy fiberglass, the city doesn't feel like it is of this world, alien bizarre, so you can't help but touch it. But when you hold it tight, it shreds you with its invisible teeth.

As if on cue, the fire alarm blared.

The air rippled hard, like corrugated metal.

Fumes. Smoke scratched the back of my throat.

Not again.

"Sister!" Bernard screamed from a window in the school's cafeteria. He waved his hands like a lunatic. "Stay there! Tell the students to get back!"

"What the fuck, Bernard?"

"There's a fire in the cafeteria!"

"What?"

"I got this. Already called 911." Bernard was panting. "They're on their way. Stay there!"

Bernard disappeared from the window. The students ran around in circles, confused. "Get back!" I snapped at them. Fleur's wig fell as she ran. Ryan Brown held on to his antlers as he galloped.

I herded the costumed students to the street.

With the kids at a safe distance, I hauled ass to the entrance of the cafeteria. Had to make sure Bernard didn't end up like Jack.

Bernard appeared at the door, holding a fire extinguisher.

Smoke started to pour through the door.

"Out!" He spat as he screamed. "Stay out!"

"Bernard," I pushed past him, "I have to do this."

I dashed inside, through the cafeteria door. There had to be a clue in there. Evidence. Or even the arsonist, hiding, watching, intoxicated by their craft.

There were no flames in sight. This fire was nothing compared to the east wing inferno. But the smoke burned my eyes and choked me just the same.

Hail Mary. Holy Ghost, give me a break, for fuck's sake.

At the bottom of the tall staircase, connecting the basement cafeteria to the school's central hall, I saw a black and white blanket in a rumpled pile.

But it wasn't a blanket.

It was Sister T, facedown, at the bottom of the steep stairs.

"Sister T!" I ran to her. "No! Sister."

Her veil was off, as was one shoe. Her black sock worn out at the big toe.

I brought my fingers to her neck. No pulse. Her left ankle was twisted, bent impossibly backward. She was motionless, as still as the ground underneath her.

My eyes rolled back in my head. I knelt with Sister T, my hand on her shoulder, praying, cursing at God. Fucking why.

How could you let this happen.

All merciful God, undo it. Take it back.

This is why everyone thinks you are full of shit.

If you are all-powerful, then unfuck this.

I searched the scene in a daze, looking for something—anything—to help fill in the blanks. I spotted a familiar shape near Sister T's battered body. My guitar pick. Must have slipped out of her tunic pocket. Or it was placed there. I grabbed it. If she had my pick, she could have been trying to frame me. Did Sister T set the fire and then fall down the stairs? But the fire was contained downstairs, and she was on the steps, face-first. She didn't smell like accelerant. And she loved me. I felt it.

Less than one *Hail Mary* later, EMTs, and a dimpled face I recognized from Sunday night, arrived.

"What's the situation?" Dimple asked.

"Sister Therese . . . she hasn't moved."

"Get outside."

With one swift motion, he eased me out of the way and began to examine her. Before I was outside the cafeteria doors, I heard him radio: *broken neck, no pulse.*

As I re-emerged into the night air, fire engine #62 had arrived, a boxy and massive red whale, alongside another truck.

Riveaux came into focus. Her head and body were out of sync, wobbling in different directions, like a bobblehead doll.

Sirens wailed. My heart hammered, a metronome set to an impossible tempo. "Riveaux!" I called.

She jogged past me, sweating through her short-sleeved button-down top, and disappeared in the cafeteria.

"Riveaux," I repeated as she vanished into the smoke.

When she returned outside a minute later, she was cursing into her radio.

People clustered in the street, as they had on Sunday night to watch flames devour the east wing like hell itself raining down. A javelin of smoke fired through the cafeteria window. What were they hoping to see, another grotesque show? Frantic parents arrived to pick up their kids from the dance. Someone had kicked over two prayer candles from Jack's memorial shrine, shattering glass.

Detective Grogan and Sergeant Decker appeared, charging into the cafeteria where firefighters were taming the flames.

In the courtyard, Riveaux's neck and chin dripped with sweat. She smelled like an ashtray and orange rinds puckering in the sun. She pushed her metal-framed glasses up her nose. As she walked back toward the cafeteria door, I followed.

"Stay outside!" Her decibel was loud, but her voice was brittle, precarious. "Déjà vu all over again. Why do I keep running into you at crime scenes? Where were you, question mark."

"Walked back to campus with Sister T. Ten minutes ago."

"See anyone else in the vicinity, question mark."

"Bernard warned us from the cafeteria—"

"He was inside?" Riveaux interrupted.

"Yes! He was yelling 'fire!' as the students were arriving."

"Those freaky deaky kids?" She pointed at antlered Ryan Brown.

"We were all in the courtyard when the alarm went off. The ball was supposed to start about now."

"Oh, good, a party." Riveaux ran into the cafeteria robotically, minimal articulation in her arms and legs. She seemed exhausted or fed up. Or both.

When I turned around, Sisters Honor and Augustine appeared.

"She's gone, isn't she?" I asked angrily. "Sister T?"

Sister Augustine's hands pressed tightly together in prayer. "The officers said the EMTs did all they could," she said, her eyes pained, streaked with red veins. She had been crying.

Standing with Sisters Augustine and Honor felt awful. Empty.

Our Order out of order.

Sister Augustine was our Mother Superior, our rock, but Sister T was the lightness that lifted us. The little sparks of reassurance I needed to keep going. The ripe figs she left on my desk. The tiny oblations she left for God at the altar, and notes of affirmation she wrote on my chalkboard, sometimes in haiku form. The hands that taught me how to bless milk.

Sister Honor shook her head. "Our Father, who art in heaven." Tears rolled down her cheeks. She was so unmoored she couldn't even pile the blame on me. "Forgive us our trespasses," she continued through her tears and thick snot, "as we forgive those who trespass against us; and lead us not into temptation but deliver us from evil."

I refrained from joining in the prayer. I rarely said the Our Father. Though I loved its cadence, I begged only Mary—only women—for forgiveness.

Fifteen minutes later, the cafeteria fire was extinguished, but brown smoke continued to seep through the windows and doors. Riveaux stalked to the cafeteria entrance, traded words with a firefighter, and then waved me over. I walked away from Sisters Augustine and Honor who were deep in prayer. Sister Honor had her hands on her knees, her tunic taut over her hunched frame. I imagined raising my generic black shoe just high enough to kick her in the ass and watch her topple. Then I quickly prayed to excise the thought from my brain.

"Kerosene was the starter." Riveaux looked left and then right and dropped her voice lower. "Ignited a giant sheath of napkins on the pantry counter."

"I need to see."

"Nice try, Sister. No dice."

"What's it like in there?" I asked, desperate to get inside.

"Surface burns only. Counter scorched. One burnt appliance, the toaster."

"Smells bad from here."

"The team will deodorize the building with an ozone treatment." She removed her glasses, rubbed her wet temples. "If the fire had been set near one of those deep fryers, with all that grease, the whole room would have lit up. This was restrained. Contained. Somebody's making a statement."

"Saying 'catch me if you can'?"

"Arrogant. The cafeteria will be habitable in a week, but we've got a firebug here. We gotta close the school down."

"Why? You said it was a minor fire."

"Low central location let the smoke spread to the other wings. Gotta treat the air in the whole school. It's a safety issue. And the students need somewhere to eat."

"They can eat outside."

"In this heat?" She tipped her head. "You're not setting these fires, are you?"

"*Me?* I'm the only one looking for clues."

Riveaux scoffed. "Or covering your tracks."

Bernard came into view with a large bandage on his forehead.

"Bernard!" I shouted. "What did you see down there? Hear anything? Spot anyone?"

"No. Nothing. Nobody. I was bringing the mop in when I smelled smoke."

Riveaux put her hands on my shoulders like a coach during a pep talk and faced me toward the convent. "Go home, Sister. Leave this to the pros."

"But I have information for you."

"What info?"

"I found a black blouse with a burnt sleeve yesterday morning."

"Where is it?"

"In my classroom. My desk—bottom left drawer. And one of mine is missing." I pulled out my red guitar pick. "And this was near Sister T's body. Someone is trying to frame me."

"You took evidence from the scene? *Twice?*" She scowled as she grabbed the pick with a tissue and dropped it into a plastic bag. She shut it tight and placed the evidence bag into another bag.

"I'm giving it to you."

"You can't—" Riveaux stopped mid-sentence. "Go home. Leave this to us. I will log the pick and get the blouse. We will examine them both for DNA, if you haven't already compromised them."

"Gloves." I lifted my hands, but Riveaux wasn't swayed. Seeing my guitar pick in her evidence bag was like getting tased. My stomach dropped. "Somebody's trying to pin this on me."

"Who?"

"Sister Honor? Rosemary Flynn? Prince Dempsey? I don't know, but I'm going to find out."

"Maybe it's your friend Bernard." Riveaux's violet eyes held gentle movement, like lake water at dusk.

"He was yelling about the fire. What king of arson calls himself out mid-arson?"

"People have reasons for everything."

"Bernard's alibi is tight," I said, "for Sunday's fire."

Riveaux interrupted me. "You already might have compromised key pieces of evidence. Stay in your lane, Sister." She hopped into her shitty truck and sped off.

She had said, *Leave this to us*, but Jack was dead. Sister T too. Both maybe murdered. Whoever was pulling the levers of terror was just getting started. Bernard was as charming as a cult leader but he was harmless. I saw the red fear on his face as he warned us to stay away from the cafeteria. Too emotional, not a stitch of hard dogma in him. Flying heart-first through the world. A bit lonely, a misfit. Walking around holding a key, waiting for it to click. Like all of us.

I walked into church and slumped into the pew, buried my face in my open hands, and wept. The kneeler bounced hard when I kicked it. Tears like a hydrant as I prayed for Sister T and Jack. For myself. Devoting my life to a God who would let this happen. Let it keep happening. Fuck this.

Hidden in the storm, you answered me in thunder. Psalm 81.

Was God the voice in the thunder and the storm itself?

Light and dark are opposite pillars that flank the gate to redemption.

You reach resolution as you pass through, restoring the order. Like cracking a case.

You have to step up, step outside yourself. But I was letting people down, even in my new life, as I had before. I sabotaged my family, my band, my relationship with Nina, and myself, bringing us to the brink of something extraordinary only to throw it away.

We were going somewhere, the band. Nina, Hannah, me, and Smiles—our lead singer earned her nickname because she never smiled. The four women of Original Sin. I chose our band name. I wrote the songs and liner notes. Smiles nailed the tough, sexy frontwoman persona and helped me land the lead guitar theater. We tore our vocal chords. We broke our bodies performing, opening for far inferior bands for the stage practice. One venue more putrescent than the next. Needles and dime bags on the gummed-up ground. Plastic cups underfoot. Paper ghosts of flyers crawling the walls.

"Holiday Walsh on lead guitar!" Smiles allowed for the subtlest of smirks whenever she introduced me on stage, which was usually in the corner of a dank dive bar.

In the sisterhood of the band, in the depraved ecstasy of our live shows, I felt a sense of belonging I had never felt before.

Maybe that's why I torpedoed it.

After a winter show at Brick, we came back into our bodies in the green room, vomit-green but scarcely a room, and it smelled like a sewer.

Nina took a breath after chugging a bottle of water. "Why is Hannah sitting on the sound guy's lap?"

"She's high out of her goddamn mind." Smiles frowned.

"You didn't." Nina looked at me with disdain flooding her mismatched eyes.

I plucked my earplugs out. Sweat rolled into my ear canals. "Just a whisper." I had given Hannah a bump of coke. "I'm not Hannah's mother. She can do what she wants."

"Holiday, yer killing me." Nina flicked her lit cigarette at me, and I ducked.

I had to focus on Smiles's unsmiling face to stop glitching. I was tweaking too. Had been hitting it hard for weeks. Months. Drugs numbed me just enough to quiet my churning brain.

"Sisters, stop figh—" Hannah was too high to finish her sentence. The sound guy, Robbie, readjusted her elegant body on his lap and sat upright, proudly, like a predatory Santa Claus.

Robbie and the other sound engineers of Brooklyn—a suspicious species of skinny-jeans-wearers—called her "Make-out Hannah," but she wouldn't touch any of them. Except that night, Hannah was as high and shaky as an old satellite, running her long pink and white French-tipped nails through Robbie's greasy hair. "Don't you *love* his hair," Hannah said, her eyes darting around the filthy room. "He looks like Jesus!" Cigarette burns pocked Robbie's flannel shirt.

"Um, no." I made a sign of the cross. "Dude looks nothing like Jesus."

"How do you know what Jesus looked like?" Nina spoke airily as she reapplied the eyeliner she had sweat off during the set. "If Jesus even existed. Listen to yourself, Hols, demagoguing Jesus. Christianity is a cult."

"Jesus was a *real* person." I was dry-mouthed from scream-singing and chain-smoking all night. "Jesus was a beautiful and gentle soul with long locks and big dreams who moved to the big city with big plans, like Patti Smith."

"What if Jesus and the saints were, like, actually aliens from outer space?" Robbie's eyes were barely open. "I mean, in all the pictures, angels are coming down on tractor beams. That's some dope alien shit."

I stubbed out my cigarette on the doorframe. "Religion is like art, we all get to make our own interpretations."

"Um, hi Ten Commandments," Nina shot back. "Ten laws for how to live, what to do, how to think. Not much room for interpretation there. Hello, Joan of Arc, burned at the stake. Welcome to the party, fiery KKK crosses. Hey, Westboro Baptist Church. Religion is evil. I cannot believe we are having this conversation *again*."

I wouldn't let it go. "A cross is a symbol. It wasn't *designed* to be burned. It's the freaks who warp religion and mutilate it for their own selfish—"

Smiles interrupted me. "We get it, we get it. You are a devout disaster, Holiday Walsh, but I love you anyway. Don't—DO NOT—be late tomorrow. Swear to God?"

"I promise."

"Repeat after me, 'I will not be late tomorrow.'"

I whispered: "I will not be late tomorrow."

"Good." Smiles kissed me on my sweaty cheek. "HANNAH." She yelled in Hannah's direction, but Hannah was on another

planet. "Get Hannah home safely. Get her home soon, *alone*"—
she mouthed—"We're not going to get a second chance from
Johnny."

The next day, we were supposed to meet at Johnny Love's
studio to record our first full-length record, *Red Delicious*.
Slaughter and salvation and queerness in the lyrics of every
song. I always felt that being queer was inherently punk rock.
You figure out your queerness as you live it. Same with punk.
And religious epiphanies.

"Don't be late," Nina echoed as she packed up her gear. "I
will carry you there myself if I have to."

"Whatever it takes to end up in your arms." I grinned.

"You're impossible." Nina threw a cigarette over her shoulder as she walked out, and I watched it land with purpose on
the concrete floor.

Typical Original Sin. Performed well on stage and nearly fell
apart backstage. Duct-taping instrument cases along with our
sanity and relationships. But we had a chance to break through
with this record.

Instead of packing up, getting Hannah sorted, and taking the
train home, I proceeded to spend the next eight hours in Brick's
green room, licking and snorting drugs off the tips of keys and
drinking Wild Turkey with Hannah and greasy Jesus.

"Blink," I instructed Hannah.

Hannah blinked. "Okay."

"Blinking is weird when you really think about it. It's
harder than breathing." I drank a half bottle of water in one
gulp. My knees bounced. Couldn't sit still. The coke was rac-
ing through me.

"Nothing is easier than breathing," said Robbie.

Lying is easier than breathing, I thought. I lied so easily. So often. Deceit was easier, safer, than sharing my own feelings and thoughts. Lying kept me afloat. The coke helped too.

It was past dawn at that point. None of us had slept. Robbie went out, somehow able to walk and talk. He returned with two bags—bagels and coffee.

I sank my teeth into an everything bagel. Food is transcendent when one is delirious.

Hannah bit into her fresh bagel. "It's so soft, like eating a baby."

"When was the last time you ate a baby?" Robbie asked.

"Don't we have to be at the studio soon?" Hannah looked worried.

"No," I lied. "That's tomorrow."

We didn't show up to record at 10 a.m. We didn't show up at all.

Was I afraid of success, or just accustomed to disappointing?

At 1 p.m. I checked my phone. Nina's quivering voice radiated through my voicemail. Through tears, she screamed, "You blew our one shot. I'm sorry I ever believed you'd change." Her words punctured the air like rusty nails, my body flinching as each one pierced.

"Forgive me," I said to myself, but I didn't call her back for weeks, instead letting the distance stretch itself out.

I said one more prayer for Sister T. The church was empty when I looked up. Just the faces in the glass, dulled by the night. Watched but alone. My destiny. A lone wolf stalking the dark.

10

THE SCHOOL WAS CLOSED for a week as crews cleaned the cafeteria and detoxified the air. Riveaux said she had fetched the burnt blouse from my desk and logged it and the guitar pick into evidence.

The week was misery. Feverish. Nabbing two or three hours of sleep a night as I turned over the events, the clues, the suspects. Surveillance was tightened. I couldn't weasel my way into the east or west wings, couldn't access my desk or my notes on the case. The Diocese, practically camped out, were breathing down our necks, bossing us around. They didn't want us to think for ourselves. Or they didn't think we were capable, like they were saving us with their divine needs, the way men have always sold women short.

Near the teeming flowers and twisted wrought iron of the courtyard gate, Sister Augustine prayed every morning. Jeremiah 17:14: "Heal me, O Lord, and I will be healed; save me and I will be saved, for you are the one I praise." Sister Augustine raised her arms high each day.

A CRIME WATCH poster was taped to the telephone pole on Prytania Street. Neighbors were scared. Parents worried. Two deaths and no arrests. I was a wreck, anxiety mixing with adrenaline—a diabolical cocktail I couldn't stop pounding.

With no classes, I could have laid low, prayed and played music in the convent, but I dashed out every morning, poking around until a police officer grumbled and asked me to "stay safe," which meant get the hell away.

Like a chickadee dive-bombing the top hawk, I tailed and harassed Sister Augustine until she finally gave her blessing and streetcar fare to visit Jamie, who was in the hospital. Lamont had already been released, but I'd track him down when classes resumed.

Sister T was gone. Jack, gone. I felt ashamed for suspecting either of them, even for one second. But betrayal and guilt were well-worn paths in the junkyard of my brain. So much time wasted. I needed answers.

On Tuesday, before I could hit up the hospital, I had my weekly shift at the Prison Birth Center. I made the solo trudge with my guitar, and CO Janelle almost gave me a hug but stopped herself. She must have heard about Sister T. Despite the metal detectors, mold, and byzantine brutality—no babies, nothing soft, only hard fluorescent lights indicating night and day—it was a strange tonic to be there. I could feel Sister T's spirit everywhere I turned.

"When's her funeral?" Renee asked about Sister T, blinking her big eyes.

"They're still investigating her death." I shook my head. "Eventually, her service will be in Idaho. That's where her family is. She'll be interred in New Orleans."

"Sister Therese was family to me," said Yasmine.

"Me too." Linda hacked a wet smoker's cough, bringing her pale hand to her mouth.

"She looked like my Grammie April." Peggy offered a rare comment.

Renee said nothing. Sister T helped comfort her during her early delivery. Helped her bring two new lives into the world, kept her together after her sons were torn away.

"I am blessed to have known her," I said, holding Renee's strong hands in my small, gloved grip.

How I appreciated Mel's easy smile. Yasmine's shaved head. Peggy's long red hair. Renee's chewed cuticles. Linda's curly blond locks. I saw myself in them too.

We all had tattoos, scars, secrets, and losses. We all wanted to be forgiven.

I left the prison with my guitar in tow, off to see Jamie. Rosemary Flynn, John Vander Kitt, and I had planned to visit the hospital together. A show of school solidarity in their minds. But to me, an opportunity to grill Jamie about what he saw the night of the first fire.

As I dug in my guitar case for the coins Sister Augustine had given me, I noticed Rosemary's ruler. I didn't remember borrowing it, but there it was, with her name labeled in her meticulous cursive on the back. The intrigue and shock of the strange find made my heart dance grotesquely in my chest. I jostled five quarters for the streetcar in the cup of my hand. The delicate weight and music of coins, metal on metal, shape in a shapeless world.

An on-time arrival, a rarity. Taking two entry steps in one climb, I boarded, dropping the money into the fare box.

The car was crowded with people. On every ride, I tried to decipher one clue about each passenger—their neighborhood of residence or job. A little sleuthing game to keep me occupied.

To my right was a sousaphone player, probably on the way to a gig in the Quarter. Two students traded gossip. I figured they were Tulane law students. After a group of tourists exited the trolley, one seat opened up near the window, and I snatched it.

Wearing my Order-issued black trousers, black blouse, black scarf tied in a knot at my throat, and my requisite black gloves, I wondered if, to any untrained eyes, I looked like a catering waitress, not a Sister on the edge of permanent vows.

The wooden seat buckled as we rolled toward New Orleans City Hospital. I liked the bass rumble of the trolley on its electric tracks. Every set of train tracks was an equals sign.

Three police cars passed us. The frequency of patrols was increasing, and so was the tension around the city.

On Canal Street, I exited, alighting on the southbound corner. The rust-red sun was still powerful as I walked the few blocks to the hospital. Phlox bowed in the wind. No power lines above. Cables and wires here are buried underground due to hurricanes and tearing gales. Everything in New Orleans is overdue, overgrown, dripping. The oak trees decked with boas of Spanish moss. Frogs creaked and peeped until the moon set. Morning glory vines strangled pink roofs and wisteria tentacles swayed in the cross breeze. A row of traditional, one-level shotgun homes: bright orange window frames, mint-green wooden shutters, and bright white columns. A cat meowed on a nearby porch.

Across the street, two familiar faces stared at me. Prince Dempsey and BonTon. I walked closer. BonTon's white fur seemed shinier. Her ears, two triangle flops. I've seen countless pit bulls with their ears maimed. People cut them because a pit bull's natural floppy ears make them look adorable. Killers can't be cute. It was telling that Prince hadn't cropped Bon-Ton's ears.

"You're following me?" I asked. "Need mentorship or after-noon prayer?"

Prince flicked his cigarette, only half smoked, into the street. BonTon exhaled through her big pink nose. "*You're* following *me*," he said.

"What are you doing across town?"

"Me and my girl are out for a walk."

"Making a run for it?"

He laughed. "Just enjoying the bonus vacay, a lil' fire break fun in the sun."

"Two people are dead. I wouldn't run my mouth if I were you unless you've got something to confess. Do you?"

"The cops and y'all have me on a tighter leash than my girl here. But ya back a dog into a corner and it's gonna bite."

"You're threatening me?" I rested my guitar case on the ground.

"Chill, Sis. Chill. I'm not starting shit. No criminal activity here, except your sorry excuse for a dye job."

"You're the one with a rap sheet."

He stretched his arms to the side, mimicking, mocking the crucifixion. "I'm a fucking saint."

"Oh, really? Sorry I missed your canonization." I couldn't look at him. "Tell me what you know about the fires, about Jack and Sister T?"

"What's in it for me?"

"Saintly cred."

"Hard pass," he said. "I've got plenty."

"Tell me, Prince!"

"Give me an incentive," he inhaled, "and maybe I'll think about it." Prince's eyes were as cloudy blue as curacao, his expression just as bitter.

He knew something.

Maybe Sister Honor was right. I thought of Sister T's body, a crinkled wreck on the floor. Jack's fiery freefall. Jamie's blood and Lamont's anguish. I steadied myself. "Tell me now, you little shit."

"Sister, you're hilarious when you're all amped up, but we got places to be," he said. Before he turned to walk up the street, he snipped, "The school's running low on nuns. Don't forget to stop, drop, and roll."

Careful that no one was watching, I shoved him hard in the back, so hard he cracked his head on a fence and fell. BonTon went berserk.

Prince turned around to face me, his eyes raging. I reached into the side pocket of my case and grabbed Rosemary's ruler.

Crack.

I lashed his knees with it. With all my force. *Hail Mary.*

"Fuck!" Prince howled and BonTon howled too. "You fucked up now. Beating up a student. A kid!" He wiped blood from his forehead. "What's that? A tire iron?"

"It's just a ruler."

"You're gonna lose your job!"

"You're eighteen, technically an adult. And I didn't beat you up."

"I'm a disabled teen." He held up his diabetes monitor with his scrawny arm.

"No witnesses."

"I'll show them my knees," he said.

"I'll say you're making it up, that you fell skateboarding. Next time, maybe you'll fucking listen to me. This isn't a game. Two people are dead and you're hiding something."

He put his bloody finger in his mouth and flinched. Maybe the copper scream of his own blood surprised him. "You're done," he said.

"Bring it." I smiled, doubling down. But I knew I had crossed a line.

Again.

Something had dislodged inside me. Pushing Prince Dempsey, knowing I could hurt him, break him even—it was exquisite. And horrible.

He spat on the dusty, cracked sidewalk, muttered "bitch" to himself, then resumed whistling as he and BonTon turned right off Canal Street.

I pivoted and walked down Saint Charles toward the New Orleans City Hospital, sun like a lit wick overhead.

God, forgive me, but I was *good* at fighting.

Even better back then. Before I opened myself to the light.

We had finished our first set. Feeling great, buzzed on whiskey but fully pinned to the moment. Playing an electric guitar isn't as much about taming an instrument as it is about riding a tsunami. A sonic palette—pushing and pulling. Thrashing power chords. Distortion, dissonance. Kinetic prayer.

Nina walked over to me, a Wild Turkey in each hand. "That dickbag at the bar grabbed my ass," she said, disgusted. "I feel a thousand percent queerer. Guys are gross."

"That guy did what?"

The whiskey went down in one gulp.

I screamed, "Who the fuck grabbed her?" and pointed at Nina.

"Don't avenge me, Holiday," Nina begged, "I'm not your damsel in distress."

But someone needed to pay. I bounded over to the bar where a tall guy in a jacket declaring him a Varsity Linebacker in red thread was looking down, laughing heartily. I poked him in his thick chest. "You fucker."

"Fuck 'er? I hardly know 'er." He erupted in laughter with his buddy who had the squat stature and good looks of a busted gargoyle. Linebacker was so tall I had to jump and punch simultaneously for the element of surprise. But I made contact. My anger flared through me, escaping from my fist as I punched his chin. With a rapid blink he touched his face. Then he pushed me with all his force into the wall.

"Fuck." The back of my head had cracked against the brick. I saw triple.

"This bitch is gunning for Jones," cackled the gargoyle.

It was futile to fight with a guy made of titanium. He was a foot taller and at least a hundred pounds heavier than me. Like everything else, though, I didn't think it through. I was dizzy with revenge and probably concussed. This predator in his starched shirt, expensive shoes, and football jacket needed to get put down. And God had my back. A dyke David to the patriarchy of Goliath.

I pivoted to the left, grabbed a full glass of beer from the edge of the bar, and threw it in his face, drenching his ridiculous jacket. His phone dropped at my feet—I picked it up and plopped it into an unsuspecting woman's vodka cranberry on ice. "Looks like you'll need an upgrade," I said, "and fuck off while you're at it."

He scrambled to fish his phone from the cocktail, spilling half of it on the bar. "Dragon bitch."

As quickly as the beer was thrown and the phone destroyed, I felt my body fly again. From behind this time. I was being carried outside of the filthy bar by a police officer whose bulletproof vest was hard against my back. His dark blue jacket sleeves carried the cedarwood cologne of winter air. I didn't kick or fight. Being carried was a relief.

"Nice and quiet," the officer said as we headed outside. "That's it. You're done."

On the curb, the racket from the bar faded as the officer placed me on my feet silently. Standing next to him was his partner, Officer Keating, a marginally attractive blond woman. I had noticed her more than once on my visits to see my father, the chief of Brooklyn's thirty-ninth precinct.

"No fucking way," Officer Keating said in an incredulous tone as she scanned my ID. "Angelero, check this out. This is Holiday. Walsh's *daughter.*"

"Do you have any idea what you're doing to your old man?" Officer Keating said. "Chief Walsh is a good guy. And you're killing him."

"At least I'm consistent."

"Consistently full of shit." Officer Angelero's gaze was an uppercut.

A small crowd had inched out of the bar, some with coats but most without, to watch the unfolding drama.

"Walsh's kid," Keating said. "It doesn't make sense. What a waste."

"Maybe the missus was screwing the milkman." Angelero smiled.

"More like the garbage man," Keating quipped.

If I had kept my mouth shut, the encounter would have fizzled out from there.

Instead, I spat in Keating's right eye. She wiped her eye with her whole hand, like a clown who just got faced with a cream pie.

Angelero spun me around to face the police car, slapping handcuffs on me. I bucked, trying to slip out of his hold, and smashed the right side of my face against the car roof. The crack of my head against their cruiser was so loud even the bar revelers went quiet. The ground quaked under my stiletto boots. Angelero pulled my hands tighter behind my back. My shoulders felt like they were going to snap.

Officer Keating grabbed a fistful of my hair and smashed my face into the roof again. "Take it easy," she said. Then she did it again. *Bam.* Fireworks behind my eyes. "Easy. Don't resist."

"Stop! She's not resisting!" Nina yelled, and I could almost feel the fire in her voice. She stubbed her cigarette and filmed the scuffle with her phone. "I'm calling Legal Aid. Everybody, look. Gay bashing!"

The police turned me around to face them and the crowd.

"Call the cops," said an onlooker whose words were glued together with sludgy drunkenness.

"Fuckhead, those *are* the cops," someone replied, frustrated.

I was faint, half there, but I could tell people were capturing the escapade with their phones. Nina continued chanting, "Gay bashing!"

Salty heat boiled at the corner of my mouth. When Keating smashed me the last time, I had bitten deep into the front of my tongue. My lip split and a tooth had broken—my upper left canine.

The officers saw my bloody mouth and jumped back.

"She ain't worth it," said Angelero, shaking his head rapidly. "I need a video of me on YouTube like I need a cherry bomb up my ass."

The officers loosened the handcuffs, turned my woozy body around. They returned to their muddy car and sped away before Keating even had her door closed.

Nina ran to me, moved blood-smeared hair out of my eyes. She kissed my cheek and I winced. The crowd thinned. Folks in skinny jeans and animal-print faux-fur coats sauntered away, like nothing had happened.

"Oh, baby," she whispered. "You never know when to stop."

In the balsam of winter air, electrified by mouth pain, we walked toward the subway. My buzz faded as fast as my mouth bled, dripping like a sacrament. *This is my blood,* I prayed, *which is poured out for many for the forgiveness of sins.* Matthew 26:28.

11

I HELD MY BREATH as I entered the hospital. It was my chance to interrogate the kid, to revisit the night of Jack's death, to understand why Jamie and Lamont were inside the school when the fire started.

The sight of white medical coats and stretchers threw me off, shorting my circuitry. I leaned against the cold wall and closed my eyes, panic roiling inside me.

"Hi, Sister Holiday."

I surfaced to see John Vander Kitt, our staid history teacher. He stood near the hospital's information desk, an undulating strip of curved wood with a mosaic stripe. He sipped from his army green thermos. "Ah, and there's Rosemary."

Rosemary Flynn walked toward us. She was stiff and distant with the students—with everyone—so it was odd to see her make an effort to visit Jamie in the hospital.

Maybe she had a hidden agenda too.

We secured visitors' passes and slowly climbed the stairs to the fourth floor, where a nurse's station—a long, counter-high, sterile island—buzzed with activity. Two computer monitors for six nurses. I noticed one waiting for a sheet of paper to emerge from the printer, his hand underneath the tray. The nurses were male and female, tall and short, and of many different races and ages, but they were all united by the same powder-blue scrubs.

The air-conditioning was severe. Rosemary's teeth chattered. For once, I was glad to be wearing gloves.

As we progressed down the hall, John slowly recited numbers—"fourteen, sixteen, eighteen"—until we found Jamie's room, Twenty.

"Mr. LaRose," John said, beaming as he saw Jamie beyond his hospital room door, which was ajar.

We made our way into the room. Close to Jamie's bedside, I focused on him and tried to ignore the wires. Cables spooled around the metal arms of the blinking monitors that tracked his vital signs. A machine beeped with a slow, persistent rhythm.

"Hey, Jamie."

Relief and dread flickered in his eyes as he tried to sit up straight in his bed. The boy who almost bled out in my arms, who needed a skin graft and blood transfusion. My hands slipping around his slashed leg. We were like soldiers who had survived a barrage, crossed a battlefield together. "How are you feeling?" I asked.

"Fine," replied Jamie, "but the Jell-O is gross. Sick of it."

"I'll bet." I sat near the window, on a brown chair brindled where the sun had bleached the fabric. I kept my gaze on Jamie to study his reactions, but in the corner of my eye, I noticed a newspaper on the ground. I grabbed it and saw a first pass at the crossword puzzle; the word *HANOI* was written in blue ink. Who was visiting his room?

With John and Rosemary so close, I had to be strategic about my interrogation. "What is the craziest thing you've seen here?" I asked.

Jamie turned away from me suddenly. "I saw a rabbit on a nurse's head, but I'm, like, trippin' on pain pills."

"No shame in that."

He yawned. "I can't tell what's day and what's night. In intensive care, I did see a guy get wheeled in with a screwdriver in his eye socket."

"He really got screwed."

"Sister!" Rosemary Flynn admonished.

Jamie flashed a covert smile. "They catch who set the fires?"

"No. The cops are incompetent. I'm the only one who seems to find any evidence."

"I'm sure the police are pleased as punch you're on the case," Rosemary needled, allowing some Southern affect to slip through.

"As punch," I echoed. A left hook to the jaw.

John sipped more coffee. "The east wing will be out of commission for two years, at least. Probably needs to be razed." He swiped his hand in a smooth, level arc. "The basement fire didn't do too much damage to the cafeteria, though. If it had hit a fryer, it would have been ..." He trailed off.

How did John know so many of the details Riveaux had shared with me? Was she telling everyone on campus confidential information?

Jamie turned his head toward the window, still avoiding my eyes. "I saw someone else that night. In the school."

"What do you mean?" John stole my question.

"I saw a person," Jamie said, "way down the hallway. I started screaming, so they'd find us, but nobody came except you."

The Holy Ghost. Jamie saw the specter too.

"Have Detective Grogan and Sergeant Decker questioned you?" Rosemary asked, giving the t's extra emphasis.

"One came in a few days ago. Not sure who." With his stubble, in his hospital gown, the cold blue of regret, Jamie LaRose looked at once more like a man than a boy, and frailer than I had ever seen him. I turned from him and walked over to the window. Steam rose from the asphalt of a parking lot, braiding the air into a tessellation.

I read seriousness knitted into Jamie's eyebrows. Something gnawed at him. He wanted to talk but didn't know how. As someone who had cultivated my skills as a secret-keeper when I was closeted, and now, as a practicing Sister, I was attuned to the emotional espionage of others. His eyes drifted to the foam tiles of the hospital ceiling that had a million perforations. No bigger than the black dots on dice. Tiny eyes, always watching.

"Tell me more about the night Jack died. When was the *exact moment* you smelled smoke?"

"It all happened so fast." Jamie's eyes were sincere, but he also looked confused. "I don't remember."

"Has Lamont been by?"

Jamie muttered, "He's with his family, I guess."

I dropped my voice. "Jamie, you can trust me. Is there something you need to tell us?"

He nodded.

Finally, we're getting somewhere.

He bit his lip. "I wanted to say thank you, Sister, for coming in like that and saving us. What you did was really dope."

"'Dope' means good," I translated for Rosemary.

She sighed, trying hard to fight either amusement or annoyance.

John left the room to get coffee. He had already drained his thermos. Rosemary soon joined him, probably to take a hiatus from me.

I leaned close to Jamie and whispered, "Hey, I think you and Lamont saw something that night. And it's totally okay."

"I don't know what you mean."

"Did you see Jack before he fell? Do you think Jack set the fire?"

He whispered. "My head hurts so much."

"What were you and Lamont doing there in the first place?"

"Talking makes my head hurt," Jamie said with his eyes closed.

"You can tell me anything." I tried to hold Jamie's right hand in my gloved hands, but he pulled away and crossed his arms. People contract when they have something to hide. The body shrinks away, tries to disappear. "I can tell you want to share something but aren't sure how. Let me help you."

"Visiting hours are over. He needs his rest," said a nurse who had marched into Jamie's room with a clipboard and paper cup filled with water. Her white sneakers squeaked as she strode about the inhospitable hospital room. "Farewell and thank you," the nurse said flatly as she scribbled quick notes on her clipboard. To Jamie, she asked, "How's our favorite patient?" But he didn't answer. His eyes were closed as if he had fallen asleep, but I knew he was faking.

■

Absence notes flowed in on Wednesday, the day classes resumed. Four students had already transferred to Saint Anne's, according to Shelly Thibodaux, the receptionist, a terminally joyful pinprick of a woman whose double-fudge brownies had been secretly lusted after by Sister T.

A police officer was stationed inside the school, but parents were terrified. Morale was low, anxiety high. Spirits were fracturing. Classes were thinning out, but daily Mass had never been so full. Father Reese added two new services to the weekly schedule to accommodate the crowds.

That morning, I sat on the church steps in the gauzy heat. The candlelit sidewalk shrine had expanded. Every day there were new candles, flowers, notes, or prayer cards for Jack and Sister T. Sister Augustine often stood silently in her office window staring out at the luminous display. Grief never goes away fully, but if it can be shared, it can be managed.

Parents showed up before classes began, holding hands, praying.

"We need assurances that our kids are safe." Ryan Brown's mother stabbed the air with her finger as she yelled.

With classes in session, the police were back. Investigator Riveaux, Detective Grogan, and Sergeant Decker stood nearby, talking quietly near a police car. They were discussing the two fires—their similarities, their differences. They didn't seem to have a clue besides the ones I'd given them. I watched Grogan's big eyes pan the school. The unblinking stare of an owl. I moved closer. Didn't need to hide myself as I eavesdropped.

New Orleans was no stranger to crime. Not by a long shot. But arson was relatively rare. "Fewer than fifty arson cases last year," Riveaux told Decker. Most of them car fires, dumpster fires, tire fires, and the occasional empty house. But Saint Sebastian's had two fires and two deaths. Notable on its own, but also potentially the start of a pattern.

SCORCHED GRACE ■ 137

"How far along in the interviews are we?" Grogan asked. "How many statements?"

"Halfway done," Decker said. "A hundred and thirty or so."

"*Half*?" Grogan was displeased. "More than a week on, and only half? Come on. Pedal to the metal."

Grogan and Decker were partners, yet Decker carried the logistical load. Typical.

"School was closed," Decker said. "Parents don't want to bring kids back here or down to the station. They're spooked."

"Apply pressure and get it done, Decker." Grogan spat tobacco juice on the ground.

Riveaux turned and noticed me standing there. "Were you here the whole time, question mark," she asked in her puzzling way.

"Yes."

She eyed me up and down, wiped sweat away from her forehead. "What do you want?"

"I want to know who did this. What *do* you know?"

"What do *you* know?" Riveaux mimicked me with an edge in her voice. "Sister Goldsmobile, Private Eye."

Sergeant Decker and Detective Grogan finished their conversation and faced me. Grogan's tall, lean build and Decker's round frame made them look like the number 10 when they stood side by side. Grogan wiped sweat from the bridge of his nose.

"I think Prince Dempsey knows something," I shared, holding the close attention of Decker, Grogan, and Riveaux.

"We've questioned him." Grogan lowered his muscular body, so our heads were on the same level. "He is still a person of interest."

"Check his alibi for the second fire."

"Same as the first," said Grogan, "the dog-walking routine."

I kicked gravel. "Prince certainly could have seen something. Or done something. He's playing games, I'm just not sure of the playbook. But he doesn't fit the typical arson-murder profile."

"'Profile,' eh." Grogan chuckled. "You're in over your head."

"All you're doing is standing around. Someone has to take action."

Decker cleared her throat. "The typical perp would be making a lot of noise and pointing the finger. A master of misdirection. Usually a misanthrope with an axe to grind and—"

"Say what you really mean." I cut into Decker's passive-aggressive soliloquy. "If you think I did it, say so."

Decker laughed with no hint of joy in her voice. She and Grogan plodded away in the direction of an officer who waved from a parked police car on Prytania Street.

"Those two are maniacs," Riveaux said, "but Homicide will crack it." With her hands on her lower back, she said, "Grogan and Decker have their doubts, but I trust you."

"Can I trust *you*?"

"If you help me," she said, "I will help you. Tag along if you want, once or twice. You tell me what you hear and see. I need someone on the inside on campus."

"I'm still an outsider, believe me. Only here a year and haven't taken permanent vows yet."

"You wanna know what I know or not?"·

"Yes," I replied, admiring her candor.

"We've got intentional fires in the school's east wing and cafeteria. We got a black V-shaped pattern on the east wing's second floor, and evidence of flashover in the room Jack fell from. We've got kerosene in the cafeteria. We got a burnt blouse in your trash. A glove in the road. Your guitar pick near that nun's body."

"Sister T. I mean Therese, Sister Therese, a human being, not 'that nun.'"

She shrugged. "You're always very quick at the scene. So, at the moment, a lot of the evidence points to you, Sister."

"But I connected *you* with all the evidence."

"That's why I'm leveling with you."

"What about the student statements?" I asked. "Anything useful?"

"Most were home when the east fire was set, apart from Jamie and Lamont. The kids getting ready for the masquerade ball say they didn't see anything."

"How *exactly* did the fire start in the east wing?"

"A tall match burned down and ignited a bundle of gasoline-soaked fabric. Didn't take more than a minute for the small fire in the corner of the history classroom to spread," Riveaux explained. "The whole second floor—gone. Ductwork let the fire run wild. This job was *clean*. Extremely precise. Someone practiced this—or researched this—very well. And I'm betting it's an insider."

"An insider?" I asked.

"Probably someone you know."

"Prince Dempsey is a circus on wheels. I wouldn't put it past him, but he is too messy to pull this off on his own. He could have had help, but he's a loner, as far I know."

"Faculty?" Riveaux asked.

"Rosemary Flynn is a scientist. A science teacher, at least."

Riveaux perked up. "Mad scientist?"

"Maybe. Thinks of herself as an underappreciated chemistry genius."

"She would understand how fire behaves—the chain reactions." Riveaux jotted a few words in her notebook.

"Rosemary is so straight-laced, though, and hates anything messy."

"This is a clean job," Riveaux reminded me. "Other teachers?"

"John is anxious, ruminates over the tiniest things."

"Interesting." She was taking it all in and scribbling quickly. I could see her mind turning, swiveling a Rubik's Cube of details and clues. "Bernard Pham's alibis checked out. Decker confirmed that his three bandmates vouched for his whereabouts on Sunday night."

"As I said." My brain went fallow for a moment. I was relieved to hear Riveaux confirm this. Despite myself, my showcase of solid-gold screwups and sordid misdeeds, it couldn't be my friend at the heart of our horror.

"You've been here how long?" she asked.

"A year and some change."

"What about your Sisters, Honor and Augustine?"

"They've given their lives to this school, our church, our Order. This is their home. My home too." But anyone would do anything to survive or start over. I was living proof. "Have you been looking into the Diocese? The bishop and the vicars, I mean."

Riveaux nodded. "Taking a torch to their own property, to swoop in and be the heroes."

"Or to keep us all in line," I added.

The fire-department radio came alive with a distant, nasally voice.

Riveaux responded, "I'm on my way. No, stay *there*, damn you."

She sprinted away toward her red truck with the assured speed of a quarter horse, sweat marks along her back. Riveaux was strong but her brain was somewhere else, perhaps two steps ahead. Or somewhere outside of her body.

Again, I felt eyes hanging on me. I detected something crooked lope into view. Prince Dempsey talked to BonTon as they approached the school, a lit cigarette between his teeth. He smiled, strolled casually.

Light coming through the leaves created a lace of shadows as Prince slithered right up to my side. He scratched between BonTon's ears. Then he dangled a rosary over her nose, causing her to nip at it. A game they regularly played, no doubt. Some of the white beads were burnt.

"Nice rosary." I leaned closer to Prince. His stringy hair held a rank funk so potent my eyes watered.

"Sister Augustine gifted it to me," he said. "She's a legit teacher, unlike you." Prince moved close to me and stared at the cross around my neck. "I'm going to get one of them big-ass crucifixes. Christ is saying 'I'm still here, bitches. Can't beat me!'" He spat as he talked. "Yes, Sis. I'm gonna get a big old cross and wear it every day."

"You should. Would be good for you."

Prince smiled and flicked his cigarette into First Street. I flinched as its heat passed my ear. "Close call." He laughed. "Be careful, Sis." He whistled to pearly white BonTon and they snaked through the sidewalk shrine, knocking over a candle. Wax spilled on the curb, into the drain.

I knew Prince's saga. Storm trauma. Family drama. Juvenile diabetes, then Type 1. Foster care. Abuse. Poverty. Blight. If he did something worthy of suspension, we were instructed to be patient and bring him back into the moment. Have him check his blood sugar. Pray. Though he had a temper like a runaway train, Prince Dempsey was a good story for the school. The fundraising committee needed good stories. Expelling him would set a bad example for one of the few Catholic schools left in the city.

Prince had an appetite for chaos, but what about a motive? Did he need one?

People were capable of anything, at any time.

Even Sister Honor, her rigidity and small mind warped by decades of stewing in solitude. She could have struck the match to pull the strings for a change. Turn it all upside down.

I had to check off every suspect, everyone who had access to the east wing, one by one. If I could only clear my head, I'd figure it out.

But I was tripping on my own shadow. Still pissed at God.

A lost soul chasing the Holy Ghost.

12

ON THE DECREPIT TV in the teachers' lounge, John Vander Kitt and I watched the Diocese, Sergeant Decker, and Detective Grogan deliver a pitiful press conference on the investigation into the deaths on campus. It was Wednesday, after the day's dismissal. The Homicide Squad and our church leaders stood in the drab lobby of the busy New Orleans Police Department as photographers clicked away with large cameras.

The unholy trinity hogged the limelight.

"In the name of the Father, the Son, the Holy Spirit," the Don chanted into the mic, so damn pleased with himself, in lust with his star power.

I could smell the bishop's stank breath through the TV screen. With their gold chains and fancy watches, the Don, the Ghoul, and the Beard could have been hitmen. My anger made me woozy, almost giddy. Our "patriarchs" held the Sisters' fate—my fate—in their dumb hands.

"This investigation into the death of Jack Corolla is ongoing," said Grogan, who was now visible after the Diocese stepped to the side. Grogan's accent was extra ropey, his open mouth so close to the microphone, like he was about to French kiss it. For Grogan's cool and collected demeanor, something about the dude unsettled me. "We have an update," he continued. "Sister Therese's death has been ruled an accident. The pathologist's autopsy report indicates no foul play. The longtime teacher and Sister of the Sublime Blood fell down the steps, and the impact of that fall resulted in her death." He ran his hand through his thick hair and stared into the camera. "God bless her," he said, as if he had rehearsed it.

I smashed the off button on the TV's remote and shook my head, sweat soaking through my black blouse. I imagined my Tree of Life tattoo crying from every inky leaf. I closed my eyes and saw Sister T's smiling face and warm eyes, replayed our last few hours together at the prison. Like the enlaced art of spiderwebs, memories could trap and nourish. The act of remembering is a maze.

"There you have it. Sister Therese was not pushed," John said as he nudged his glasses up his nose. "That should make us feel safer. It was a sad accident, not murder."

"She was *thrown* down those steps. I'm telling you. Sister T was nearly eighty but she was one boss bi—" I stopped myself from cursing. "The violence of it. Her shoe was off. Her legs backward and ankles all contorted like a rag doll."

"Shouldn't we trust the cops? They know what they're doing."

Without saying a word, I gathered my papers into my bag and ran outside into the balm, leaving John muttering to himself, sipping his hot coffee in the hot air.

John's bumbling innocence was cloying. Or was it an act?

Someone was trying to frame me.

Or screw with me.

It could be anyone.

I worked so hard to let people into my new life. But when you don't know or trust yourself, how can you give anyone else the benefit of the doubt?

Riveaux's shitted-out pickup truck was parked in front of the school. She was cursing at a stack of paperwork in the driver's seat when I opened the passenger door. Tiny vials spilled out. Too many to count.

"Careful!" she scolded like a ritzy shopkeeper. "Grab those! Save them!"

As I slipped into the stuffy car, I had to move a few bottles of what smelled like palo santo, lemon, and bergamot. There was a pillow in the cab, the half back seat. Had she been sleeping in that sad old truck? Sweat stippled on Riveaux's chin.

"What are these?" I held up a vial the size of an eyedropper.

"I make perfume."

"Fancy."

"Keeps my nose alert. Keeps me at peak performance. Keeps me learning." She pulled a vial from her front jeans pocket and held it up high. "Scented molecules are my specialty."

"All I can smell is smoke."

"What do you want, Sister?" she asked, studying the clear liquid.

"Get me back in there," I said. "The east wing. The cafeteria. To review the scenes."

The car was running, the air-conditioner dial turned on high. But only hot air piped through the vent. Riveaux reeked of cigarettes and citrus deodorant that didn't work. Like rum and the viscous froth of putrefied lemons. Maybe it was one of those homebrewed perfumes knocking about in the truck.

The heat was solid, wet, and thick. A zephyr tousled the treetops, whipping up clouds. Riveaux wiped her cheek with the back of her hand. "You're on a mission."

"Damn right."

I removed my scarf to use it as a sweat rag.

"That hurt?" She pointed to my neck tattoo—my white bird, a fledgling dove.

"So much. That's why I did it."

"A white dove doesn't seem like your style. You're more of a unicorn meets honey badger. A creature that is hard to explain and—"

"Impossible to forget." The truck's sideview mirror caught a glint of my gold tooth as I smiled.

She rolled her eyes. "You can walk with me only if you answer my questions," she said as we exited the truck. She left her keys in the ignition. The old red Chevy was a trash can on wheels, but to leave your keys seemed far too trusting. "Convenient that you were at both fires exactly as they started," Riveaux said.

"I live here and work here. With lots of other people. Including two who have been murdered."

"Keep your trap shut and follow me," she said. "Put these on."

We slipped blue plastic booties over our shoes to prevent disturbing the crime scene. I bent under the yellow police tape in front of the east wing entrance. Riveaux stepped over it. Right leg, then left, holding her lower back as she stepped. She opened the heavy main door with a master key, and I followed her in.

We slowly ascended the stairwell. The air became more poisonous with each step. Through it all, I smelled Riveaux as she walked in front of me, her lemon sherbet scent of decay. Heat had melted the blades of the ceiling fan in the hallway, "the antechamber," as Jack used to call it. He liked using specific words. The blades all pointed down like a wilted sunflower. The bulb had shattered.

We were about the same height, but Riveaux marched with her shoulders lifted, back straight. Some days her body held conviction and precision. Some days it seemed she was slowly dismantling. Consistently inconsistent. Maybe she was just tired from sleeping in her truck. I remembered how my old man wore the invisible scars of police work. Late nights on a cold case. The ticking clock.

The second floor of the east wing was carnage. Every shade of darkness, from charcoal to slate to bird-eye black. To nothing, the color of vacancy. The wall had flaked off in layers.

"This building's old ductwork helped the fire spread." She pointed up to the exposed vent. Then she nodded toward burnt wires dangling from the wall, sickeningly half eaten and half intact, like regurgitated noodles. "Rock would be reading you the riot act for all these code violations."

"Who's Rock?" I asked.

"My judgmental husband. Been riding his last nerve for years."

"No surprise there."

I liked knowing Riveaux had a partner, that she wasn't alone. But it was obvious that the ground was shaky. Maybe that's why she was muddled sometimes, depleted. Trying to keep things together. Riveaux had high walls, as did I. But, like most people who didn't take my shit, she was slowly growing on me.

We walked into the black husk of a history classroom. I reached out to touch the burnt wall. "Don't touch anything!" she chided.

"I'm wearing gloves."

"Observe *without* touching. Grogan and Decker will tar and feather me if you move even a fleck of dust. Believe me, Grogan will know. He notices everything."

"Decker suspects me, I can tell. Look." I pointed to paint strips on the windowsill and floor. "The air-conditioner. The unit was painted in at some point. Must have been moved. And where's the cord? It's not plugged in."

"Huh." Riveaux nodded. "Good catch."

"Nobody would last very long in a classroom without AC."

She inspected the floor, then looked out toward the fire escape. "Maybe this is how the firebug got in. They used the fire escape to get to and from the street. Betcha the cord is out there." Riveaux tightened her ponytail. In the strange light of the burnt wing, everything and nothing felt like a clue.

"Or that's how Jamie and Lamont got in," I said. "Could be a red herring."

She laughed like a six-year-old. "What do you know about red herrings?"

"Served up plenty of them when I was closeted," I explained.

"Closeted?"

"Long story."

"Will have to take a rain check for story hour. Look, the biggest burn pattern is right here." She pointed her bony finger to the wall. "We found remnants of a bundle of fabric soaked in gas." Her expression was half excited, half scared, the naked intensity of a base jumper. She stepped carefully, trying to avoid piles of debris. She readjusted her left bootie, which had started to fall off. "See here? This is where flashover started."

"Flashover?"

"The transition from having a fire in the building to having a building on fire," she said.

The classroom window frames were splintered. Glass shards everywhere, like the building had been bombed. Some light-bulbs had been deformed but didn't shatter. The air inside the charred wing was sweltering.

"How did you know it was arson so fast the night of the east wing fire?"

"Crime scene investigations and forensics have changed fire science, I can tell you that."

Riveaux recited key pyrology milestones, comparing them to breakthroughs in her perfume-making practice. "Proust said smell is the human sense most connected to memory. Like time travel. 'The immense edifice of memory.' Reading that shit made me want to understand science."

"Reading mysteries got me into this mess."

I knelt in a pile of ash and examined the ground.

"This old history room is the point of origin," she said.

That meant more clues were hiding. Maybe something was stashed here before the fire.

I heard Riveaux crack her back. I stood.

"Fire, like everything else, has a story. You have to listen to it. Take your time. Observe." Riveaux was getting elaborate. Her expertise so fluid, like she was born knowing every fact. It was far more interesting than the science diatribes I had to endure from Rosemary Flynn. "The odor of smoke gives you clues. What it sounds like gives you clues. How it moves along the wall, ceiling, or ground. Ask the residue questions. Treat it like it's a person with something to hide. Watch its behavior closely."

"Sounds like a fun date," I said.

"Rock and I are always too busy for date night."

Riveaux was letting her guard down. Maybe she felt she could be herself with me.

"What's Rock's story?" I asked.

"Rockwell has many stories," she said, tilting her head and blinking at the wall like it was a mirror, "and each story has many chapters."

Riveaux turned toward me, held up her phone, and showed me a picture of her husband, Rock, flipping the middle finger, sticking his tongue out.

I held her phone and looked at the photo, surveying the dude who had clearly failed up. Classic bad boy. A tatted-up white guy in a Hawaiian shirt with so much cheap ink he looked like a dive bar bathroom stall. The type of faux-woke white guy who thinks marrying a Black woman exonerates him from any infraction, from having to think or evolve.

I glanced at the scumbag again. "Is he a chef or something, with all those tattoos?"

She laughed without smiling. "Nah. Rock can't boil water. He was a tech with NOPD. That's how we met, he harassed me until I went on a date with him. Now he's one of those traveling IT guys, setting up networks and server farms. Wish he could get paid for all the video games he plays. Such a man child."

"Love is a distraction anyway," I said, returning the phone.

"That why you're a nun?"

"Clarity is an extra benefit."

"Look." She pointed to the corner where fire had devoured the bookcase. "Textbook arson." She chuckled, enamored with herself. "But seriously, what fire takes can tell you as much as what it leaves behind. Get a whiff of that."

"Revolting."

"A particular kind of acrid. Like decaying flesh. Probably from the insulation."

It was so nauseating in there I had to stop myself from gagging. The air had a sickly sweet undertone. It had been more than a week since the fires, but the smoke was still alive. I could still feel that ember in my eye.

Riveaux fidgeted like she was saying too much.

"If there is no question that both fires are arson," I cut her off, "why is the investigation taking so long?"

"More work to do. And there's no clear motive yet," Riveaux said.

I pushed back. "Isn't it your job to figure that out? Plenty of students hate school," I said. "Teachers too."

"Enough to burn it down? Risk arrest? Death?" Riveaux clasped her hands. "Arsonists strike for revenge, control, or money."

"What about boredom?"

"Nah. They'd just troll their target online." Her words cut with sharp edges. "Even if a student was mad about a grade or bullying or whatever, emotions are not motives."

"Emotions are the root of motives. Think of all the school shooters, their manifestos."

"Fire is different," was her annoying reply. "Arson motives are almost always insurance fraud or revenge. Therefore investigations take time and expertise. Therefore you shouldn't even be in here."

"You let me in. I need to make sense of this."

She laughed. "'Sense.' Don't waste your time trying to make any kind of sense."

"Time is the only thing I have."

13

THURSDAY MORNING WAS QUIET. Panicked parents continued to keep their kids home from school. The upside was that my usually rowdy classes were manageable.

After the bell, students clipped their guitar cases shut and slung backpacks over their shoulders. They moved through the door slowly, in a cluster. I eyed each of them carefully, as if one would drop a clue out in the open.

I needed a break in the case.

And just a break.

My teaching-sleuthing double act was hard to keep synced. Constant threat of a trap door opening before the curtain.

"You need fire extinguishers in every room and every stairwell," an officer on patrol that day told Sister Augustine.

The NOPD brass patrolled the campus during school hours to reassure worried parents. They had concluded their locker search during the closure. A tedious process, surely, but I doubted they could be any slower. Besides, the kids were too smart to leave anything incriminating in their lockers.

Rosemary Flynn was discussing an exam grade with a student at the other end of our shared classroom while I collected a tall stack of papers from my desk—my office.

"Ms. Flynn," I yelled, "lock up when you're done."

"Some people dare to say 'please,'" she projected like a thespian.

"Good to know. Lock up when you're done."

I raced out of the classroom into the loud hall, weaving between entranced texting students. Every dent in every locker seemed to shine. Saint Sebastian's was on the scrappy side, no doubt about that. The building was about the same age as Sister Augustine—eighty. Parents were paying for Christ's blessing, not lavish amenities. Funds were tight without the safety net of tax dollars. The Diocese loved toying with us, telling us what funds or programs would be up next on the chopping block. The select families who could pay full tuition kept the lights on, poor kids like Prince Dempsey in attendance, and our cafeteria stocked with frozen pizza and tater tots. But our academics were top-notch—the best in the state—thanks to Sister Augustine's high standards. Rosemary, John, Sister T, even Sister Honor and me, were all excellent teachers, if not crackpots.

Sister Augustine's voice on the intercom announced a faculty assembly at 4 p.m. that Thursday. I resented the interrogations, police presence, canceled classes, student whispers, and meetings with homicide detectives, especially Grogan, whose syrupy kindness was starting to feel out of place. Before the arson rewrote my rhythms, I worked hard to accept my daily patterns as a Sister of the Sublime Blood. Mass, meals, teaching, praying, sleeping. Repeat. It took more than a year, but I grew to appreciate the sameness. Purity of ritual. I wanted it back.

I turned left toward Sister Augustine's office. I needed permission to read Prince's school files.

"Is Sister Augustine in?" I asked Shelly.

"I'm so sorry. You just missed her. As you know, Sister, the Lord's work is never done." Her toothy smile made me anxious.

The phone rang and Shelly sprinted to her desk. "Been ringing off the hook. Parents are all sorts of upset. Pardon me, Sister. 'Saint Sebastian's principal's office, this is Shelly speaking. How might I help this blessed morning?'" She put her hand over the phone receiver and lifted her chin to me, "Sister Holiday, why don't you come back in an hour? She should be back by then."

I nodded, but as Shelly turned from me and riffled through the outgoing mailbox, I backed up and placed my gloved right hand on the doorknob of Sister Augustine's office. I walked in to find not my principal but Investigator Riveaux sitting at the desk.

"I was a miserable failure of a student." She lifted her legs and rested her feet on the desk. Her shoes were scuffed black leather.

"Smart people get bored quickly."

"Right." Her violet eyes perked up. She swiveled away from me to look out the window behind Sister Augustine's desk. "I gotta step outside and talk to Decker. Stay here. Don't go anywhere, Sister Goldsmobile." Riveaux tapped her left canine.

My gold tooth was my calling card, an ever-present reminder of my previous life.

"You're a gorgeous disaster," purred Nina after my tussle with the cops. She reached over the arm of the mocha loveseat that had most likely been there since CC's father opened the pharmacy in 1982. She kissed me softly on my battered left temple.

"What day is it?" I remember touching my sore jaw. Deep, raw pain. So familiar. Sometimes I wondered if I fell in love with it, the steady drumbeat of pain.

"Days are arbitrary," Nina said. "Calendar-makers invented day names to keep us addicted to buying calendars."

"You know everything." I put my hand on her thigh and we kissed. Though it hurt, her mouth on mine also felt good. Her lips tasted like sweet trouble, like whiskey and coke.

"I know that I love you, Holiday Walsh, private eye."

Nina cleared her throat. I knew she was gutted I didn't say it back—that I loved her. I couldn't say the words *because* I loved her. More than flames love to climb walls. More than the dusk loves to dismantle day. I made a dumb joke instead. "Private Dick. That's what old school PIs were called. Short for *private detective*."

Nina played along. "A private dick is what a queer lady keeps in her bedside table."

We both laughed. My concussion and fresh hangover irradiated my skull like the jagged teeth of lightning.

I put my head on her shoulder, breathed in her sandalwood as I kissed her neck. Her skin was soft and warm. "We won, didn't we?"

"We did win," she said. "We're getting more exciting with age. Like a fine wine."

"More like an unpaid parking ticket."

Nina wrapped her hands around mine, her gold manicure, the color of sand on a sun-drenched beach, a strong contrast to my black leather pants and CC's drab sofa.

Though it hurt my face, I smiled at her. Dazzling Nina.

It seemed impossible now that we hadn't been in the same room in over a year.

My pal CC—pharmacist by day, amateur dentist by night—gave me the gold crown. "You're fucking kidding me." He didn't hide his irritation at my presence in his office. His heavy, black-framed glasses covered most of his face.

"Gold tonight, buddy. Then we're square. Promise."

"Follow me."

Riveaux rapped her knuckle on the door as she returned to the office.

"Have something to confess to your Mother Superior? Guilty conscience?"

"Just praying that someone will solve the case this century."

"We're looking at everything and everyone. All students, staff, teachers. What do you know about Rosemary Flynn?"

"Besides her chemistry expertise, matching twinsets, and stick up her ass?" I shrugged. "I'd say watch her."

"You watch her." Riveaux glared at the large crucifix on Sister Augustine's wall. "See what you discover."

I nodded.

Riveaux's radio chimed to life with an address, "14 Renaissance Village," followed by a string of jargon and numbers.

"What's that?" I asked. "What are they saying?"

"Chill!" Riveaux enjoyed directing me. "Copy. 217. Now?"

"Copy that," said the radio voice.

"Over." She raised her eyes from her radio to me. "That's Dempsey's last-known address, a FEMA trailer in a mobile home park in Metairie. Our guys are heading there now. There's a warrant out for Prince's arrest." She jumped up then straightened.

"For the fire?"

"No, no. Vandalism. The cathedral downtown was tagged last month. He somehow managed to crack open two of the oldest tombs in the city and spray-painted the shit out of them."

"If the warrant is live, why hasn't Prince been picked up already?" I followed as she walked outside.

"Just issued. Too much crime, not enough cops."

Riveaux and I jogged to her pickup, the keys still in the ignition. I slipped into the roasting vehicle. "I'm coming with you."

"Like hell you are," Riveaux said, as a trail of sweat rolled from her left eyebrow. She wiggled in her seat again, knocking a perfume vial to the floor. "You do your job, I'll do mine. Amen or whatever. Goodbye."

Riveaux was a pond of sweat behind the wheel.

"You need me," I said. I didn't wait for an answer from Riveaux and fastened the seat belt around my waist, the metal of the buckle lightning hot.

Riveaux laughed heartily, so hard her eyes watered. "You just want to see us take him down."

I wouldn't mind seeing Prince knocked down a rung, I thought. "I want to see how he reacts," I said, "what he gives away. He knows something."

Prince Dempsey was a loner, like me, and a survivor. He knew how to hide and when to get away.

Riveaux turned the key and the truck coughed to life with a loud rev. "Are all Sisters this spiteful?"

"Not spiteful," I said. "Thorough."

"You're never going to leave me the hell alone, will you?"

"No."

The truck's hazy heat made me panic. I readjusted my seatbelt and looked at myself in the flip-down mirror. Any chance

I could get, I stole a moment with the mirror and the stranger on the other side.

She muttered, "I'm going to log this shit as a 'ride-along.' Put in a good word for me upstairs."

"I'll make you a saint if you get on the damn road. Let's go!"

The air-conditioner was on full blast but wasn't producing cold air. It was a wind tunnel of scalding heat like a blow-dryer. A cough tickled the back of my throat. I kept it contained.

Riveaux was driving in the middle of the road. She was bobbing and weaving from lane to hard shoulder. At seventy miles per hour, we joined a cluster of NOPD cars with their sirens blaring. All the other cars had pulled to the side of the road to let us pass.

Five minutes later, as we arrived in Prince's trailer park in Metairie, the motorcade slowed, looking for his unit. The number 14 was barely visible in the weeds that grew so high they curled in front of the doorframe. Finally, the car ahead radioed and the dispatcher confirmed. They'd found the trailer. As we were parking out front, Prince jumped into a car and sped off. The crispy NOPD radio relayed second-by-second details as the deputies attempted to pull him over. Riveaux and I were a few beats behind in the steamy truck. But Prince forced the NOPD into an eleven-mile chase that ended downtown, and we were forced to follow suit. During the drive, I was sure that we were about to die.

Holy Mary, Mother of God. Let the afterlife have central air and hot women.

Each hairpin turn dished out a centrifugal force so strong it pushed me against the passenger door. My seatbelt sliced into my neck. Riveaux slowed, stopped, tailgated, and sped back up abruptly.

"Your driving is a sin. I hate it."

Riveaux shook her head. "Nuns are supposed to be forgiving."

"I'm nuanced." Bile burned the back of my throat. "Dear Lord," I said aloud, "keep me alive long enough to kill Investigator Riveaux for her shit driving, then resurrect us both for Mardi Gras." I kept my eyes closed, trying to push the nausea down.

She wiped sweat from under her sunglasses. "You're the one who begged to join."

The fractal of New Orleans spun as we drove. Crimson gladiolas. Diamond blinks of flax. Dabs of lemon on a canvas of hunter green leaves.

When deputies finally forced Prince's car to the side of Erato Street, Riveaux and I arrived right behind, her siren squealing, the truck wheels searing pavement, scoring the asphalt with rubber tire marks. We were both raining sweat. My fingers pruned inside my leather gloves.

Detective Grogan and Sergeant Decker's cruiser was behind Prince's vehicle. Interesting that the Homicide Squad was there to execute a vandalism warrant.

Grogan exited, rolled up his beige sleeves, and swaggered toward Prince's car. Through a megaphone he barked, "Exit the vehicle now."

Through the open window I saw Prince, shirtless, and Bon-Ton, her fur as white as fake snow. They remained in the car.

"Now the real danger begins," Riveaux said, "trying to extract a guy from his car. A vehicle can be a deadly weapon."

But the situation diffused quickly.

Two NOPD officers dragged him out of the vehicle. An image of the Statue of Liberty giving the thumbs up was tattooed across Prince's back, which was slick with sweat. On his right bicep was a tattoo of a heart with an arrow going through it and *THE STORM* in filigree cursive across it.

Sergeant Decker said, "Prince Dempsey, we are arresting you on an outstanding warrant for felony vandalism of the Eau Bénite Cathedral. You have the right to remain silent," she chanted. "Anything you do say can and"—she lowered an octave—"*will* be used against you in a court of law. You have the right to an attorney. If you cannot afford an attorney, one will be provided for you."

Prince flailed in the gravel and tried to swing a punch as she recited the Miranda warning. "Don't touch my dog," he snarled.

"Don't fight, Prince," I shouted as I crossed the street. "You'll only make it worse."

"Came for the show, huh?" Prince sneered.

"I'm trying to help you," I said, but I was winding him up even more. He tried to kick Sergeant Decker, who easily brought him to his knees.

"Sister, move back behind the police car," Grogan told me. "This is the scene of an arrest."

"Prince, did you have anything to do with the fire?" I was desperate to know one way or another. I searched his sweaty face as I darted toward him.

But there was nothing in his eyes. Nothing but fear. Maybe he was just a messed-up kid. A vandal and irritant, but not a murderer.

Prince spat at me. "If anything happens to BonTon, I will burn you alive." His hands were cuffed behind his back.

An officer reached into the car and led BonTon out onto the side of the road.

"We'll be gentle," the cop said. "Riveaux, call Sharon at Animal Control. Big white pitty."

BonTon's floppy ears were flattened against her head in raw fear. She whimpered and blurted a single *woof* as they dragged Prince off. BonTon was a mountain of muscle, but she was devoted to her human. A softie with a tough exterior.

"BonTon," he screamed, and she barked, her pink nose high in the air. "Don't worry, baby!" Prince turned, his eyes were desperate, furious. "No Animal Control. It will stress her out. My mom will take her. Or Sister Augustine. If you put my dog in a pound, I swear to God, I will gut you."

"The hits keep coming today," the officer mused, still holding BonTon's leash. "Add 'threatening an officer' to the young mister's charge sheet."

"Let him call his damn mother," I said.

Another officer took BonTon's leash and led her into an NOPD truck, where I could hear her squealing.

Across the street, an officer held Prince's phone to his ear as he yelled at his mother. When he finished, he shouted to me, "Hey, Sister Holiday." He kissed the air. "You're a bitch."

Before I could bring more shame to the Order, Riveaux grabbed my elbow. A cop led Prince into the back seat of the NOPD squad car and the vehicle sped off. A truck with Bon-Ton drove in the opposite direction.

"Well, Merry Christmas to me," Decker said. "Good thing Judge Galvez granted us our search warrant because looky, looky."

In Prince's trunk was a red leash and a gray duffel bag fraying at the seam. Inside the cheap bag was a Smith & Wesson M&P 9mm. I knew the make and model because my old man had one.

"Check if he has a gun license," Decker announced into her handset.

Sweat rolled down her wrists, from under her plastic blue gloves, as she carefully pulled objects from the bag to examine them. Besides the gun, they extracted a spent can of red spray paint, a small pocketknife, one pack of cigarettes, three bricks of cash, and an empty can of kerosene.

"That fuel can looks exactly like what we stock in our school shed," I said. "Maybe Prince stole it."

"Common brand." Riveaux wasn't impressed. "Probably in every garage in the parish."

Photographs were snapped and the items in the trunk were logged by a tall NOPD officer who looked young enough to be one of my students. He swallowed loudly.

Riveaux's thin eyebrows pinched together as she stared at the money. "Where's this kid getting that kind of coin?"

"Babysitting and paper routes," I said.

Riveaux stifled a laugh, then spoke in radio code. Though the terms were different in New Orleans, from growing up with a cop for a dad, I worked out that Prince had been arrested on the outstanding vandalism charge, along with the possession of presumably stolen cash and a handgun without a firearms license. On top of that, he had resisted arrest.

Riveaux and I walked over to the other NOPD cruiser where two officers sat sweating in their steaming vehicle. A noxious cloud of body odor wafted out. Riveaux popped her head in the open window of the passenger side and spoke with an NOPD colleague, his skinny face contorted in the reflection of her aviator sunglasses. The officer in the passenger seat was counting the cash from the car.

"I'll trace the serial numbers next," the other cop said.

After two minutes of silence in which I said the Hail Mary ten times in a row, Riveaux finally spoke loud enough for me to hear. "How much we looking at?"

"Six thousand dollars." The officer yawned as he handed the money to his partner. "Riveaux, who's that?" He stepped out of the police car.

"That's *Sister* Holiday," Riveaux said smugly, "from Saint Sebastian's School. One of Prince Dempsey's teachers. She agreed to help ID him."

"No way." The cop guffawed. "HER? A nun?" He pointed at me. "She looks like the gutter dykes I arrest in the Bywater. One tried to cut me with a broken bottle today."

"Maybe the Lord should cut you." I smiled at him.

"You can't say that! You're a damn nun." The cop tripped backward, and I marched to Prince's car, feeling taller, stronger. Hard as an axe handle.

"What happens next?" I asked Riveaux.

"Prince will be booked. The arresting officers will take his details." She looked me up and down. "Want to know what I think?"

"No."

"Some part of you likes the chase."

"I just want to help," I lied.

I loved the chase. Even Riveaux's insane driving. Not just the velocity but the violence of it all. I liked speeding through red lights. Headfirst to the edge. Scraping enough skin to burn not bleed. Sleuthing was impossible sometimes, a doomed quest. It was godly, really. A gorgeous curse. Like a plague of locusts. Like kissing a married woman.

As the forensics photographer fished out his camera lens to capture the scene, I peered into the car for another moment and a whip of jealousy seized me. Years ago, a can of spray paint, a knife, fresh smokes, a handgun, and bricks of cash would have been irresistible. If self-denial brought you closer to God, I craved a little distance.

14

FRIDAY'S MORNING MASS was packed. No empty seats left in the long pews, so parishioners spilled into the aisles. If the Diocese had any shred of decency, they wouldn't displace the congregants. But there they were, front and center. Father Reese devoted his "homily" to facing fear, not letting the fire control us. The Don's puppet. Sister Augustine sang with particular strength, though. Light spilled through the stained glass, abstracting the holy scenes into a projection of vivid color. I thought of my mother in church, the way she belted out hymns, embarrassing Moose but inspiring me. Mom's voice was crap, too nasally, but she sang with such conviction, with her whole self, baring her soul, her essence, flawed and rare as a gemstone born in subterranean fire. I remember being eight years old, wearing my white Communion dress. Frilly disaster, like a giant doily. But sitting next to Mom was magic. We sang together and I felt my core shift. It was the first time I prayed. Really prayed and felt my words connect to God, following Mom's conduit to the Divine. When I prayed that Friday morning, for Prince Dempsey, Jack, Sister T, and even Sister Honor,

I felt Mom again. Things were different. God wanted—needed—me to be here. To keep a wise heart. To solve it.

■

Up, down, I spun across the classroom a dozen times as I showed each student—except absent Prince Dempsey—their problem and its correction so they could improve. Their playing was tentative, guarded, and clumsy, but still a glorious noise. The guitar strings helped bridge my old life and new life.

In our shared classroom, Rosemary Flynn and I avoided small talk.

"Jonah, what's the distance between the Earth and the sun?" Rosemary asked one of her students.

Jonah looked through the window, and I followed his eyes to the neon sun. "Uh, super far."

"We covered this last class." Rosemary bowed her head.

Rosemary was a good teacher but that didn't mean her students were good learners.

"It's an average distance of ninety million miles," I exclaimed from across the classroom. Students on both sides of the room craned their necks in my direction.

"How did you know that?" Rosemary asked.

"You covered it last class. And it's right there," I pointed, "on the poster you pinned up on my wall without asking." Rosemary's solar system poster looked like it was from 1955, vintage but without being cool.

"Indeed," said Rosemary, who, in her tight black-and-white-striped cashmere sweater and white pearls, reminded me of the trust-fund girls I hated back in New York. Her strawberry-blond hair was knotted in an aggressive bun. As I scrutinized the lift of her shoulders—was she curious or annoyed?—I stopped breathing. Like a strong hand had gripped my throat, the base of a thumb on my windpipe. My reaction confused me. I had spent so much time trying to ignore Rosemary Flynn.

Trying to ignore her body.

But our bodies *are* holy and meant to be shared, for a time, at least. Jesus was given to us in the form of a human. During Communion, the wafer transforms into Jesus's body and blood on our tongues. Transubstantiation. Inking my body was also holy. Sure, the needle hurt sometimes. But it should hurt. Salvation required sacrifice. "Pain is temporary," Sister Augustine always said, "but God is everlasting."

Rosemary wrote on the board, chalk scraping with each stroke. *Solar irradiance, watt per square meter (W/m2).* I studied her handwriting to see what it might reveal, besides her grating perfectionism. Handwriting analysis was like a Rorschach test. Low tech, no doubt, but it could tease out personality traits, tendencies, habits, criminality. Rosemary's script was uniform. So controlled. As I watched Rosemary at the chalkboard, writing with tremendous focus, her back astoundingly straight and dangerous as a cast-steel dagger, I grew more suspicious and turned on by the second.

"Warm-up routine." I dropped an easy exercise on my kids to occupy them for ten minutes so I could rewrite my suspect list. I pulled the list from my desk drawer and got to work. Making lists wasn't enough. Rewriting them bore the content into my brain, like reciting a prayer over and over to memorize it, to metabolize it.

I tried to order the names of the suspects from most likely to least likely, but I was stuck. Treading water in a sea of potential culprits. Jamie and Lamont saw or did something, but were staying tight-lipped to protect each other. I'd swear on the Bible. Prince Dempsey was still in custody after the chase. He was galling, a serial offender, and his alibis were unverifiable. It was the teachers and the Diocese with the most to gain from framing me. Sister Augustine fought for my placement, but Sister Honor and Rosemary Flynn would have *loved* to see me shipped back to Brooklyn or doing time in the slammer.

But murder. Who among us would dare cross that uncrossable line?

■

Later that day in the staff lounge, among a storm of papers and cups of half-drunk, cloudy coffee—Sister Honor's special brew tasted like ground-up crickets—teachers were discussing the book of Judith for the Big Read, our campus reading program. Every year a text would be read by the entire school. Then we would gather to discuss its contemporary relevance and debate its interpretations. The Diocese offered Saint Sebastian's a grant for the Big Read, but we chose the title. One of the few outside funding sources we had left.

It was a momentary relief, to hear about something other than the fires.

To me, Judith was the quintessential riot grrrl. It was a deuterocanonical book, but who could deny its feminist legacy. Judith beheaded Holofernes to save her people. A stone-cold badass.

I stood and stretched my arms as John summarized the book for scruffy Bernard, who was kneeling on the carpet repairing the drum in the clunky printer.

John recounted, "As you might have guessed, the story is about Judith, a brave widow."

"Single and ready to mingle." Bernard winked.

I nodded my head. Bernard chuckled and Sister Honor glowered at us.

John continued. "Judith knows the opposing army wants to destroy her hometown, so she leaves with her loyal maidservant. They walk to the camp of Holofernes, the general in charge of the enemy army."

"That takes major balls," Bernard contributed.

"Bernard!" Sister Honor clucked.

"Well, she certainly *is* brave," John improvised, taking some liberties with the story. "They approach Holofernes. He's attracted to Judith. She makes him trust her. Judith is then allowed into his tent one evening, and she feeds him wine. There he is, stewing in bed, in a drunken stupor."

"Been there once or twice myself." Bernard and I again exchanged smiles.

Sister Augustine sat quietly, marking a stack of quizzes. Or filling out paperwork. It was hard to tell from across the lounge. Next to her, Sister Honor squinted at me, observing my every movement with triumphant scorn, as if I was a furry spider trapped behind glass.

"As Holofernes lay there, drunk, wine staining his lips, Judith, with the help of her maid, decapitates him!"

"Call 911," Bernard joked. "Dude's gonna need a Band-Aid. A big one."

"Then Judith takes his severed head back to her fearful countrymen!" John was giddy as he sipped from his thermos. "A trophy."

I exploited the group distraction to investigate the first-aid kit near the coffee filters, a box I often pillaged for aspirin when Ryan Brown or Prince Dempsey made my head throb. Rosemary side-eyed me as I stood and walked across the room. The roll of gauze was missing.

Another reason to believe the culprit was a teacher or the Diocese, though anyone in the building could have taken it.

Another reason to keep searching for answers.

My sleuthing method? Look at everything. Exhausting? Sleep when you're dead.

"Even Prince Dempsey may be inspired to read this text when he learns how graphically violent it is," Rosemary said.

"Like he can actually read," I muttered, causing Bernard to crack up.

"Sister Holiday!" Sister Honor sprayed saliva as she spoke. "How dare you disparage a student!"

"Rosemary Flynn literally just implied that Prince is illiterate."

John wiped sweat from his brow and continued: "The Assyrians, having lost their leader, flee Israel." He raised his voice, almost to a shout. "The town is safe. Judith wins!"

"Does she win?" Rosemary pursed her lips. "She dies alone."

"She was not *alone*." Sister Honor made the sign of the cross. "She was attached to God!"

"Maybe Judith was more interested in spending time with her maidservant, if you know what I mean?" I said, nodding at Bernard, who smiled like a jack-o'-lantern. "Using her feminine wiles to trick Holofernes while the ladies polished off the wine together in bed."

I knew what queers had to do to survive. You have to pass. Suck it up. Suck a dick. Whatever it takes. A means to an end.

"Stop!" Sister Honor charged me, backed me against the wall. "Judith was not a *lesbian*"—she gagged at the word. "Judith was a true believer!" She yapped in my face, her corpse breath stained the air and my soul. "Judith would do *anything* for God!"

I lifted my chin and curled my fist. "Anything?" I hit back, cracked my gloved knuckles. "Like burn down a school?"

Sister Honor brought her grizzled face to mine. Pure hatred in her rot-brown eyes.

"My *Sisters*," our principal begged. "Please."

With her teeth clenched, Sister Honor hissed at me. "Don't you *dare*—"

"What? Finally call you out? What are your alibis for both fires?"

A switch flipped. She was always a buzzkill, but this was unbridled aggression. Maybe she was capable of setting the east wing on fire. Pushing Jack through a window to his fiery death.

"Filth!" She pushed me. How angry she was, red-throated as an ember.

Startled, I stumbled back but quickly regained my footing. It was so glorious to feel Sister Honor unhinge. *Hit me*, I thought. *Do it first so I can return the favor.*

"Sister Augustine should never have let you come here." In one swift motion she ripped off my scarf, revealing the beating wings of my dove tattoo. "Poison! That's all you are!"

I grabbed my scarf from her sweaty hands.

"I am your elder. I've devoted my life to the Order, to the Word!" She scuttled backward. "You will never know the sacrifice."

"Stop this right now," urged Sister Augustine with the firm delivery of a mother refereeing a sibling bust-up in the back seat of the family car. "How infelicitous, beneath our Order."

"She's implacable!" Sister Honor wiped her brow, her anger renewed. "Instigating me!"

Sister Augustine calmly placed her hand on Sister Honor's solid shoulder. "I know you are protective of the Word but, please, we all deserve redemption. We are on the same team."

"I'm not on *her* team." Sister Honor screeched. "Judith did what God asked of her." Her chin sagged, gravity pulling her down. "When God speaks, we *must* listen."

Sister Augustine nodded. "Sacrifice."

I looked over at them, then everyone in the musty lounge. "Everyone, share your alibis. For my investigation—"

"Your obsession," said Sister Honor.

"My *investigation*," I straightened my back. "Don't you want to know who did this? Alibis. John first."

John pushed his glasses up his nose. He spoke hesitantly. "Okay, well. I . . . I was with my family the night of the first fire."

"I was with John too," said Rosemary, a wobble of urgency or fear in her voice, "remember?"

"Of course." John smiled. "I gave Rosemary a ride home after our Sunday night meeting before I joined Kath and the kids for supper."

"During the cafeteria fire, I was in our library," Rosemary added.

"Same here," John echoed, "I was in the school library too."

Weird, I thought, *their synchronicity*. Though not out of the realm of possibility.

"We were worshipping at Church during both fires," said Sister Augustine, pointing to Sister Honor.

"Fires, worship, yes," said Sister Honor. She was barely listening, too busy hamming up her saint routine. She smiled condescendingly. My fists tingled, I wanted to hit her in the face so badly. I also felt pity. Sister Honor was unbending, but underneath the veil she seemed unstable, a scared child crying alone in the dark.

That's how it was to live two lives. In the convent, in the classroom, on stage, you are the flawless avatar, the saint, the superhero. But inside we're all the same. Hearts that want to belong. Some people would do anything to feel less alone. Haze. Praise. Hate. Decapitate. Whatever. It was pressurized in my new home, the city where magic and trauma coexist. If it's not a hurricane washing us into the Gulf or the mass incarceration of Black people, it's fire ants and termite swarms. Marsh monsters fighting back.

"Sunday night, I was home, with my band," said Bernard, "as I've already gotten confirmed by the police. And you all saw my valiant efforts to extinguish the cafeteria fire."

But Bernard's words were lost on the group as they started chatting about the Diocese's impending visit.

"I'm gonna get a Judith tattoo," said Bernard as I sat down next to him, my hands like live wires, electrified from the scrap. "Her name. Right here." He placed his index finger on his chest, near his heart.

Speaking softly, I said, "I would ink *Judith* on my heart too, but I have no bare skin left." I retied my scarf. "No money either."

"Oh, please," he said. "I got your back. Always."

15

THE REST OF FRIDAY was a blur of rage streaked with righteousness.

I was juiced up from my cage match with Sister Honor. So on edge I snapped two guitar strings. The last thing I wanted to do was sit through a faculty assembly, but the Lord works in mysterious ways. Or something.

Sister Augustine had arranged the event after a heated conversation with the Diocese. Time to update the campus community on the status of the investigation. It had been nearly two weeks since the first fire. The police had finally wrapped their interviews: 260 students and 18 staff members. And Prince Dempsey was still in custody on an outstanding warrant.

After dismissal, we reluctantly filed in and took our seats in the auditorium.

I noticed Rosemary Flynn sitting by herself, and I sat next to her. "Hello." I removed my gloves to peel a satsuma.

"What do you want now?" asked Rosemary, barely moving her lips, her eyes fixed on my ungloved hands and tattooed knuckles. Her red lipstick was as loud as she was quiet.

"Just saying 'hello,'" I said, as she opened a textbook, *Chemical Principles*. "Now it's your turn to say 'hello' to me. That's how it works."

"Hello."

Rosemary Flynn, the only cold front in New Orleans.

I leaned in and asked, "Come here often?"

She collected her books—"I need less noise"—and moved to a seat three rows up.

I traced my gold incisor as I watched her relocate. Once seated, she turned back in my direction. We quickly darted our eyes away from each other.

John Vander Kitt sat on my right side, sipping coffee from a mug he had brought down from the lounge. He was never without his coffee, even in the swampy heat.

Bernard plopped down to my left and slid his toolbox under the seat in front of him. "Aloha," he said. His denim coveralls were rolled up at the sleeves. His long black hair was pulled up. "How's Kathy?" Bernard leaned over me to ask John.

"We made the switch to a new 'smart wheelchair,'" John replied, his face glowing. "This new contraption is like a car, let me tell you. It's connected to the internet. Kath can control it with her voice. And you can even listen to music through it. I can't quite operate it—almost crashed on a test ride in the hall. But Kathy just loves it. Kath and me, we make the best of it," he said. "What else can we do?"

"Right on," said Bernard with an earnest nod. "Right on, bro. Keeping it positive. Keeping it chill." He tried to give John a fist bump, but John didn't understand, and instead held Bernard's closed fist with two hands, inches from my face.

John's wife, Kathy, had ALS. Their son and daughter, Lee and Sam, fraternal twins, had moved back from budding careers as location scouts in Hollywood to help with Kathy's care. John Vander Kitt could talk about anything—could talk a starving dog off a meat truck—but he especially loved talking about Kathy.

Grogan, Decker, and Riveaux had arrived and sat in the row in front of us. Sister Augustine walked up to them, carrying a stack of papers in her willowy arms.

"What else can we do to help with your investigation?" Sister Augustine asked Riveaux, fatigue straining her voice.

Riveaux thought about it for a second. "Anyone else we can interview? Part-timers? Subs? Coaches?"

They hadn't made any ground at all.

"I believe you have seen everyone," Sister Augustine replied. "And we don't have dedicated coaches anymore. No funds. Low enrollment."

"Depressing state of affairs," said Grogan, "folks losing their way, raising kids without Jesus."

"Well, if anyone else comes to mind, let us know," Decker said sharply.

From the way Sister Augustine nodded, she seemed to like Decker's conviction. "We will make sure that you and your team have everything you need."

"She's a pro," Grogan said to Decker after Sister Augustine had walked away. "Been principal here since the dawn of time, since I was a kid."

"Here," said Bernard under his breath as he placed a thick roll of dollar bills in my satsuma peel.

"What's that for?" I asked. "Must be a hundred dollars at least."

"For your Judith tattoo."

I swallowed, almost choking. "I was kidding."

"I wasn't." He looked angry, blinked his black eyelashes, so long they cast shadows on this face under the fluorescent lights. "We made a deal. I got mine during my lunch break. When he tugged his coveralls down, revealing the skin of his chest, I saw the puffy outline of cursive letters spelling *JUDITH* under a transparent bandage. "Now you have to get yours, Sis."

I stuffed the money from Bernard into my bag. "We'll discuss this later." Sister busybody Honor was within earshot, so I didn't want to elaborate.

"They sure are taking up a lot of our time." A ringlet of coffee steam fogged John's thin metal-framed glasses.

"The arsonist will slip up soon," I said. "I can feel it. At some point, they'll crack."

"Forget school sleuth," Bernard beamed, "we've got our very own Judith on campus!"

On stage, Riveaux seemed confused by the microphone. "Does this thing work?" Her voice squealed. "Testing."

Someone shouted from the back of the auditorium: "We can hear you!"

Then Sister Honor erupted with a comical sneezing fit.

"Most of y'all have seen me by now, we've been going at this for a while. But for the unacquainted, I'm Fire Investigator Magnolia—Maggie—Riveaux from the New Orleans Fire Department."

"Please get to the point!" Sister Honor interjected. "Parents are scared, and we have district exams for which we need to prepare."

Riveaux cleared her throat. "We've got two fires here on your premises. Two dead bodies. Someone on your campus knows something, and has chosen to stay silent. Even if it seems small, tell us. You could be sitting on invaluable evidence for our investigation. Detective Grogan and Sergeant Decker from Homicide are working around the clock to—"

"She's certainly loquacious," John whispered as Riveaux meandered.

"Ladies, gentlemen, Sisters, brothers," Sister Augustine, who had stepped onto stage, calmly took control of the mic. "Please give our law enforcement your full attention."

It was Sergeant Decker's turn to take the mic. "Thank you, Sister. The NOPD and the bishop are recommending a campus curfew until we have more clarity."

Grumbling cascaded through the auditorium.

"Listen, we don't want to scare you. But we've received a credible threat," Sergeant Decker said. The audience gasped. She continued, "The promise of another fire. For everyone's safety, from dusk to dawn, until we apprehend the arsonist, no one should be on this block. After dark, stay inside unless it's absolutely necessary."

Bernard sprang to his feet. "This is *New Orleans*. We need to be free!"

"We will not reveal the exact nature of the threat, but just know we are treating it seriously."

"We should fight this," Bernard said sincerely.

I grabbed his arm, pulling him back into his seat. "A curfew is good," I said. "People are terrified."

"Why now," Bernard whined, "like two weeks after the fires?"

"Again, the curfew applies only to this campus. Make no mistake, an arsonist is targeting your school, your church, your convent and rectory, and potentially the whole Catholic community of New Orleans." Detective Grogan spoke into the mic with a mellifluous voice. "Catholic schools and churches are at risk, y'all, and it's what your bishop requested," said Grogan, tapping into his folksy roots. Code switching. I knew it well. "The threat we received is real. Don't take nothin' for granted. Not one iota of detail."

"Any questions?" Riveaux pointed at the assembly crowd from the stage. "Questions? No? Great. Stay present. Keep your eyes open. Stay strong and start telling the investigators what you know. That's a wrap." She descended the seven steps of the stage stairs with Sister Augustine.

I caught up with John, needed his ear before we parted ways. "What was the school like before the Diocese took the reins?"

He considered it for a moment. "Oh, the halcyon days. There was real energy then. Such possibility and pride! Sisters Augustine, Therese, and Honor had great successes with the scholarship program and—" he paused. "They've always been on their social justice kicks, your Sisters. They've organized for reparations, gender equity, holistic healing, the ozone layer, climate change, and caretaking for AIDS patients! Rabble-rousers, right here at our school! Sisters Therese and Honor were arrested after they handcuffed themselves to the parish jail!"

Badasses, I thought. "What were they protesting?"

John corkscrewed his face as he reflected. "That time? Oh, they might have been demanding prison abolition. Or protesting brutal conditions and the death penalty." He spoke excitedly and urgently, like he was recapping the best scenes from his favorite movie. As he continued listing the Order's achievements and brushes with the law with gusto, I let the idea settle: The Sisters of the Sublime Blood help people. I was part of something good.

Someone was fucking with us, and I was going to fight back.

As John prattled on, I reached for a cigarette in my pocket, not to light it, just to feel it. Sometimes the potential of a thing was better than the thing itself.

Saint Sebastian's would host a series of prayer circles and a rally in the coming days. More of Sister Augustine's endless efforts to keep spirits high. In the hysteria, faith was needed again. Prodigal children circling back for shelter. Direction. A compass only God could provide.

16

AFTER THE POLICE ASSEMBLY on Friday, the campus curfew went into effect.

We sat at the convent's long dining table—me and Sisters Augustine and Honor.

Sister Honor said grace and dedicated our devotion to the Lord, Jack Corolla, and Sister T. No music played. The ceiling fan whirred. I scanned the walls, all empty except for a large cross. The convent, like every classroom in the school, was painted white with the faintest hint of wheat, like a Communion wafer.

I passed around the loaf of bread, baked by Sister Honor after school. Sister Honor was a traditionalist in every sense. Joined the convent when she was twenty years old. What was it like to spend nearly sixty years without having sex? Sister Honor hated me because I had a life before the convent. Or because she thought I was an imposter. Or both.

I placed a thick slice of bread on her plate and smeared it with soft, golden butter. Sweat burned the corners of my mouth.

Sister Honor took the plate. "That Bernard Pham has been acting most unusually. His outrageous display whence being taken to the police station. His outburst at the assembly." She sucked her teeth. "Troubling."

"I mean, he did lose one of his closest friends." I spoke with my mouth full to annoy Sister Honor. "A comrade."

"Bernard is an eccentric, that is true," said Sister Augustine, after praying over her food a second time. It was a rare moment of doubt. "But the wayward need our love most of all. It is our task to lead him to the righteous path."

"That's what Sister Therese believed." Sister Honor blessed herself. "Sister Therese said every child of God was worthy of love."

"Why are the police so sure that Sister T fell? How can they know for a fact that she wasn't pushed down those stairs?" I asked, trying to probe a reaction from Sister Honor. *Take the bait*, I thought. *Take it.*

"The only thing we can know with true certainty," Sister Augustine's voice was level but impassioned, "is the love of our Lord. We must honor the perfection of the Gospel. He is depending on every one of us." She winked at me, her eyes singing like crystals.

I was never an easy sell for the Saint Sebastian's community. A one-minute Google search produced my perverse song lyrics, images of me and my band topless at the WYMXN'S PUNK FE$T, and who knows what else. Parents were up in arms, but Sister Augustine made a strong case to the Order and the bishop. Miraculously, the Diocese allowed my entry. "All will be absolved," she often said. "We practice tolerance, redemptive progress, and deep faith in our Lord. What we practice, we become."

What the students and parents at Saint Sebastian's seemed to have forgotten was the Sisters of the Sublime Blood were a progressive Order. Sister Augustine had been in handcuffs more times than me, protesting everything from the death penalty and police brutality to the post-storm FEMA trailers laced with formaldehyde. The kind Prince Dempsey lived in.

That Friday night, it was my turn to wash the dishes. I filled the basin with soapy water and soaked the utensils. As I washed the salad bowl, I looked over my shoulders, tracking my Sisters' movements. I could hear Sister Augustine singing a song down the long hall. Sister Honor slumped on the sitting-room sofa reading the Old Testament, occasionally talking to herself.

"You have already read this passage, Sister Honor!" She lectured herself, her voice a squall. "What a silly thing to do! You know better. Right? Right."

How sad.

Sister T had been about the same age as Sister Honor but so different. Joyful.

I moved to the convent library, a giant bookshelf in the hallway between the kitchen and living room. To solve the riddle of Sister Honor, I needed more information. Context. History. I flipped through a dozen books searching for details. *Sisters of Purpose. Crusaders of Christ. Jesus Was a Feminist. Sisters in Christ: A History of Women Religious.* Then I found it, *Revolutionary Grace: Saint Sebastian's Living Herstory,* written in solemn font, a treasure trove of historical accounts about our school and convent.

In the book, there were black-and-white pictures of Saint Sebastian's faculty from the school's golden age in the 1960s and 1970s, when the student waiting list was longer than our total current enrollment. There they were, young *Sister Augustine Wójcik* and *Sister Honor Monroe*, standing side by side in the first row of a dozen nuns in a picture with the caption *Sisters of the Sublime Blood, 1966.* I hadn't seen their full names before, not even on mail or school ID cards. They were twenty-five and twenty years old, respectively, in that picture. Hard to believe Sister Honor was ever young. How spritely they looked. Their bob haircuts, kitten-sweet eyes, plucky but respectful expressions. Fervent believers, newly matriculated, eager to learn and lead. They must have met teaching here, decades ago.

Sister Augustine became the youngest principal in the school's history when she took the helm. *A devoted Sister from Marblehead, Ohio,* the 1966 photo caption stated. Like yearbook photos, Sister Augustine added her mantra: *The wayward among us have the most to gain from the divinity of the Holy Spirit. I lost my parents when I was just a girl, and God's love became my everlasting family. We must honor the sacred potential of all pupils and believers of Christ our Lord.*

Lost her parents as a kid. Poor Sister Augustine. Maybe that's why she took a shine to Prince Dempsey. To save his sorry self the way she was saved.

Our obsessions, our fetishes, our pet peeves, and passions always have personal roots.

Sister Augustine built herself up from tragedy to rise to leadership, then the rug was ripped out from under her. The patriarchy's specialty. But she remained a beacon of light.

Under her own picture, Sister Honor had written: *I believe with the utmost conviction that living God's truth means finding redemption in each and every soul.*

Hard to believe the rude Sister Honor I knew now had ever felt so alive, so devoted to individual promise and the sensational complexities of life. Maybe it jaundiced her, having the men push their way into Saint Sebastian's after the Sisters had led it well, for so long. Maybe that's what broke Sister Honor, ground her down into a dispirited doomsayer, afraid of change. Drove her to fight—scorched-earth style—and destroy whatever got in her way, including the school. The same trigger can launch two people in staggeringly different directions. Like me and Moose. Riveaux said it, *Arsonists strike for revenge, control, or money.*

▪

After Sister Honor retired to her room for the evening, I detected a familiar sound through her open door. Pounding bass, shredded guitar. Bikini Kill. I popped my head in the doorway. She quickly turned off the boom box.

"Are you playing my mixtape? Sister Axe?" I asked her. "On my old boom box?"

"Well, I discovered it in the closet, and," she stammered, "I was trying to understand the motivations of the youth."

I didn't believe her. She was trying to decode me, understand what made me tick, size me up to fit the frame tighter. She was playing me, but I'd play harder.

"It's all right if you like it."

She abruptly stood and shut her door.

The curfew was on, but I needed fresh air, so I crept outside slowly and hid myself behind trees until I reached the convent garden bench. I sat in a tiny ball and closed my eyes. Voodoo hopped onto the bench and purred on my lap. She slow-blinked, a sign of safety. I was grateful to feel another mammalian heartbeat. Feral cats were as common in New Orleans as gale-force winds that tore up the Gulf. They belonged to no one. Even Voodoo, who came to rely on us for food and affection, would bounce away after a minute of human cuddles, drawn to the call of the wild, even in the subtropical steam bath.

New York felt like an eternal winter by comparison. I remember slogging to the train in subfreezing temperatures, traveling to the instrument repair shop and where I taught guitar lessons. Two layers of denim, a parka, wool hat, gloves that extended to the elbow, and I still froze in the sleet. Each frigid drop sharp as a razor. Even the designer dogs of New York, jaunty dandies in the warm months, begrudgingly did their business on the arctic pavement and sprinted immediately back inside. The sun seemed to set as soon as it rose. I often slept so late I missed daytime altogether.

But darkness cannot exist without light. During New York winters, the world's only color seemed to hum in my gold cap and lipstick. The gray sky a prison. Skeletal trees. I would be happy to forget Brooklyn altogether. And most of the memories that were tethered to it.

Like the night my mother told our family her news. The news.

I remember lighting a cigarette, leaning against the yellow banister of the subway entrance as I called my mother back. While it rang, I heard the banshee squeal of my train sailing away in the distance.

"Hey, Mom."

"Holiday," my mother replied in a flat tone, our family cat, Marple, yowling in the background. "Meet us for dinner." I could tell more words were forming, but she pushed them down.

Family dinner. Something was wrong.

Later, at my parents' apartment, Mom emerged from the bathroom looking uncharacteristically made-up. As a girl I had longed for a mom who knew the best ways to blend eyeshadow, master liquid liner, and extend eyelash length. But much to my irritation she was never one for makeup. Mom had spent a decade as a Roman Catholic nun in Brooklyn—said it was the happiest time of her life. Mornings of ecclesiastical study and afternoons of Worship. Pure. Simple. Perfect. Our names reflected Mom's devotion. Gabriel for the angel, the protector. Holiday because every day was a sacred gift, a blessed holiday. This irony was never lost on me. A retired nun with a gay son and a lesbian daughter. Her crosses to bear.

When I told my parents I was gay, they both sobbed. Then Moose came out too. Always trying to steal my thunder.

"You're our only kids," Mom wailed, gesturing at us, as if we had forgotten the family tree. "Why are you doing this? To hurt us?"

"This is who we are," I said.

"I left the Order for *this*?" Mom cried. "I left my *life* for this? You're both selfish."

"What do you want us to do?" I asked angrily. "Play pretend?"

"Our only kids. Two queers." Dad thought I'd shrink like Moose and beg for forgiveness. He didn't know me, though. He didn't know me at all. "Two selfish brats who have no respect for anyone or anything."

"Just love us for who we are."

Heat tore through me. I looked at Moose, his body as slack as a bunny's in a terrier's jaws. Another alloy in our trauma bond, me and my brother.

"Give it back then, your Communion money." My father was smug. "Your Confirmation money. The names your mother said would keep you blessed. Give your names back too. You already do that stupid 'Moose' and 'Goose' thing to annoy us."

"I hate you both!" Something cracked inside me then that would stay broken for years. "I wish you'd die!"

That was decades ago.

Now I was a Sister of the Sublime Blood. Worshipping God, teaching music, sleuthing. Nothing more. I didn't need love, outside of God's and my Sisters'. I needed prayer. I needed structure.

I came here because I wanted to make better decisions. If we can't make our own choices, we're nothing more than marionettes. And after six months of dedicated service at the convent, and six more teaching music, New Orleans finally felt like a real home.

The same way I'd board up the windows before a storm rolled in, I would find the arsonist and protect my home. My new family. My new life.

17

BRUSHING MY TEETH WITHOUT a mirror was doable but still felt strange. I gargled mint mouthwash, spit, and walked to my bedroom on the second floor of our convent. In front of my door, I tripped as my foot met soft resistance.

Voodoo lay on the threshold of my bedroom. "Sorry, kitten. I didn't see you there." She must have followed me in from the garden, slipping through the convent door as it briefly opened.

A velvety black cat, save for a tiny white diamond on the top of her head. Like the hundreds of cats roaming New Orleans, Voodoo was wild but self-assured with a persnickety air, a sense of humor that I found endearing.

Now she was perfectly still, pitch-dark.

She was dead.

"Oh, God, no."

There was no blood on the ground. No open wound that I could tell. Eyelids fully open as if pried apart. Even her fur looked wrong.

"Voodoo," I yelled. "Fuck!"

Sister Honor stormed into the hallway. "Sister Holiday, we are trying to sleep! Are you physically or simply mentally unable to allow us one moment of peace?" Sister Honor's bright white hair glittered like snow globe flurries without her veil.

"She's dead. Voodoo's dead." I flapped my hands, twirled my palms, as if the rotation could rewind time itself.

From the staircase at the opposite end of the hallway, Sister Augustine floated toward me. "Sister?"

"She's dead. Voodoo. Somebody put her dead body in my doorway!"

"Slow down." Sister Augustine dropped her voice as she moved closer.

Sister Honor knelt, looked at Voodoo. "Mangy thing. Riddled with disease and worms, I'm sure."

"She's one of God's creatures, like all of us." Sister Augustine stepped over the lifeless cat, into my room. "Sit down, Sister Holiday. You've had a fright."

Sister Honor scoffed, walked into her room, and returned with a trash bag. She threw the black plastic at my face. "Get that thing out of here."

My hands shook. "I can't just throw her away. She was my friend."

"Tough Sister Holiday," Sister Honor laughed. Then sneezed. "Not so tough after all."

I looked at my two Sisters. "Someone killed her to terrorize me."

"This is a sad accident, Sister." Sister Augustine looked younger. Though we lived together, we rarely saw each other during interstitial moments. Vulnerable hours without the armor of our black, Guild-issued garb. "You have a big heart," she said with a comforting smile.

"Did you do this?" I scowled at Sister Honor as I beat back tears. I didn't want to break in front of her, but everyone has a limit.

"I want you to take a deep breath," Sister Augustine said. "Can you do that?"

I nodded.

"Let us pray for this cat, for all of God's creations," Sister Augustine said. "God delivered her to *you* for a reason, Sister Holiday, to test your mettle." She gave me a hug. "I know you are strong, but you're learning how resilient you truly are."

"She needs to be buried," I said with a sign of the cross. "She deserves at least that."

"Hideous things," Sister Honor said. "Cats. Detestable. Bringing disease wherever they go. Devilish varmint. Don't bury it. Burn it."

"No more fire, please," Sister Augustine blessed herself. "Do what you need to do to put the poor creature to rest, Sister Holiday," she said calmly, then walked away, into her room. But I wished she would help me, hold me, tell me it would be okay.

Alone again, I closed my eyes, letting silent tears escape. I didn't want Sister Honor to hear me. I held my breath as I knelt, picked up Voodoo in my towel. Her blue-black fur was rigid. Her body too light.

The moon was a silver locket as I carried death in my arms. Two police cars circled the block. With the campus curfew in place, I couldn't be seen. I had to work quickly. I took Voodoo to the far corner of Saint Sebastian's garden. Past the satsuma tree. Behind the mayhaw tree with its tart berries, too many to count. Behind Sister Therese's rain barrel, compost bins, and mulch. In a patch of dry ground that felt discrete, I put the towel down. A hush of mist floated up from the silver moss, like rain in reverse.

I pulled back the cloth to see Voodoo one last time.

She looked fake. So irreversibly dead she could never have been alive in the first place.

I went to the utility shed for a shovel. Flicked on the light. It smelled of lawnmower gas. The shovel was easy to find despite the clutter of Bernard and Jack's haphazard organizational system. Tools and bags of nails and toppling towers of bagged mulch. Refillable gasoline containers with Smart-Fill spouts. Batteries stored in empty coffee cups from Crescent City.

The surreality of the moment cleaved me in two. I dug the hole deep enough for me to stand up to my knee. Hyped with fear and confusion, the head rush of whip-its mixed with the hard sink of sorrow. I prayed for my little familiar. Three friends gone. *Hail Mary. Our life, our sweetness, our hope. Amen.* I wrapped the towel tight and placed Voodoo at the bottom of the hole. Returning her to the earth. I sat on our bench, hoping the cops wouldn't notice me.

The Lord is near to the brokenhearted and saves the crushed in spirit. I was broken, crushed, and it brought the Lord closer to me.

Again and again. *Save me. Stay with me, Lord.*

Across the street, the church windows glowed like gems lit from within. Amethyst, garnet, emerald. Jack's favorite seraphim. I thought about the stained glass of our family church. Sitting in the hard, cold wood pew, next to my mother, staring at the windows, how they both held and changed the light. Mom must have thought I was daydreaming, a million miles away, ignoring Father Graff. But really, I was finding a foothold. Burrowing in.

"Holiday," Mom nudged me gently with the back of her hand, "pay attention."

She was usually measured, about matters small and large. Even as she delivered her death sentence.

It happened in the family home in Bay Ridge, our rent-controlled two-bedroom apartment. I remember opening the fridge to search for a beer—Dad usually had a Guinness tucked away—when my mother's voice cut through.

"I've gathered us together to announce—"

"You're going back to the convent?" I interrupted her, thinking it would make her smile.

"Stop." I recall Pop's lips twisted in anger.

Moose shook his head and made the hand gesture of zipping his lips.

"Your mother has fucking cancer," Dad said as I stared at a jar of French's mustard.

"Jesus, Pop." I closed the door to see Moose and my parents holding hands.

"Language." Mom sighed, eyes downcast.

Pop and Mom blessed themselves and, in unison, muttered a quick prayer of forgiveness under their breaths.

We sat down and listened to the details. Moose leaked stoic tears into his beard and the collar of his flannel shirt. He wiped his nose with his sleeve.

Mom said she had popped into her doctor's. An ulcer, she thought. Like Aunt Joanie. Too many spicy takeout dinners. But after weeks of prodding, poking, an MRI, waiting on hold lines for follow-up appointments, she learned she had pancreatic cancer. Stage four.

I didn't even know where the pancreas was. Mom was sixty-two years old, a former Glorious Love of Mary nun. By all accounts a saint. A face so plain you couldn't describe it to a sketch artist. Her face was every face. Sure, every summer, she whisked us to a woodland Catholic Leadership Camp, the Catskills equivalent of a Siberian work camp, but she did what she did for us. Mom was a drill sergeant to keep us safe from the madness of New York. She once broke up a knife fight on the subway with her bare unmanicured hands. She once ran into a burning apartment to save an older neighbor's photo album. How could my mom of *all* people in this world get cancer? Somebody had got it wrong.

It was too easy to dent the kitchen wall. I hit it twice. Then I folded at the knees, like genuflecting at the altar, and sobbed. Kohl eyeliner melted down my cheeks. Mom stooped down and put her arms around me. Moose and Pop, both used to my histrionics, continued talking at the table. Tears streamed out of my eyes. My *lost* knuckle tattoos coated in thick white dust from punching through the drywall.

Mom had three months to live.

She tried to calm me but I remained crumpled in an inconsolable puddle.

"Don't touch me."

Mom was dying and I had no idea how to feel. How to tell her that I loved her.

Moose pleaded with me to stay but I left, descended the stairs, two at a time. I wanted the wet cold of the night, the dark of it, to swallow me. I unlocked my bicycle and rode home, weaving recklessly through tangles of traffic.

The month that followed was a fog of calls and plans. Meals of plain white rice and clear broth from the Chinese restaurant on the corner. Dad was constantly scrambling. Moose screamed at me in the kitchen and then tearfully apologized at least once a day. We shopped in bodegas and Duane Reades at all hours. For odds and ends. Or to pretend everything was normal for five minutes. Remarkable how soothing it is to buy Q-Tips and ziplock bags when everything else is shit.

No one was sleeping except for Mom, who slept longer and longer. Then one day she stopped getting out of bed entirely. About five weeks after the news, she went quiet. Moose and I took her to the doctor. We kept her favorite TV shows on 24/7. *Matlock. Perry Mason. The Price Is Right. The Golden Girls. Law & Order.* Mysteries that were easy to solve. Sitcoms she loved but never laughed at. She didn't eat. Hollowing out.

"She's forgotten who she is," I whispered to Moose near the sink as he washed dishes and I dried, "and she's forgetting who we are. Let me take her out for a ride. Change things up."

"Don't be dramatic." He was losing patience. "The last thing she needs is a joyride out in the cold. Here." He handed me a wet plate. "Dry."

That was the day before the fire.

It has passed, it is the past. But the memories are close, stitched into me like tattoos. Intricate. Painful. Screaming back to life every time I pray.

18

THE WEEKEND COLLAPSED UNDER the weight of chores, four Masses, and Sister Honor's evil eye during meals. I couldn't stop perseverating about, well, everything. Particularly Sister Augustine's quote in the book about Saint Sebastian's. I wanted to understand her better, as a human being, a Sister, a leader, to learn from her. The loss of her parents as a girl. It was almost too much to bear. I could ask Sister Augustine, but a partition remained between us. She was my mentor; I was her charge. She hadn't broached the topic during my year in New Orleans, so I should probably take the hint.

We were yoked by loss and loneliness, me and Sister Augustine. God's second chances.

On Monday, using our green phone in the convent kitchen, I called the librarian of the only library in Marblehead, Ohio. I had asked Bernard to look up the phone number on his cell phone.

"Public library," said the loud voice on the other end. I thought librarians were supposed to be quiet.

"Hello, um, hi." I stammered, so out of practice talking on a phone. "I'm calling to . . . I need obituaries. To read, I mean." I felt like I was bombing on stage. "Can you access obituaries of Marblehead families?"

The librarian laughed loudly. "We just might be able to help you, but I need to know which family and when first."

"Right, right. When. Who."

I was sitting under the wall phone with the Saint Sebastian's book in my lap. I flipped to the picture from 1966. No idea how to pronounce Sister Augustine's last name, so I spelled it out: "The letter *W*. An *o* with the accent mark. Regular *j*. Then *c*. Then *i*. And *k*. The *Washsick* family."

"Wójcik!" She pronounced the name like *VOYchic*, stressing the *voy*. "What a *tragedy*. Mrs. Wójcik was my kindergarten teacher."

"Yeah, so so sad. Oh, then, do you remember what happened? The year? The circumstances of their deaths?"

"Oh dear dear, that was a real, real sad story, that." The librarian liked repeating words. She whistled. "Hold a moment while I move over to the microfiche room."

"Okay."

Twenty minutes later, after I had reread the pages in front of me three times each, the librarian returned to the phone. "Here we go. Mr. Robert Edward Wójcik perished in 1955."

1955.

I ran some light math in my head. Sister Augustine would have been fourteen years old then. "Okay," I said. "Did Mrs. Wójcik die in the same accident?"

"Oh, dear. No no. I do know she lived a good long long life. Well into her eighties. Nineties even, come to think of it. Gave everything to her students—three generations at least. Such a lovely, lovely woman, Mrs. Wójcik."

"Huh? No. Maybe we are talking about different people. Maybe there was another set of Wójciks in Marblehead?" My face warmed with the instant heat of confusion. Or embarrassment. Remarkable how the body doesn't lie the way the brain does.

"No. Only one Wójcik family, a pillar of the community. Until Mr. Wójcik hanged himself in the family's front yard and—"

"He what?"

The librarian sighed. "Mr. Wójcik took his own life. It's not in the obituary, dear, but Marblehead is a small, good old-fashioned town. Everybody still knows everybody. We talked about it for years, Mr. Wójcik. Poor poor soul. Hanging from one of those old maple branches. They said it was the drink that got him, like so many veterans back then. The Greatest Generation, those men, and that's a fact!"

Too stunned to utter *thanks*, I stood and hung up the heavy phone.

I was shaking, my vision a hazy whirlpool. The sound of the book as I slammed it into the wall was hard and monstrous, like Jack's bones breaking as he landed on the unforgiving ground. Like trust breaking.

■

Thirty minutes later, Sister Augustine asked me to accompany her to the courthouse. Prince Dempsey was being arraigned.

Why did she lie about both of her parents dying? What was she trying to hide?

I was as skilled a liar as the rest—it was survival. But Sister Augustine was a hell of a lot godlier than me. If it was all an act, what hope did any of us have?

But I still needed definitive proof of Prince's innocence or guilt, so I sucked it up and agreed to go to the courthouse with her.

We walked four miles in total silence. I prayed and played the call with the librarian over and over in my head. *Mr. Wójcik. Poor poor soul. Hanging from one of those old maple branches.*

The courthouse was across the street from the jail. I stared at Sister Augustine, then the razor wire, its sharp shark teeth, and thought of Sister T. Her easy smile. Her intrinsic light, a stark contrast to the dehumanization of the cruel facility.

I missed having a Sister I could trust completely.

In the lobby, Sister Augustine stood next to a vending machine that was empty except for one wet-looking oatmeal cookie. She leaned against the wall holding her rosary. I wanted to pull back the curtain. Get answers.

I was surprised to see Riveaux in the courthouse. Maybe she was testifying in another case. Or maybe she was, like me, convinced Prince knew more than he was telling. We were both chasing the big bad, me and Riveaux. One case to solve, two scores to settle.

She lumbered over to me with a curious expression, a leather bag slung over her shoulder and *The Times-Picayune* in her hand.

"When it *arraigns*, it pours, eh?" she deadpanned. Sweat beaded at her hairline, and her russet ponytail was tight. Her blouse hung loosely over her shoulders, her arms thin as drink stirrers. I hadn't seen Riveaux since the assembly. Now, she seemed elsewhere, her head in the turbulent storm clouds. Things with her husband must be deteriorating. She left without a wave or parting word, jumping into conversation with Sergeant Decker down the hall.

Sister Augustine approached, her rosary wound around her wrist like an invasive vine. She put her hand on the small of my back to straighten my posture. "Prince needs us today, needs us to stay positive." She smiled an easy smile that normally would have calmed me but on that day enraged me. "Now is the time for prayer and steadfast love." She delivered her words like Commandments.

I backed away. She inched forward.

A tall, unfamiliar woman powered through the main entry doors of the courthouse. She was a smudge of scarlet. Red sunglasses, red hijab, red Gucci purse, red leather briefcase, and a pair of striking red high heels that my old self would have loved to wear. She stood out against the beige marble of the courthouse. Perfume emanated from her like she had fallen into a vat of it. It made my eyes water. Unseen but painfully present, like speaker feedback.

I watched the tall woman share a few quiet words with Sister Augustine. Two women, two veils. One Catholic. One Muslim.

Twenty minutes passed. My lower back tightened. I needed coffee.

There were two water fountains next to each other at staggered heights. A faded flag and large city seal occupied the corner. Two NOPD officers walked by, and one stopped abruptly to spit chewing tobacco into the shorter water fountain, the one kids drink from.

To Protect and to Serve, the police motto. Yeah, right. My dad worked hard, but I had seen too many rogue officers delight in beating down queer and trans kids at the Chelsea Piers. Was it a few bad apples, or the system itself that was corrupt, a tree rotten at the roots? Nina would say burn it to the ground. Start over. But even if one person could make a difference, dig deep, tilt toward the light, that person wasn't my father. He looked the other way, cocooning his officers in a law-and-order narrative that excused their odious actions.

Sister Augustine continued chatting with the scarlet woman who was typing with red manicured thumbs on a red-bedazzled phone. Words—"lost," "compassion," "second chances"—escaped from Sister Augustine's lips. I avoided eye contact with them both.

Riveaux returned, flanked by Grogan and Decker. "Hold up!" Riveaux paused, closed her eyes, and sniffed the air. "Who is wearing Chanel No. 5?"

The red-clad woman raised her hand.

"Nothing like it in the entire world," Riveaux said. "An olfactory symphony. You can almost hear that scent. Timeless yet forever *now*."

Perhaps Riveaux was more aware than I realized.

"Who are you?" Decker looked at the woman's headscarf.

"I'm Attorney Sophia Khan from McDade, Khan, and Haheez."

"The uptown firm?" asked Grogan. "What brings you all the way downtown, Attorney Khan?"

"I represent Mr. Dempsey. A pro bono case. Sister Augustine called us."

Riveaux shook her head and wiped sweat from her eyebrows. "'Pro bono.' We have thousands of people getting properly beat down—wives fleeing abusive husbands, kids kidnapped, old ladies robbed—and you're wasting your time on this cretin."

"Mr. Dempsey has constitutional rights," Attorney Khan said. Riveaux and Grogan smiled. Decker rolled her eyes.

Grogan said, "He doesn't have the right to vandalize property or resist arrest. We have video footage of your client opening two tombs and defacing the oldest cathedral in New Orleans."

"Technology is not secure," Khan interrupted. "How do we know the video feed wasn't manipulated?"

"As clear as day, the video captures him defacing crypts and spray-painting the oldest historic site in the city," said Grogan. "All the while with a white pit bull loyally by his side."

Khan readjusted her scarf. "Why is Homicide here today?"

Decker wiped her nose. "There was a suspicious death at your client's school."

"Prince Dempsey hasn't been charged," Khan challenged.

"Not yet," said Decker, "but—"

"Which means you have nary a scrap of evidence." Khan had the snappy delivery of a TV lawyer. "I will be asking for Mr. Dempsey's release on his own recognizance."

Grogan yawned. "He's a flight risk."

"He's annoying and verbally abusive," I said, "but I don't think he's a flight risk."

"Oh, great, here she is," Decker gestured toward me, "Sister Holiday, the wolf in nun's clothing."

"Wait," Attorney Khan seemingly noticed me for the first time. "Who are you?"

"Ignore her," Riveaux said to Khan. "She's nobody."

Nobody?

19

INSIDE THE COURTROOM, Prince's arraignment convened. Attorney Khan sat at the defense table next to Prince. Detective Grogan and Sergeant Decker sat at the back, near the door. Seated in the front row, next to Sister Augustine, I pushed the tip of my tongue into my gold incisor. Riveaux's nostrils flared as she sniffed the air beside me.

Khan calmly flipped through a manila folder.

The assistant district attorney, Michael Armando, blinked. He was balding and had a beer gut that reminded me of my old poker buddies in Brooklyn. I emptied their wallets every time. I knew how to hedge a bet.

"Your Honor," ADA Armando said, "the basic facts surrounding the nature of this unlawful conduct are repellent to the good people of New Orleans."

The arraignment judge was a middle-aged woman with a smart haircut. Not one wrinkle on her skin. She peered over her thick glasses and said in a lilting Louisiana twang: "Assistant District Attorney Armando, can you please summarize the charging document? Keep it short."

"Can do. Your Honor, the state alleges that on August seventh, Prince Dempsey was captured on a security camera damaging historic tombs and spraying red paint on the Eau Bénite Cathedral in Jackson Square in New Orleans in the Orleans Parish of Louisiana."

"Glad to hear the city hasn't moved to Alabama," the judge said.

"Your Honor?"

"Sarcasm, ADA. Look it up. Continue," she said.

He laughed nervously. The air was tensile. Maybe Khan was intimidating him. Strong women have that knack. "As I was saying, the State is charging Prince Dempsey with one felony count of vandalism as he engaged in the intentional destruction and defacement of property. He damaged two of the oldest tombs in the cathedral cemetery. We seek a felony conviction here."

"*Felony*," I groused to Riveaux. "I thought it'd be a misdemeanor."

"Damage exceeds five thousand dollars," she said precisely.

"And the charge of resisting arrest?" the judge said, with her nose in a folder.

The ADA stammered. "Yes, yes. One count of resisting arrest. And possession of a handgun without a firearms license."

I watched Prince closely, waiting for any change in his expression. How would he react to the words? I would be his human polygraph test.

But he didn't flinch. Didn't hold his breath or fidget. Nothing fazed him.

The judge closed her folder. "Attorney Khan, what is your client's plea?"

"Not guilty, Your Honor," Prince said.

"There is no direct evidence connecting Mr. Dempsey to any crimes. Prince was *not* resisting arrest," Khan stated. "None of the exhibits from the car trunk belong to Mr. Dempsey. He had no knowledge of their presence in his vehicle. They belonged to friends whom he kindly provided transportation to earlier in the day. Additionally, my client has Type 1 diabetes."

"As do I," said the judge.

"On the day of the arrest, Prince Dempsey was suffering from low blood sugar. Any erratic behavior and inconsistency observed resulted from his chronic illness."

Prince sighed audibly.

"Your Honor," ADA Armando bayed. "We have a *sworn affidavit* from the city's surveillance technician, who claims that we have high-resolution, timestamped video footage of the defendant vandalizing a protected edifice on the historic registry."

"Your Honor"—Attorney Khan smiled as she interrupted him—"if I may?"

"You may."

Attorney Khan spoke, "Your Honor, I testify to the profoundly decent character of my client, Prince Dempsey. Please look closely at this young man." Prince looked doleful, his blond hair brushed and tucked behind his ear. "While Prince Dempsey is no choirboy, he is a young man with a harrowing past. In the courtroom here today are nuns from my client's religious community at Saint Sebastian's." Khan pointed to Sister Augustine and me. I leaned back in surprise. "My client's favorite teacher, Sister, er . . ."—she flipped through pages of notes on her legal pad—"Sister Holiday, and the principal at his beloved school, Sister Augustine, are both here today to support him, as spiritual leaders and guardians."

Favorite teacher? If she meant favorite teacher to torment, then yes.

The judge glanced at Khan. "Does your client have a job?" she asked.

"Sister Augustine testifies that she will give Mr. Dempsey a part-time job as a groundskeeper at the school. Prince Dempsey has deep community ties both in the city and the parish. He rescues dogs and volunteers at the animal shelter. He poses no flight risk."

The judge tucked her chin to her chest and looked at Prince over her glasses. "Young man, we're going to release you today on your own recognizance," the judge said, her voice the timbre of cigar smoke. "But it's up to you to stay out of trouble, and you cannot leave the state."

"Understood, Your Honor." Attorney Khan smiled and Prince nodded.

With one gavel smack, the judge said, "This session is adjourned."

Prince caught my eye, and, like looking into a mirror, we blinked at the same time.

20

AFTER THE ARRAIGNMENT and Prince's release, Sister Augustine left with Attorney Khan. I was relieved I didn't have to look at Sister Augustine or walk back to the convent by her side. Instead, I begged Riveaux to drop me back at the campus—I needed to know what she knew.

But, as we drove, she spaced out. Answered my multi-clause questions with one-word responses. We parked in front of Saint Sebastian's east wing.

She yawned. "Even when I'm smoking a cigarette, I need a cigarette." She shifted in the driver's seat. "What's that about?" The pillow that usually occupied her back seat was absent.

"Addiction," I said.

The sidewalk shrine for Jack and Sister T now felt like a permanent fixture. Someone had added a few tea lights and taller votives. Their fires were small, contained in glass, but they spat and sparked with fussy wicks.

Even in Riveaux's truck, I felt watched. By someone, or something—a shadow with no body.

"Gotta go," Riveaux said with no emotion as she turned the key, killing the car's ignition. "Hop out. Tonight's perfuming experiment is my take on Dior Dune. A classic, like a gentle ocean breeze. A coastal storm. Not a hurricane storm, a—"

"Stop and actually talk to me for a minute."

The skin inside my gloves was wrinkling. Riveaux readjusted her rearview mirror and stared hard at something. "Make it snappy. It's two hundred degrees."

"Let me back into the east wing for another look."

"Nah. Scenes long tagged. Evidence is logged. There's nothing left to find." Riveaux's voice turned gruff.

Two police cars idled on Prytania Street.

"There's always more to find."

"I'm too tired to fight with you," she said with a frown. "If I tell you more—stuff that will be available to the public and press soon enough anyway—will you leave me the hell alone?"

I made the sign of the cross.

"We have evidence all right, but none of it links to anyone specific, except Bernard."

"What evidence?"

"The glove. It's still at the lab."

I sighed loudly. "Still? And the blouse and pick?"

"For your own safety, drop it," she said stonily. "Get out." She reached over me to push the passenger door open.

I left the smothering heat of her musty truck for the blasting humidity of the street. The sky pulsed with veins of blue-gray, like spoiled milk. Riveaux drove off, her taillights disappearing down First Street. I turned into the alley, toward the east wing.

Riveaux had told me to drop it, but Saint Sebastian's was my home. I needed to be alone in the school, to hear it breathe, feel again where secrets were hiding. Every building is like sheet music. In the same way that the space between musical notes creates the song, I knew how to look for clues between the obvious.

Since the first fire, I had felt a presence lurking. Pupil-less eyes. Shadows behind and in front, anticipating my next move. I turned the details over in my mind. The east wing classroom where I found Jamie and Lamont. Jack's falling body. My burnt blouse. Sister T at the bottom of the stairs. My guitar pick near her tunic. The precision of it all. Chemistry, calculus.

Two cops were on duty but distracted, perhaps drowsy from the considerable heat. Both transfixed by their phones. I looked over my shoulders, lifted the yellow crime-scene tape, and opened the door to the charred building. I would notice more if I searched alone. I followed the misshapen lightbulbs, like fingers pointing to the fire's origin.

My eyes wandered over the burnt books, wet ash, insulation torn from the walls like a singed, eviscerated stuffed animal. I traced specific paths but couldn't *see* anything. No new clue, no new detail.

Off the entrance to the Spanish classroom, Sister T's room, was the janitor's closet. It was a narrow door in the hallway. Surely Grogan, Decker, and their crew had scoured it a dozen times, but the closet warranted a second look, at least. I tested the knob—unlocked. I opened the door and heard it click closed behind me.

Inside the closet, the air was thin, reeking of solvents. Materials designed to cleanse often smell the most poison-ous. Against the wall was a four-step ladder. I opened it, blew dust off the steps, and climbed to see what was on the higher shelves. But all I saw were boxes of jumbo trash bags, soap, old crusty batteries, and industrial-size rolls of paper towels.

Then a pop. The lightbulb burned out.

Total darkness.

As I descended slowly, I heard a metallic sound. The sound of a lock turning over. Dear God. I held my hands in front of me, feeling for the doorknob.

Finally, I found it, prayed while turning it. But it was locked. I tried another slow turn, pulling the door into myself and lifting up, the way I wrangled finicky doors in Brooklyn. Nothing.

"Help," I screamed. "Anyone? Anybody here?" I slammed a broom handle against the door. "Hello!"

The cops outside would never hear me.

Hail Mary. Don't leave me. Holy Ghost, cut the shit. I cracked my forehead against a pipe.

I sat on a buckled ladder step in darkness, for what seemed like an hour, though it could have been three. I exhausted myself with my screaming. Dehydrated, weak. I ran my hands over every surface.

Dear Mary, I know I'm a fuckup. Just give me a light. I don't want to ask for too much. Just a light. I'll handle the rest.

As I felt around in the darkness, my hand grazed a cool metal box. I took a breath and opened it. The items inside were familiar. Matchbooks. Dozens. Hundreds. The box brimmed with them. These matchbooks felt new with hard paper covers. They had somehow escaped the relentless New Orleans humidity.

Hail Mary. I plucked one from the box, slid open the cover, felt the comblike arrangement of matches. I tore off a paper match like I had done so many times before. All the fires of my life, infinite as stars. Pressing the tiny bulb of the match head against the abrasive strip, I struck, igniting a pop and two quick sparks as it crackled to life.

In the bead of new light, I quickly scanned the shelves of the dusty closet. Why did Bernard have a box full of matchbooks? Or had they been Jack's?

The match was burning down fast, but I blew it out before it could sear the skin of my thumb and index finger. Plunging back into the blackness, I tried the doorknob again.

Locked.

I tried to conjure something bright but calming to ground myself. A lustrous flicker of memory. The chancel candle of my Sister Antonia tattoo. The chalice before Communion. And mom's smile.

At the end, she was so frail she practically slipped through my arms when I hugged her, her arms cold and thin as paper clips. We lived less than two miles apart in Brooklyn, but I hated visiting. It dredged up the rot of my past. Tiny reminders of my misspent youth: the same carpet I vomited on, same wall I headbutted, same damn Chandler novels I reread when I was grounded every other month.

My parents were second-generation Bay Ridge, Brooklyn Catholics with Irish heritage on both sides. Our family went hard on drink and suppression and light on conversations. Most exchanges were three words or less. Mom's years in the convent carried real-world consequences for me. I wasn't allowed to bring boys home. Little did they know that the ever-revolving door of my school "girlfriends," warmly welcomed by my parents, were my vehicles for sex, drugs, and rock 'n' roll.

I was closeted until I was sixteen. Most of my youth was blurry anyway. A plot smeared, stuck in fast forward. Growing up in New York accelerated everything. Some people recall memories from as early as two years old, but I always felt like

I sprang from the unknown into the speeding subway train of adulthood.

Nina was like that too, as if she raced past childhood—a stone skipping across the skin of a pond. What would she think of me now?

After the wedding, the happy couple bought an apartment on West Fourth. When Nicholas traveled for work, some academic conference, we never missed an opportunity to hook up.

One night, Nina and I had such gymnastic sex we broke their expensive wedding registry bedframe. We pulled each other's clothes off so sloppily that Nina's shirt button got stuck in my hoop earring and almost ripped my earlobe off. My black dress draped over the bathtub ledge.

"Don't stop." She was underneath me, digging her nails into my shoulder and arm. My back rained sweat. "Harder."

"Your neighbors hate us right now."

"Fuck the neighbors. I want you to break me," she growled.

She kissed the tiny white bird under my jawline, then palmed my nipples until they were hard enough to crack a tooth. She pinched them both.

"Ow. Bitch!"

"You love it," she said.

I did love it. I loved her. Nina knew what I wanted before I did.

She put her hand on the center of my sternum, on my Sacred Heart of Jesus tattoo. "This one is creepy as fuck." The burning organ was pierced by thorns, surmounted by the cross.

Rays of divine light emanated from the tattooed heart. The heart's fire, the transformative power of love. Fury of a resurrected body.

"The Sacred Heart was popularized by nuns."

"Give me the TED Talk later." She kissed my neck, touched my cross necklace. "If you're wearing this to keep me away, it's not working." She blinked slowly, put the cross on the tip of her tongue, like she was testing to see if it was poison.

"Don't." I pulled the cross away.

"Your religion can't save us. We're monsters," she said.

"Beautiful monsters."

She grabbed my arms and pinned me.

Men fucked like grammar schoolteachers diagramming sentences: This goes here, and now that goes there. I'd rather die than be restrained by a dude. But women were unpredictable, like trying to tame a flame. When Nina held me down and looked at me like she wanted to tear my heart out with her teeth, it was ecstasy. We fit together like two clasped hands, slick with sweat.

A police siren blared.

I rolled us so I could be on top, leaned on my elbows, rocked until my abs burned. I ran my tongue along her fingernail, her ruby-red nail polish. She opened her legs wider. I lifted her hips, slid my tongue inside.

"I'm going to come."

"Wait." I jumped up and reached into her bedside dresser.

Fetching a strap-on hit the brakes. Stopping the action to reach for the leather. I usually strapped it on with Nina, though. She liked it but I needed it. She housed her many expensive sex toys and accoutrements in an antique metal box with a faded print of *The Treachery of Images* by René Magritte on it. *Ceci n'est pas une pipe.*

She smacked my thigh hard and the pain sang down my leg. "Give it to me."

Then she was on top of me. A storm of her hair fell into my face. I planted my feet flat on the bed, propped myself on my elbows for leverage. One corner of the fitted sheet popped off. A naked woman straddling you, muscles tense in her stomach, riding you. Wanting it so bad you thank God to be alive. Naked except for our jewelry and manicures. Champagne too warm to drink, lipstick-smeared glasses on the dresser.

"Yes yes yes yes yes. I'm going to—"

The bedframe buckled. We tumbled to the edge as the right side of the mattress slumped. We froze, swimming in sweat, then erupted in laughter on the sloped bed. With my face in the crook of her wet neck. Nina stacked books underneath the frame, but the bed never gave her—or Nicholas, apparently—a good night's sleep after that night.

I tortured myself with the memories for an hour.

Stuck in a closet. Again.

When I joined the Order, I made a choice to free myself. I hunched over, pressed my palms against my upper thighs, and screamed into the darkness.

Then I felt it, throbbing like light.

In the front pocket of my Guild-issued black trousers. A guitar pick. I pulled it out of my pocket and slid it into a seam between the door and the frame. I bent it the opposite way, forcing the lock to go back. The pick was short but the right balance of pliant and stiff.

I leaned against the door and tried again. Pushed all of my weight into it while bending the pick. Just when it was about to snap in half, the lock popped open. I tumbled out. Light scorched my eyes. I searched around for someone, anyone. But I saw nothing. Not even a shadow.

21

THE NEXT MORNING before Mass, high on sleeplessness and rage, still gasping from the closet's chokehold, I looked for Sister Augustine. To ask her about her family, to ask her why she lied. Make her stare it in the face.

She was praying at the sidewalk shrine.

"Sister Augustine, *why*?" My voice was so wobbly and high-pitched it scared me.

She met my eyes with hers. "Why what? Ask me anything you wish."

"In the book about Saint Sebastian's, *Revolutionary Grace*, I saw what you said, about losing your parents when you were young."

She collected herself and shrugged. "We all have burdens, mine are not heavier or lighter."

"But it isn't true! Your dad offed himself, but your mom lived into her nineties. I don't understand why you'd lie."

"Sister Holiday, no," she said, pity flooding her face, her silver eyebrows crinkling. "You've misunderstood."

"Bullshit! I talked to the librarian who read me the obituary. Told me the whole story."

She snapped her spine straight. "I said I *lost* my parents, not that they both died."

My stomach sank.

"After my father's death, my mother was lost," Sister Augustine continued, her voice taut. "She threw herself into teaching and sent me away. She couldn't hold together the pieces of her old life. She didn't trust in the Lord to guide her."

Fuck.

My trigger-finger temper.

Again and again. So convinced people would fail me, I failed them first. Got it out of the way.

"I'm so sorry." I pressed my hands in prayer position, hung my head. "So sorry."

"I know you know about loss too," she said. "It's never simple or straightforward."

No idea what to say next, I hugged her, felt her fragility.

"I'm sorry. I will pray for your father's soul, and for you."

"Don't pray for me. My pain is my gift—suffering is Jesus's ultimate test of love. My hardships help me see more and do more. We are more resilient than we think we are." She smiled and sent me on my way to Mass.

Sister Augustine, always demanding, asked questions and gave back too. What drew me to the Sisters of the Sublime Blood—besides the fact that it was the only convent in North America I thought would consider my candidacy—was its mission statement: *To share the light in a dark world.* I had seen my fair share of darkness, but Sister Augustine made me feel welcome. She tried to keep one foot in tradition but her eyes on the future. Think religion is bullshit? Punitive? Join the club. I thought that too, even as a believer. But after what happened in Brooklyn, everything changed. I needed a way to make all the contradictions of my life fit. God helped it fit. Sister Augustine knew more about that than I had realized.

I ducked into the school's mailroom. An officer was already standing guard in the west wing. I gave him the stink-eye as I walked past, sighing as I saw Sister T's name on her mail slot. In the chaos, no one had thought to remove it. Her shelf overflowed with envelopes and student papers.

My mailbox was also full, but immediately I knew something was wrong. All the envelopes that were addressed to me—Fleur's extra credit paper on deep listening, a notice from the Diocese over-architecting my permanent vow process, a letter from Moose, another from Nina—were all ripped open.

I walked briskly to the staff lounge and dialed Riveaux's cell phone, which I had memorized. It rang four and a half times before she answered.

"Detective Magnol—"

"I need to talk to you. Can you meet me at school?"

"Who is this?"

"Don't fuck with me," I whispered.

"Oh. It's you." She coughed. "Sister Goldsmobile." Her voice was disembodied. She sounded drunk or half asleep. Each word punctuated by a long breath. She reminded me of myself after a bender.

"You high or something?"

"Naw, Goldsmobile. Just exhausted by the constant clusterfuck."

"I need to talk to you, in person."

Rosemary Flynn walked into the lounge with her fine teacup, ruby lipstick on the porcelain lip. She waved in my direction, like she wanted to talk to me. Odd.

"You need something?" I asked Rosemary who smoothed her pencil skirt. She had a bizarre look. When her eyes held the light, they looked like the sage leaves Sister T loved.

Rosemary blurted out, "Bernard was cleaning and he—"

I cut her off with my open palm.

"What?" I asked Riveaux through the phone's handset, which smelled like bad breath and bad luck. "Just swing by. I need to talk to you before our staff meeting."

"Oh, what the hell," Riveaux groaned. "I'm not far away. I'll be there at 9 a.m." Her voice was subdued on the other end of our connection. She was probably hungover. Her delay and audible ache were familiar to me. "If you aren't outside at 9 a.m., I'm leaving."

"No need to worry, I—"

She hung up.

Across the lounge, near another THE BIG READ poster, I heard Rosemary sigh. She was always disappointed by something. She lamented the quality of student work (unexceptional) and the heat to which she could never acclimatize (unacceptable), even though she was a New Orleanian, born and raised in the Seventh Ward.

I was about to see what Rosemary Flynn needed to complain about when I noticed the clock—ten minutes until nine.

"Can this wait?" I asked her.

"Fine," she replied as she cooled her tea with her breath.

■

Riveaux's piece-of-shit truck rolled up to the convent at exactly 9 a.m. "Get in."

I opened the passenger door and slid in. It was broiling, hot enough to barbecue catfish. Moldy and musty air. Did she leave her windows open during every rainstorm?

"Good morning to you too," I said.

The sound of Riveaux's fire department radio changed from audio snow to mumbling. Then mumbles to words. "Dispatch to 217," said the deep voice on the radio.

Riveaux sighed, hit the radio button with her right hand. "217 here."

"ABT 289," the radio voice said. "70114. We have a female on the side of the road with the 289."

"Repeat," Riveaux said, "coordinates."

The dispatcher's voice cleared its invisible throat. "Okay, 217. That's an ABT 289 in the 70114. Tchoupitoulas and First. School bus." The voice paused. "Female driver okay. With medical. The street's sealed off. It's on fire. Repeat: *live fire*."

"Get out." Her voice was loud and severe. "There's another fire."

"I'm coming with you."

"217," said the radio voice. "Confirm your coordinates."

"Fuck it." Riveaux flicked her cigarette out of her open window.

Before I had a chance to buckle my seat belt, Riveaux sped down Prytania Street and cut a sharp right. She exhaled a cloud of smoke into the fast air.

"You're in the thick of it now," she said. "Behave yourself at the scene." She wiped sweat from her earlobe. A green parrot flew past the windshield. "What the hell was so important that you had to tell me in person, anyway?"

"All of my mail was opened," I said.

"Don't get paranoid. It was probably a mistake."

"Every single piece of mail? Letters from my brother over-seas. My ex. The Diocese. Someone locked me in the closet, dumped my own shirt in my trash. Dead cat on my doorstep. They are trying to intimidate me. Frame me. Opening another person's mail is illegal. We should report this."

"We?" she laughed. "*We* got bigger priorities at the moment." Saint Charles Avenue unfolded beneath the pickup truck. The black trolley cables gathered into high webs over the shady intersections we sped through. "Who else has regular access to the mailroom?" she asked.

"Everyone."

"Right, right." She itched her left eye. "Teachers?"

"Of course."

"Janitors?" she asked.

"Yes."

"Students?"

"Sure," I said. "When they deliver late homework or assign-ments, which is very often."

"So, literally everyone at Saint Sebastian's has access to the mailroom. You've missed your calling. Should have been a gumshoe, not a nun."

I stole a glimpse of myself in the passenger mirror. Next to Riveaux, I looked like a carnival freak. She had dark, clear skin despite her cigarette addiction. I was a mosaic of puzzle pieces that didn't fit but were cobbled together anyway. Gaping holes here and there.

As we drove through a red light, we passed an apartment for rent—2-BDRM, 1-BTHRM, NOT HAUNTED—and a charm parlor. ODDITIES AND ECCENTRICITIES. LOVE POTIONS ON SALE. I thought of

Sister T. A man in a white cowboy hat and oversized denim overalls blurred past. I thought he was walking an exceedingly long dog until I registered that the animal was an alligator. The creature, its face frozen in a smile, winked at me with one of its wet eyes.

"This is taking too long," Riveaux said. Too many cars for us to make a clean pass. She turned on the car's top-mounted siren. It blasted a few cars out of the way. "And it's hotter than a billy goat in a chile patch."

"Doesn't bother me," I said.

"You complain about everything *except* the heat. Even with those gloves. What's the story with all that?" she asked.

"I'm incognito."

"Gold tooth and neck tattoos are real incognito. Don't need to wear 'em around me. Your secrets are safe."

"Everyone's got secrets, and none of them are safe."

Riveaux dug into her pocket and pulled out a prescription bottle. She fumbled with her left hand as she tried to open it.

"Jesus take the wheel," I said, sparking a loud laugh from Riveaux.

She finally put the bottle into her mouth, bit down, and popped the white plastic top off. She dropped one pill on the middle of her tongue and swallowed it with no water.

"A bit early for recreational drugs."

She chuckled. "My migraine won't quit. I can't believe you are on a dispatch call with me. Again."

"You said I could tag along if I shared what I saw and heard on campus."

"Dish the dirt then."

"There is no dirt," I said, my voice practically drowned out by the siren. "No one is saying anything."

"You're of no use to me then."

We sailed over a speed bump. Airborne for a terrifying second. I pressed the door lock for the thirteenth time and tightened my seat belt.

Driving with Riveaux gave me whiplash, but the severity of it was divine. I closed my eyes as my heart sped up. Riveaux cranked the car's speed. The siren wailed. I palmed my cross. *Hail Mary, full of grace.*

The car squealed to a stop as Riveaux parked hastily, twenty feet behind fire engine #72, which had an American flag painted on the back.

A skewer of smoke sliced the firmament in half. In front of the fire engine on the left side of Tchoupitoulas Street was a classic yellow school bus spewing wild flames. The letters on the side of the bus read SAINT SEBASTIAN'S CATHOLIC SCHOOL.

"Ain't that a sight." Riveaux licked her lips and ran to four NOFD colleagues in helmets, bright green suspenders, and fire coats. They ran with fire hoses from a supply engine with a water tank. There were no hydrants nearby. "Where's the driver?" she asked. "Students?"

"Driver's with our EMT and she's doing fine. No kids on board. Driver said it started in the back of the bus. Out of nowhere. No warnings."

I blessed myself and kissed my hands to the sky.

Fire raged through the two rear windows of the bus. It was eating a hole through the metal roof.

The soundscape reverberated as if a bomb went off. Two tires on the bus's left side blew, causing the vehicle to teeter. As firefighters pounded the blaze with water hoses from east, west, and south, fire and smoke poured through the passenger door of the bus, silent as lava.

Headlights shattered. I stared at the bus's circular reflector light. Saw myself double in its orange refraction, like a giant amber eye, before the heat cracked it in half.

In the shock of red ruin, my body shut down, my brain offlined. I stared at my useless hands. At a flattened water bottle with no wrapper.

Another eruption of tires.

My voice climbed back into my throat. *God exists and God is good. God exists and God is good*, I chanted.

"If we don't get this puppy contained," a firefighter hollered to Riveaux, "the whole thing is going to blow. Mags, suit up and get her out of here," he pointed to me.

"What are you going to do?" I coughed and followed Riveaux, who was walking backward.

"Get in there to help the crew tame this shit." Riveaux suited up in a pair of extra boots, a helmet, pants, and a long black coat. "You need to get back—way back." She looked at me, then the fiery bus. "It's on."

Heat from the fire boiled the air. Black smoke unspooled through the bus windows.

"Mags, move your truck!" A firefighter needed Riveaux to reverse her pickup. Another engine was waiting to park.

"Sister, move it for me!" Riveaux shouted.

She was about to throw the keys to me when I said, "I can't drive stick. I'm sorry."

"Shit, Sister. No time for this." Riveaux, coughing and cursing to herself, jumped into the driver's seat to reverse her truck.

Fire danced as it ripped through the back of the school bus, throwing the back door sideways, leaving it dangling by one blackened hinge.

A bite of sun through the smoke cast a wicked glow on the flames. If fire isn't possession by the devil, then nothing is. Fire crawled without legs—a viper. Pure inhabitation of a demon force.

O Lord. You have mercy on all, take away from me my sins and mercifully set me ablaze with the fire of Your Holy Spirit.

What was once a school bus was now a carcass, a burnt façade. The empty windows gaped open, making it look like a startled skeleton. The fire, insatiable, started to tear away chunks of Tchoupitoulas pavement.

Riveaux started the pickup and hit the gas, but instead of reversing to make room for the new fire engine, she shot forward. Into the back of engine #72. Two men fell off the truck.

"Riveaux!" a firefighter shouted. "What the hell?"

From the side of the road, I watched her body thrust forward, as if thrown by a giant hand. Her head struck the windshield with such force the glass cracked with two thick, intersecting lines. Like a cross.

22

"**WHY DID YOU GUN IT** in 'drive'?" I asked Riveaux in the hospital after her crash. Her neck brace practically covered her whole face. Her glasses rested on the bedside table. "You could have killed your men," I said. "Or yourself."

"I'm not leaving that easily. Gotta stick around to annoy you."

"Level with me." I tried to hold her gaze. "Were you drinking? I'll absolve you."

She rubbed her right temple. Then her left. "Just worn out."

"Up late making Eau de Dumbass?"

"More like tired from dealing with your dumb ass."

We sat in silence. I let her win that round of banter.

She needed a win.

After Riveaux was rushed to the ER, she had an X-ray, an MRI, and an abdominal exam. Nothing had fractured despite her trouncing. A rib contusion, serious concussion, and whiplash. Relatively lucky despite her stupid mistake.

Riveaux requested a different doctor when she heard that Dr. Gorman, a young female resident, would be caring for her.

"Don't change doctors," I said. "It'll delay everything."

"I've known Dr. Turner for years. Get her," Riveaux demanded. Her voice was hoarse but determined. She put her glasses back on as I shuffled out to the nurse station to placate Riveaux.

We waited for the doctor and more test results. A subdural hematoma was still a possibility. I shivered at the sight of the mechanical bed's remote control. The tissue boxes, rubber gloves.

Riveaux powered her phone on, and it buzzed for a minute. An avalanche of texts seemed to pour in. She scrolled through a few and laughed, then slid the glowing rectangle under her skull-white pillow. "Rock's doing the baby-man thing again, having all his boys tell me how much he worships me, not to leave him."

"Listen to your gut."

"I should have left years ago," she said.

"Being in a bad situation doesn't make you a bad person. Though your fashion is another story."

"You're one to talk. Ragged cat burglar over there."

I grabbed the Bible stashed in the side table. The Word was always close by. "Ever read this?"

Riveaux squinted at the Bible and laughed. "Get that away from me. Pray for me to win the Powerball so I can quit this fucking job and open a perfumery."

"You know the whole point of the Bible?" I asked.

"Didn't realize it had a point."

"It's a compass."

"Can't believe you're pushing the Bible on me *now*! I thought you were different." Riveaux readjusted, as if trying to get comfortable.

A nurse materialized, placed her clipboard on an empty chair, and removed the neck brace gently. "Merci," Riveaux said.

The MRI showed no bleeding in Riveaux's brain, but she still had to "take it easy." She said "yes, dear" to all of Dr. Turner's orders, dressed, marshaled her strength, and picked up all her medicines.

We walked outside, into the extruder of 100 percent humidity. The marbled sky threatened rain. The air smelled like old dust and burnt paper. A police car rolled by.

"They're increasing the frequency of the patrols," Riveaux said.

"The arsonist is ten steps ahead of us. They'll probably burn the whole church down while we have our meeting tonight."

The air churned. I needed to get back to the convent.

Riveaux opened the passenger door of a taxi, slid in, then leaned out of the window. "I've seen investigations unravel too many times to count. Stay objective. Don't get emotional. I'm going home to rest while the truck's in the shop."

"Tell them to fix the air-conditioning."

"Some things are beyond repair," she said through the window.

Detective Grogan appeared as the taxi's taillights disappeared. Sergeant Decker was nowhere in sight.

"Mags is off in a hurry," Grogan said as he ran his sausage fingers through his blond hair. His right cheek was packed with chewing tobacco.

"Restless, that one," I said, and turned to walk back to the convent, the long trek up Saint Charles in the fierce heat. Grogan's hand landed on my left shoulder. He spat his shit-colored juice as he spun me to face him.

"Sister, I know we have differences of opinion. Your lifestyle and all."

I stepped back. "Lifestyle?"

"Where we all agree is that you need to stop getting in the way. Leave these investigations to the pros." He moved closer. His chin hovered above the top of my head.

"The pros?" I laughed. "I don't see 'the pros' doing much of anything."

"Why are you so fixated on this case?" His eyes traveled along my face, as if he were tracing the outline of my jawline and chin.

"Saint Sebastian's is my home."

He brought his hand slowly to my neck and pulled at the knot of my neckerchief. It loosened. He lifted my left hand, peeled back the wrist of my black glove. "Never did see a nun with tattoos before. And you sure have a lot of 'em." I jerked my hand away from his. "They everywhere on your body?"

"Yes."

"Desecrating the body don't seem too holy, if you ask me." He leaned so close I could feel his breath on my head. "Ain't the body a temple?"

"Yes. A temple that wants to be adorned. Like a cathedral, amplifying the glory of God, with painted ceilings and stained glass."

"Are you stained, Sister Holiday?"

I tried to back away from him but there was nowhere to go. People milled about the street seemingly oblivious to the two of us. Grogan smiled. His shirt collar and tie were perfectly pressed. Up close I could see that his eyes were young, but his skin was leathery. Too much time in the Louisiana sun. "So many tattoos," he repeated, and touched my scarf. "Where do they stop?" He spit onto the street. A trace of the warm liquid landed on my cheek, and I quickly wiped it off.

"Grogan," Sergeant Decker called to her partner through the open passenger window of their cruiser as she pulled up. "Chief needs us downtown. Want to get in?"

My legs shook.

"Shame we have to cut this short." He opened the car door and slipped in.

"Shame."

23

THE CAMPUS DUSK-TO-DAWN CURFEW remained in effect. Unlike the cops, the curfew made me feel safe. Any building on our campus—the east, west, or central wings, the convent, the church, the rectory—could burn at any moment.

Back at the convent, I washed my face and tied a clean black neckerchief over my throat, pulled on my gloves. I went to retrieve my rosary, but I couldn't find it. It wasn't at the foot of the bed where I had left it. I looked under the bed. Nothing. Not on the windowsill or desk. Finally, its familiar shape caught my eye. My rosary was looped around the doorknob. I hadn't left it there. Perhaps I dropped it and one of my Sisters returned it. Or someone had moved my things around when I was in the bathroom.

Or I was losing my mind.

I looked for evidence of someone poking around my room, but found nothing.

I replayed Riveaux's crash. And Grogan's puff-up, baring his teeth, trying to scare me. Maybe he locked me in the closet. Maybe the cops were colluding, covering up some procedural fuckup—or something bigger?

Despite the high alert, the Saint Sebastian's faculty and staff would be holding a prayer circle to discuss keeping Catholic education alive and combating dropping enrollment.

Before joining the meeting, I crossed the street and ducked into church to bless myself with holy water. I needed the reset. I was surprised to see Prince talking to Sister Augustine near the church altar. BonTon stood by Prince's side. Sister Augustine waved to me. Snippets of their conversation carried to the back of the church.

"Good to see you back where you belong," Sister Augustine said to Prince. "Back at church."

I stood in the doorway listening, the same spot I stood every Sunday and heard the tears and trials and joys of our congregants. Touching their faces nervously. Blessing themselves. BonTon turned her head in my direction and bayed.

"I will be right with you, Sister Holiday." Even though Sister Augustine spoke quietly, her voice filled the church. House of worship acoustics were better than any club I'd ever played.

Prince flicked his lighter on and off. "This school is killing me."

Sister Augustine sighed. "Put your lighter away. You look tired, Mr. Dempsey. Are you resting? Monitoring that blood sugar? No serious highs or lows?"

Prince shrugged.

She said in my direction, "We are already behind schedule. Let's make our way." Sister Augustine left the altar and joined me at the back of the church.

Prince walked to the middle of the church and BonTon followed, dragging her red leash dutifully. He took a seat in a pew and knelt. I had never seen him pray before. Was he putting on a show for our principal?

BonTon barked. One fast, hard bark, like a gunshot.

"Damn, I'm thirsty," Prince yelled.

"You need water?" Sister Augustine asked. We walked over to him.

"Water. It's hot in here. It's wet!" Sweat poured from Prince's hairline.

"He seems wasted," I said to Sister Augustine. "Prince, have you been drinking?"

Prince's face twitched as he fell out of the pew, onto the aisle's carpet, the red hue of a brush burn. BonTon nosed his face, licked his lips, then yowled so loud I had to cover my ears.

"It's hypoglycemia!" Sister Augustine's voice cracked. "Low blood sugar! Good Lord, stay with us. Prince, stay with us." She ran to the doors and cried out, "Help! We need help in here."

I heard a student at the door.

"Call 911! Tell them we have a diabetic emergency with a male student, aged eighteen."

"Damn. Okay." The student dialed and on speakerphone she said, "Hey, 911! Help! We need an ambulance at Saint Sebastian's Church. Hurry. Some kid is on the ground."

Sister Augustine spoke quickly. "Run across the street to the school. Tell Shelly to call Prince's mother immediately. Her number is on my desk."

The student said "okay" and dashed off swiftly, like she was covered in Vaseline.

"We need his emergency kit. He's in shock." Sister Augustine blinked, then said clearly. "Lord help us! Sister, get an insulin kit. The red case. There's one in the fridge in my office and one in the nurse's office fridge. Don't get the one that has expired. *Run.*"

"Where is it? How do I know which case?"

"I'll go." She started to sprint. "Hold him. Keep him awake."

"Wait!" But she was gone.

BonTon hopped and barked. She rooted her nose into the crook of Prince's neck.

I crouched down. BonTon growled like mad as I rested Prince's greasy head in my lap.

"Prince," I yelled. "Stay with me, you bastard."

His eyes twitched, like he was stuck in purgatory. Between here and there, wherever there is. His stubble grated my hand as I opened his mouth to make sure he wasn't biting his tongue. I put two fingers in his mouth, pressing down his tongue to make sure the airway was clear. His lips were warm. A few of Prince's teeth were cracked and rotting. Dead breath, so sour I almost gagged. His saliva on my hand.

I cradled his draping body. I felt the eyes of Jack's seraphim watching us.

We are all like stained glass, beautiful and complicated and fragile as fuck. We all need care. And some of us don't get what we deserve.

Prince's body was warm as I prayed over him. *Hail Mary. Good Saint Anne. All the angels and saints.*

Sister Augustine returned with the medicine quickly. She had run the length of the school's central wing, but she didn't seem winded.

"He's fading." I put my ear on his heart and heard a faint beating. "Prince." His head was still in my lap. "What do I do with the syringe?"

Sister Augustine opened Prince's eyelids. His eyeballs were milky. "I'll do it. We need a clean injection site. Check his stomach." She opened the red plastic kit, removing the needle and vial of insulin.

I leaned down, lifted his shirt, but his stomach was a network of scars. Cross-hatched. He was a cutter, apparently. Or he let the dog scratch the hell out of him. Masochistic fun. Pleasure-pain. I knew it well.

"His stomach won't work."

"Try his behind or his thighs." Sister Augustine spoke quickly but with authority.

I unbuckled Prince's belt, turned him on his side in my lap. BonTon watched quietly, with intense focus. I pulled down his filthy jeans so Sister Augustine could inject his butt cheek. Sister Augustine inserted the syringe into the vial and carefully withdrew its liquid. She swiped his skin with an alcohol swab and injected him on his right cheek. I applied pressure to the site for a moment, then we rolled him back over in my lap, pulled his pants up.

Prince's eyelids pulsed. The medicine was working. BonTon barked.

"Bonnie, Bonnie," Prince bleated.

BonTon yelped, slobbered over his forehead. She panted, dug her nose into his ear. She licked his cheek so hard his head fell off my lap and onto the ground, where it landed with a thud.

"Owww," Prince groaned with his eyes still closed.

"Praise Jesus! Praise." Sister Augustine had tears in her eyes. "Thank you, Lord."

The EMTs, now familiar faces to me by that point, had arrived.

Sister Augustine told the medics the details of the insulin. "Ten minutes ago, he got confused, numb, and he passed out. Not sure if he's eaten today."

"Roger," said the medic.

"Where am I?" Prince asked.

"At church. You will be just fine," Sister Augustine said. "The Lord is always watching over you. Praise Him! Thank you, Lord, for your everlasting love."

The EMTs carefully loaded him onto a stretcher to take him to New Orleans City Hospital, where I had just been with Riveaux. Where Jamie spent about two weeks recuperating.

"BonTon?" he whispered as they wheeled him outside.

"She will be by your side at every turn." Sister Augustine handed BonTon's leash to a medic, then she pivoted to me. "Sister Holiday, God has blessed you. You helped save Prince."

24

WITH PRINCE'S GREASE STILL on my hands, I stopped at the sidewalk shrine for a short prayer, asking Sister Augustine to start the staff meeting without me. I needed a moment alone with God, with myself.

When I joined our meeting in the faculty lounge, Sister Augustine abruptly left to take a call from the Diocese. Sister Honor gleefully took the reins, blabbing on and on about moral rectitude.

I turned to John seated next to me at the table. "Why are your hands shaking?"

"Oh, that? I graded so many papers this morning. A cramp in my right hand like you would not believe. Trying to work it out."

"Give them all A's and be done with it," I joked, but wondered if John was developing Parkinson's or something. I hoped he trusted me enough to share.

As I looked at the cross on the wall and revisited the hell of the past two weeks, I silently ran through my list of suspects, like mouthing song lyrics before a live show in Brooklyn.

"Earth to Sister Holiday." It was John's voice, a light whisper underneath Sister Honor's drone.

"Sorry," I replied. "Praying for a rewarding meeting."

"Undoubtedly," said Sister Honor, outing me for talking during the meeting. She was an old bat, but I shouldn't have been surprised by her sonar-level hearing. Usually, I was the one shaming Prince Dempsey for talking during class. Sister Honor brought a white cloth hankie to her nose and wiped it. "Avarice. Selfishness. Always praying to be rewarded."

"Ignore her," John said to me softly. "Focus on the positive. Before you walked in, Sister Augustine told us how you both saved Prince. Quite a feat."

"Thanks." I cracked my gloved knuckles. "Prince's diabetes is getting really bad."

"Worse than usual?" Rosemary asked.

"He's extra volatile lately."

"That's unfortunately the nature of the disease," said Sister Honor. "Bless his malcontent heart."

I stared at Sister Augustine's elegant script. She had written *Christian Values* on the chalkboard before leaving for her call.

When I looked away, I caught a silent signal—a shared, piercing look—that strung an invisible rope between Rosemary and Sister Honor.

"I haven't told her yet." Rosemary directed her words to Sister Honor, knowing full well I could hear.

"Told her what?" I asked.

"You're the sleuth," Sister Honor chortled, "you work it out."

"Not a very quick one," Rosemary said slyly.

A thin smile crept across Sister Honor's face, her cheeks sagging. "It was likely rat poison that killed Voodoo. When

Bernard was cleaning, he found traps that Jack had laid out months ago. He told us they were empty, picked clean." Sister Honor practically whinnied, reveling in the macabre detail.

"Makes sense," I said flatly, envisioning Voodoo's tiny nose. I balled my fists and ground my molars to beat back tears and feel the familiar sting. That sweet little cat came to me as she was dying. She came to me for comfort, and I didn't find her in time.

Another failing in my lifetime of mistakes.

"I was going to tell you this morning," Rosemary said, "but you had better things to do."

Sister Augustine reappeared and rattled off new protocol from the Diocese. I stared through the window. I could take in only some of the courtyard from my viewpoint, but it was enough to distract me. Magnificent flowering trees. Fountained weeping willows. Night rivers of jasmine. The cleanliness of the convent leveled me, saved me.

The Sisters of the Sublime Blood had not abandoned me, despite my temptations and sins. I was trying to follow their lead—praying, teaching, giving, making amends.

Prince needed me. I'd had my fingers inside his mouth, his saliva and cells were still on my hands. He had no choice but to trust me and Sister Augustine.

Like me in the back of the ambulance, my eyelids held open by the EMTs.

Moose in some distant land, patching up wounds.

How scary and sacred it is, to place your trust in someone. To ask for help. Almost like love.

Everyone I loved I could visit only in my mind.

Jesus. My parents. My brother. Sister T. Nina.

I let my mind rest on Nina. Our countless hours together. Staring at her wedding ring, imagining it had been from me, and that she was my wife. The torturous futility of it.

I replayed one morning with Nina after a wild night while Nicholas was away. I knelt at the foot of her broken bed, as if I were praying. I pulled her to me. Her legs wrapped around my waist.

"I'm going to get my shit together," I said. "Starting today."

"You say that every time I see you." She tilted her head, looking at me quizzically. Brought her hands to my face. She pressed her fingers into my cheekbones. "You're so clean."

"I just showered."

She traced my eyebrows. "In all these years, I don't think I've ever seen you without makeup."

Nina moved her hands along my collarbone and neck, stopping at the Eve tattoo. She lifted my chin and turned my face right and left, silently, as if she were a scientist trying to classify a new species. She opened my mouth and touched my gold cap. "Hmm."

"What are you doing?"

"I want to see what you do when you cannot hide."

I traced the lattice of veins in her left wrist. She touched my necklaces, earrings, and hand tattoos. We always did that, marveled at one another, worshipped each other's bodies.

"You should go," she said. "Nicholas will be home in two hours."

I climbed on top of her, loved feeling her underneath me. Closeness I craved.

"What is this?" she tilted her head. "What are you doing?"

"Making up for last night," I said.

"Surprised you remember anything about last night."

"Sorry I didn't text," I said. "That was selfish and dumb."

Nina was still pissed. "Apologize."

I lowered my head. "I'm sorry."

"Sorry for what?"

"For being good at sex and bad at love."

"Stand up," she instructed.

I stood in front of her.

She loosened my towel and it fell to the floor. She trailed her fingers from my sternum to my navel, over a network of overlapping tattoos. "This is why I can't stay mad at you. You're too hot to be mad at for long."

I straddled her on the bed. She put her hands on my ribcage. She slipped her shirt off and tossed it on the rug. She followed the lines of my thigh muscles with her red fingernails.

I shivered at her light touch and laughed.

"Why are you laughing?" she asked.

"That tickles," I said. "Stop. I am trying to be sexy."

"Trust me, you are," she said. "And stop trying to be anything. Just be yourself."

"I don't know what that is."

She grabbed a fistful of my damp hair. I kissed her, put my right hand on her left cheek, my thumb resting lightly on her throat.

As we kissed, I opened my eyes quickly to look at her. Her brow was furrowed, streaked with creases, thin as knife marks.

"You okay?"

"Yes." She lay back, her head on the pillow, her hair an electric contrast to the dull white sheets. I kissed her stomach then opened her knees. She closed her mismatched eyes. I pressed my thumbs on her hipbones. Her skin was taut where bone met muscle. She tasted elemental but new. Like minerals forming.

Rain at the edge of the slate city. She curled her left hand into a fist, bit her thumb knuckle to stay quiet. I wanted it to be agonizing, for both of us to suffer in that sublime way. To bring her to the cliff, leave her there for a while, then hurl us over. Her taste changed, from sea to living metal. Her body tremors made her seem possessed.

I recall the softness of her skin as I rested my face on her stomach. I let her pulse burn into my cheek, sealing the memory in place. The abdominal aorta pumps as the heart beats, like a secret heart. But every heart holds a secret. Something nested inside that can never reveal itself.

We lay like that, Nina breathing heavy, us saying nothing. The morning—bike bells, clicking high heels, beeping cars—rammed into high gear. Sunrise loved to bounce off mirrors and windows of the apartment buildings. New York's light show. Nowhere to hide, except in plain sight.

25

AFTER THE WASTE-OF-TIME MEETING, Rosemary and I walked the long corridor and down the steps.

I said, "Bye," making my way toward our shared classroom.

"Bye," she parroted, like an accusation.

Then we both walked into the room at the same time, bumping arms. She was several inches taller than me, so her elbow jabbed the tender part of my bicep.

"Oh." Rosemary was startled. "I need to be in here now, *alone*, to grade quizzes." She pointed at the stack of papers on her extremely tidy makeshift desk. "I have midterm projects to plan."

"More like another *fire* to plan?" I stared, trying to read her.

"You cannot be serious."

"So the fires aren't serious to you?"

"You're seriously annoying," she replied, exasperated. But I sensed heat.

"I need the room now to prepare a lesson." I pointed to my desk, my office, crowded with books in sloppy piles, papers,

CDs, refuse. It looked like the domain of an indulged, ignored child.

"Fine." She sat at her desk. From a large silver cup, she regarded three, four, five pens before deciding on her preferred instrument.

"Whatever." I tried to lance her with my sharp tone, but, like a boomerang, it shot right back to me.

"Whatever," repeated Rosemary. I could tell she was smiling, secretly smirking at me, though I didn't confirm it with a glance across the classroom.

She graded quizzes methodically while I studied my notes on the case.

The silence was annihilating. I itched for a cigarette, stared at the old linoleum floor patterned with triangle clusters, brown as dried blood.

All I wanted to do was go home. Pray and sleep. I walked outside to the hallway for a drink of water. In the silver basin I watched my reflection shake as ripples bent my image.

Back in the room I was restless.

"Can't you sit still," Rosemary suggested, a futile attempt. "You need to be shot with a tranquilizer dart."

"You would like that," I said, putting my hands around my covered neck. "Watching me stagger and fall."

"Could you be more dramatic?"

At that moment, Sister Augustine popped her head into our room. She must have sensed disagreement in the stale air. She blinked. "God wants us to face our challenges *today*, with radical grace."

As she turned and left, her veil looked to me like a fin that guided a way forward.

It was getting late but neither of us made attempts to leave. Rosemary and I sat on opposite sides of the room. Through the classroom window, the night sky turned blood orange with the setting sun. New Orleans looked more like a silhouette than a city.

"I cannot believe I have to share this room," Rosemary quibbled, "with *you*. Music isn't a real discipline and it's not a district requirement. Music won't help our students advance in their studies and it certainly will not help them secure good jobs."

"I used to be a musician, not that it was a *great job*, but—"

"Your clutter certainly sets the scene," she announced as she walked over to one of the dozen music stands and tapped it.

"I was an artist, I mean. Now I'm—"

"Annoying," she said. "I hate art. Art is for the rich and the afflicted."

She seemed wealthy and tortured, I thought but didn't say. "Maybe you *think* you hate art because you don't understand it, like religion. People do themselves a great disservice when they write something off because it's new to them." I leaned in my desk chair. Sweat dripped under my breasts, over my *deified* and Sacred Heart, down my stomach. The air swirled with murky heat.

"You sound like Sister Augustine," she said.

I thought of Sister Augustine's pain, losing her father like that. Me losing my mom. All of us holding secrets, hiding our wounds. How I doubted her. "She's been a lifeline for me."

"For all of us," Rosemary said. "I admire Sister Augustine. Her professionalism and reliability."

"She keeps us sane." I crossed my knees and lightly shook out my left foot, which was pulsing with pins and needles.

I looked at Rosemary, but her eyes were elsewhere, in a distant place, far away or somewhere deep inside of her. She leaned against the front of my desk, the way so many students did as they itemized the reasons they didn't practice.

Our classroom was double lit—the flood of fluorescent light softened by the diffuse glow from nearby buildings.

Because I was sweaty, or because I temporarily lost my judgment, I removed my gloves and scarf. Rosemary took notice. I didn't want her to stare at my tattoos. I didn't want her to look away, either. I pulled my cross out from under my blouse and laid it flat over my chest.

"Flashing your crucifix to further your confounding agenda?" Her voice was sharp.

"It's a cross, not a crucifix." I straightened my posture. Fighting with Rosemary wasn't going to get me anywhere. We'd never understand each other. But I *wanted* to spar. "A standard, perfect, Catholic cross. Used to be my mom's."

She moved closer to me, leaned down, and took the metal between her thumb and forefinger. Inspected it slowly. The way her heart-shaped mouth held red lipstick made her seem wise and old, like a portrait from WWII. "Why do you wear a cross instead of a crucifix?" she asked.

"The cross is a symbol, the crucifix is a moment in time," I said. "Jesus is present on the crucifix, but his absence—his shadow—is on the cross. For me at least. A constant reminder of suffering to come, or the suffering of the past, what he was willing to endure for salvation."

"Hm." She turned it over, leaning down so close I could feel her warm breath on my chin, could smell her rose-scented hand lotion. She inhaled tensely. "The opiate of the masses."

She let the gold cross rest on my blouse, over my burning Sacred Heart. "Religion is the opposite of science," she mused as she touched the necklace again, then traced my gold chain with her fingertip. Her skin was cool and soft. "And science is the enemy of religion. It's an unending battle."

"It's not a battle," I said. "Just different ways of understanding the world. And how we fit into it."

She hesitated, then smiled. It was magnificent. I hadn't seen her truly smile until just then, in the amber light of our classroom.

"Why are we whispering?"

"Feels appropriate."

"We should lock up and go now," I said.

"There are a lot of things we should and shouldn't do right now." She readjusted her hands, interlacing her fingers. It was hard to decode Rosemary's expression. Her breath paused the way it does before you say something important. But she didn't say anything else. Neither of us did.

It would have been so easy to walk over to her, press her against the wall of our ugly classroom, and kiss her. I wanted to, so badly. But I didn't. I bit my lip until it bled, until I tasted salt and metal.

Did Sister Honor orchestrate this whole thing? Put me and Rosemary in the same room, tempting me to forget my vows? Distract me?

Or was Rosemary Flynn breaking bad in her weird way? The chemistry savant wasting her talents in the underworld of high school education, finally claiming her rightful power by setting fires? Making a move—throwing red meat my way—a signature femme fatale play.

I didn't take the bait. I shut my eyes and imagined myself disappearing.

■

Before supper, I showered and changed into a fresh pair of black pants and a black blouse. Savored an extra moment alone as I brushed my hair, which, at that point, was long enough to pull back in a miniature ponytail.

The curfew limited my movement, but I needed to be outside. Careful not to catch the attention of a cop on guard, I slipped into the convent garden. Late summer heat had scorched most of the grass, and a carpet of fallen petals had softened the earth. I touched a new jasmine blossom. It was small and innocent in the way of a growing thing. I should have left it alone so it could grow, but I broke it off and stuffed it into my pocket, where it would never open.

I walked to a bench, smoked one of Ryan Brown's contraband cigs and sipped one of his confiscated peach schnapps shooters.

I thought about Rosemary. Was she moving the chess pieces, trying to set me up? Her hatred of organized religion was palpable, and yet she worked at a Catholic school. *Why*?

Or was it Sister Honor betting against me, judging me as weak? Sister Honor despised me, that much was irrefutable, but she didn't seem to hate Jack or Sister T. Nor Lamont or Jamie, so gruesomely injured. The red eye of Jamie's wound, a blood tunnel that wouldn't release me, like stigmata.

Unending instigations from Prince Dempsey. His loose alibis. So eager to fight, but was it a front? Sister Augustine was clearly protective of him. And me.

Lamont was MIA; he hadn't returned to classes. Jamie was holding something back, afraid or guilty or both.

Nothing added up. Nothing made sense.

My second chance was slipping away.

I buried my face into my gloved hands, screamed into my darkness.

Kneeling on the grass, I prayed for all of us. But no matter how much I prayed, I couldn't escape the flames, ever since that night in Brooklyn, no matter how fast and far I ran.

It was the last night I spent with my mother. Late October. The wind, honeycomb-sweet, shook the trees. The sidewalks had turned into rivers of orange, gold, and red leaves. I was on Mom duty because Dad was on patrol and Moose had a work mixer.

"I need fresh air," said Mom. "Take me for a drive."

"Moose said it's a bad idea."

"Please," she pleaded, weakly. "Let me see the city I love in my favorite season."

I shook my head. "Pop will kill me."

"I don't have much time left."

"Okay." I relented. "Let me see if I can borrow the band van."

It might be the last time she can leave the apartment alive, I thought. Mom could hardly walk. She needed a break from the agony of sameness. Being locked in that stuffy, cramped apartment. A night drive with Mom seemed incredibly stupid but doable. I didn't have a car, so I asked Nina if I could borrow the band's van, our beat-up junk heap that we bought for five hundred bucks from her brother, Steve. The van was registered to Nina, but Original Sin used it for tours. Not that we toured widely, but we hit Philly and Boston throughout the year. Lugging amps, instruments, bongs, incense altars, illicit drugs, and cases of beer. Somehow, we managed to keep the thing intact despite the years of abuse and reckless driving. The theatrics and antics of punks who refused to grow up. We never rotated the tires, checked the alignment, or changed the oil.

An hour later, Nina drove the van to Brooklyn. She texted: *Van parked in the usual spot but needs gas. Take Toni somewhere nice. I'm going to Dobranoc if you wanna join later. Luv xx*

The van always seemed to be on *E*. I had a key on my keychain. Miracle I hadn't lost it.

I brushed my teeth and helped Mom down the steps carefully in her nightgown, robe, and slippers. She was lighter than a rosary.

After fueling up the van at Exxon, eking out extra gas by shaking the nozzle a few times, we drove slowly through the labyrinthine Bay Ridge streets. Mom sat in the passenger seat.

"Nothing prettier than the city at night." She let her head rest against the glass.

I readjusted the passenger wing mirror to catch brief glimpses of her eyes, to see what she was seeing.

Brooklyn was crackling with energy and action. Airscape of sirens and traffic. A couple in matching red motorcycles sped past our van and cruised by a stop sign, almost hitting a biker in the designated cycle lane.

"Bike lanes in Brooklyn," Mom whispered. "Never thought I'd live long enough for that."

I parked in front of the dive bar where Nina said she'd be. We sat for ten minutes outside the bar, van engine idling.

"What do you think *Dobranoc* means?" I asked Mom. In all the years I had patronized that bar, I never thought to ask about the name.

With her eyes closed, she said, "It's Polish for 'good night.'"

How on earth did Mom know Polish? What else did she know? I was too self-absorbed to ask.

"Let's go into 'good night,'" I said, "for a mother-daughter drink."

"I'm fine right here."

"Just one drink," I whined. "It'll be fun."

"I need to rest," she said. "I want to stay and watch my city." She smiled but it was forced. Her face was being slowly erased. "Go ahead."

I pulled up the van's emergency brake, and cranked up the heat. "I can't leave you here alone."

"I'm not alone," she patted the cross around her neck.

I put a blanket on her lap and turned on WNYC, Mom's favorite radio station. She loved listening to real, unedited voices. Said it was holy. I locked the van doors.

Nina was dancing inside the bar as I walked in. A riot of bronze hair with messy bangs above her cat-eye makeup. She danced alone in the corner. Spinning around and around, fast and warped, like a vinyl record so good it loses its shape. Nina never gave a fuck when Nicholas was out of town. Madcap Nina.

She waved when she saw me. "Holidaaaaaaay!"

"Hey."

"You came! How did it go with your mom?"

"She's outside."

"Jesus, Holiday . . ."

That night, with Dad on overnight duty and Mom locked in the idling van, I drank. One whiskey turned into two. Then four. Drink after drink. Nina went outside every ten minutes or so, to check on Mom.

"How is she?" I asked, with my head on the bar. One eye opened, one eye closed.

"She's okay. Sleeping." She put her hand on my shoulder. "She's curled up like a beagle. Seems peaceful. At least she's not stuck in that bedroom."

"This shit is so hard." I did a shot. The whiskey tasted dreadful, uninspired, like it was tired of performing. I rested my forehead on my wrists. "Doesn't help that I'm a fuckup."

"You're wasted, hon. But you're beautiful."

I smiled.

"It's good to see you smile for a change." She kissed me. Her warm lips on mine. I opened my mouth and she lightly traced my bottom lip with her tongue. I remember how she tasted, like green olives and vodka. She put her hand on my right bicep, on my tattoo of SISTER ANTONIA. My mom's name when she was a nun. The cursive letters coiled around a red chancel lamp on my arm. Mom told me about the lamp, its ever-present flame, when I was ten years old. Its incandescence symbolized pure light. It was one of my first tattoos.

"I need another drink," I said.

The bartender looked at me with curiosity—or pity—in her raised eyebrows.

I leveled my head as if it could make me sound sober. "I need a house whiskey and put extra alcohol in it." Straight liquor like a sandblast to eat my brain. That's what I needed.

"Sweet pea, you don't want the *house* whiskey," said the tall bartender as she flipped her filthy towel over her tattooed shoulder. "It's like lighter fluid."

"Lit lighter fluid." Nina shuddered.

"That's exactly what I want."

"Here, love." The bartender slid a glass my way. "My treat."

"She's into me," I told Nina.

"Dear Lord." She rolled her eyes. "Stop."

I leaned over the bar. "Hey!"

"What's up?" the bartender asked as she rinsed a glass.

"Want to make out later?"

Nina pulled the back of my shirt and I careened onto the bar stool. "You are the fucking worst."

"What did I do?"

"I'm sitting right here."

"What's the big deal? We're not dating. You married Nicholas, remember?"

"You have my name tattooed on your arm."

"I have lots of names on my arm," I said. "And room for plenty more."

"Forget it. I'm done. You can check on your own mother," she said. "Do what you want to do."

"Thanks for your permission."

After another shot, I stepped into the storeroom where I enjoyed a hot and heavy makeout session with the bartender on a vintage pinball machine that was out of service.

When I emerged, it was 2 a.m. Nina was chatting up a hipstery waif who looked like Ariel from *The Little Mermaid*, minus the tail. Nina broke their deeply intellectual conversation to ask me, "How's your mom?"

"Great," I lied. I hadn't checked on her at all.

I felt my pockets to make sure I had my wallet and keys when I noticed two people standing at the door.

A man at the window shouted. "Fire! Something is on fire!"

Nina stood quickly. "Oh, fuck."

The van.

Mom.

We pushed our way through the bar, but it was jammed with people. When I spilled onto the street, I saw it. Fire. Liquid red.

Our band's van was ablaze, with my mother locked inside.

So drunk I could barely stand, I tried to run the few yards to the van, but everything was in slow motion. I needed to open the door, pull Mom out.

The heat shoved me back as I reached the burning vehicle.

"Help! She's in there!"

"Who?" asked a cop who was sprinting toward us.

"My mom! She's in the van."

"Get back." The cop snapped. "The engine's gonna explode."

"Mom!" I raged. "Someone help her, goddammit!"

"There's nothing we can do."

"My mother!" I slapped the cement over and over, so hard I tore the skin of my palm. "Get her out!"

No screams from inside the van. Only the sound of my voice breaking. And murmurs from horrified onlookers.

With the cop holding me back, I watched helplessly as Mom burned alive in the locked van.

Seeing but not seeing. Unable to take it in. Mom's immolation.

Three police cars and two fire engines had arrived and quickly worked the scene.

It was a cold autumn night, but the fire was so intense, everyone was sweating.

The thunder of water from powerful hoses. The van drowning.

My father and brother stood in front of Pop's cruiser. Dad wouldn't look at me.

Moose couldn't stop crying. Tears soaking his beard. My broken kid brother, now shattered beyond repair. Because of me. How he shook and fell hard, so hard, his insides giving out, spilling out of himself like a human Chernobyl.

Side by side we watched the incineration, its tremendous light and embers streaking and popping in the periphery. Cracks of tiny whips.

Pop fell too, sobbing.

"It was an accident! Pop, please. Please talk to me."

A fireman turned to me. "That your van?"

"It's mine, technically," said Nina through tears.

"A fuel leak. Or a power-steering leak," the fireman explained. "Get it serviced regularly?"

"Been years," Nina said.

"You gas up the van tonight?"

"Yes." I cried.

"Maybe it was running rich."

"What?"

"Too much fuel." He spat.

"Fuck."

"And you parked over dry leaves." He pointed at the ground. "Looks like the fire started beneath the van. Some drunk could have thrown a cig. Or a match. It went up. Fast."

"Holiday." Nina tried to hug me.

I pushed her. "I can't accept this." I paced, muttering, "This isn't happening, this isn't happening. I take it all back."

My old life ended that day.

I spent months scrapping and searching. I would join the convent, like my mother had done. I would devote myself to the liturgy. Atonement. My penance.

Six months after the accident, after Dad got me and Nina off the hook for endangerment and negligence (first and last favor he'd ever do for me in my lifetime), I canceled every music lesson I had scheduled. Stuffed my old life—driver's license, wallet, phone—in an old Dr. Martens box and gave it to Moose. I sold my jewelry, my acoustic Fender, and my electric guitar. My baby. My graphite Stratocaster. I would have sold my gold tooth too, if I could. With that seven hundred dollars, I took a taxi to JFK airport and bought a one-way ticket to New Orleans. Sister Augustine had agreed to meet with me—no one else would. People traveled to the Crescent City to get lost, find love, hide out, reinvent themselves. I needed more. I needed to be reborn.

26

I WALKED INTO THE CHURCH and was surprised to see Jamie, asleep in a pew, near the Nativity glass. His silver crutches were leaning against the dark wood. Under his head, like a lumpy pillow, was his backpack.

I read conflict in his troubled face as he woke.

"Oh, hi," he said groggily.

"Glad you're back," I said.

"I actually was hoping to talk to you," Jamie said. "I saw you."

"Me?" I was confused. "Where?"

"In the east wing, on the night of the fire."

"Of course you saw me. I carried you out."

"No. I mean, the person I saw in the hall. It was you, Sister. I even told Lamont."

"It wasn't me," I said. "I was in the alley, smoking."

"I saw you," he insisted.

"I swear on the Lord's name, it wasn't me."

Jamie exhaled slowly. "Then who was it?"

"I'm not sure. But I saw a shadow too. The Holy Ghost?"

Jamie didn't respond to my rhetorical question, and I pictured Sister Honor floating down the hall like a Macy's Thanksgiving Day Parade float. Her veil, collar, and tunic with her generic blouse underneath. Then I imagined Rosemary and her vintage twinsets, her own modest uniform. Every teacher at Saint Sebastian's followed a visual script, same as me. Everyone wanted to be invisible.

"Why were you and Lamont there in the first place?" I asked.

"I'd been sleeping there." Jamie looked down. "In the old history room."

"*Sleeping* there? For how long?"

Jamie sank into the pew. "A week. Since school started."

"You climbed the fire escape and moved the second-floor air conditioner."

"Yeah." His cheeks flushed.

"Did your parents kick you out," I asked, "because you and Lamont are together?"

"You a mind-reader or something?"

"Just attuned to the ups and downs of queer life."

Jamie scratched his neck, then tugged on his earlobe. "Mostly downs for me."

"Sorry to hear that."

"I couldn't sleep on my friend's sofa anymore because her parents are getting divorced, and her mom needed the sofa back."

"Jamie," I met his twitchy eyes, "I'm sorry that happened to you."

"Can I sleep in the convent? Or here, in the church?" His voice was brittle. One strong gust and he'd shatter.

"We'll need your parents to come in and discuss all of this."

258 ■ MARGOT DOUAIHY

"My folks don't care about me. My mom caught me making out with Lamont in my room. She totally freaked. She went nuts. Crying and screaming. My dad kicked me out. Called me a faggot and a disgrace. They said if I went to some conversion camp in Arkansas, I could come home. Lamont's been at one of those gay jails for a week."

The details poured out. Now was my chance.

"I know you didn't set the fire—there have been two more while you were laid up. But you saw something, and I need to know. Was it Lamont?"

"What? No." His voice was low. "I was just sleeping at school. We were trying to get into the room where I was crashing."

"The fire had already started?"

"Yeah. All my stuff was in that room. My clothes and my wallet. Everything I had. I lost it in the hallway. Jack heard me freaking out and—"

"And he thought you started the fire."

Jamie nodded. "He went nuts. We were saying *no no no* but he was so mad. He threw me down into a pile of glass."

"The transom glass in the hallway."

"Yeah. Lamont lunged at Jack, protecting me. Never saw him like that. Then Jack and Lamont were swinging at each other. Jack spun them into the burning room. Lamont fell when his ankle cracked."

I cleared my throat, as if that could make me see better.

"I don't know why but Jack tried to stomp out the fire. Made it worse," Jamie continued.

It all made sense then. The fireball of flashover thrust Jack through the open window, the oxygen source. That explains why Jack was so badly burnt.

"Why were you in the religion classroom?" I asked.

"Lamont crawled, dragged me in to get us away from the smoke."

"That's when I found you." I blessed us both, then put my hands around Jamie's.

"Me and Lamont, are we going to hell for what we did?" Jamie wept, the open-mouthed sob of a child.

"No, no. Jack would have tried to put out the fire no matter what. His death isn't your fault. But we have to tell the cops everything, immediately."

I put my hand on Jamie's arm again. The light from the stained glass cast a gentle spectrum across his face. We were in it together. Me and Jamie. Lamont. Moose. Misfits and castaways, all wounded in different ways.

Amid the sloppy crying, Jamie asked, his face swollen, "Can I stay with you in the convent? I stayed in the shelter once and a drunk guy said he was going to dig out my eyeballs."

"I will ask Sister Augustine if you can stay a few nights. Come into the church after evening Mass. You can sleep in the sacristy tonight. No one will see you there. I will tell the cops you're the lead altar server this week. But you can't leave from dawn till dusk. Curfew is still on."

He squeezed my gloved hands as the tension lifted from his limbs. "Thanks, Sister. You're saving me again."

"The situation with your folks isn't forever," I said. "They may come around, in time. People can surprise you. And God can too."

27

"YOU STILL LOOK LIKE *YOU*," Nina said. Her voice was incredulous, and her eyes widened as she looked me up and down. "You look like the *old* Holiday, minus the makeup."

"What? You thought I'd be wearing a Bride of Christ sign?"

It was early Thursday morning, after I spent most of Wednesday night on the phone with Riveaux, filling her in on the details from Jamie. I wanted more time to revisit my earlier interaction with Rosemary. She, Sister Honor, and the Diocese were now my primary suspects, and I was running out of time to piece it all together. But as usual, Nina commanded my attention. She was a rough-cut crystal I couldn't drop, healing or stabbing or both, depending how I held her in my heart, in my hands.

I tried to contain my excitement at seeing Nina, but the second I saw her I ran to her. We hugged tight in the arrival area of the Louis Armstrong Airport, saying nothing. Too nervous to squeal. It had been more than a year since we had seen each other. Since I left Brooklyn. Since Dad drove me to the airport in his NYPD cruiser, with Moose already gone, signed up for medic training. Whatever Dad thought about the new chapters of our lives, he didn't share. Or didn't know how to articulate.

Nina was a masterpiece—extreme and adorned. Her lipstick was firebird red.

She held one of my hands. "What's with the gloves? Handling fancy artwork?"

"More like hiding it," I said. "My ink is too artistic for the convent."

Nina moved her hand to my right hip, leaned close, and brought her lips to mine, but I quickly turned my face away.

"Don't," I said.

"Fucking seriously? It's not like I'm going down on you in front of TSA PreCheck."

"Nina, don't say that."

"*TSA* or *fucking*? Can't even curse around you now? What a fun trip this will be."

Nina slid her gold sunglasses on. Inside the airport, everything about her radiated confidence. The kind of person I used to be before I became invisible.

"Be yourself. Nothing's changed," I said.

She laughed and shifted her purse from her left shoulder to her right. "*Everything* has changed. You're a nun."

"You're still you," I said, "and I'm still me."

"No, you're not."

"Sixty seconds ago you said that I'd hardly changed."

"Whatever." She had more to say but stopped herself.

"Maybe I *have* changed. That's a good thing. We should all be growing and evolving and changing."

"An existential nun, too." Nina pulled a Camel out of a black hard pack. She tapped the cigarette against the box to tighten the tobacco. I loved the sweet, nutty cologne of fresh smokes.

The ritual of it. "So how are we getting out of here? I'm assuming you don't have a car. Is it a horse and buggy situation?"

The contact high of seeing Nina wore off quickly, replaced with the sobering reality of logistics.

She could sense it. As she pulled a lighter out of her pocket, she sulked, "I knew this would be a mistake."

"Then why come?" I asked. Seeing Nina on the verge of a tantrum reminded me of the old days. The maddening dance we played.

We loved each other but settled for crumbs.

We had only crumbs to offer.

"The band's playing a show at the Fair Grounds tonight," she said. "And I've missed you. You don't call. Or email. You've vanished."

It's true that Nina had written a dozen real letters, often asking if she could visit New Orleans. She wrote every month. I never responded. How could I? And yet, when Nina called the convent at dawn Thursday morning, after a fitful night, and announced she had arrived on a plane in from New York, my heart flipped—with fear, with excitement—as I raced to meet her.

"My buddy Bernard is here, circling the airport. A piece of work but he's sweet. He gave me a lift here and will take us into town."

Nina and I left the arrivals terminal, she in her glamor, me in austere black—scarf and gloves. We picked our way to the arrivals line through hordes of travelers rolling suitcases, families crying amid hurried hugs, and zombie teens.

She fidgeted as we waited for Bernard to circle back. A man near us tried to read the *Times-Picayune*, but it was so humid, the paper kept collapsing like a wet noodle.

"Welcome to N'Awlins," said Bernard from behind the wheel. "What do you have planned in the Big Easy?"

"Playing a show tonight," Nina replied as she slipped into the back seat. I rode shotgun. "I wanna see the French Quarter," she continued, "and have some crawfish and a Sazerac and turtle soup."

"Give the turtles eternal rest, O Lord," I said, and made the sign of the cross.

"And I want to see where you teach"—Nina tapped me on the left shoulder—"and where you live."

"Cool cool cool," Bernard said, always agreeable. "Getcha a slice of spiritual life."

"Not a good idea." I needed to shut it down quickly.

"Ashamed to be seen with me?" Nina asked harshly from the back seat.

"Of course not," I lied. "Police are permanently stationed at the campus now, and they're not fond of visitors. Or me."

Her voice dropped. "Guess I can't crash with you, then?"

"Stay with me!" Bernard piped up. "Humble digs, but I put up musicians all the time."

Nina muttered a halfhearted thanks as she chewed her thumbnail. The air in the car was stifling.

On the ride into town, Lake Pontchartrain glowed like a new moon to our left, a black magnet absorbing our wishes. Bernard, jittery, turned around every few minutes to look at Nina in the back seat, causing the car to swerve slightly onto the shoulder. Nina was supermodel gorgeous, so I didn't fault Bernard for taking a shine to her, but I didn't love it either. I caught Nina's what-the-fuck look in the rearview mirror—her big, agitated eyes asking, *Why is he here*?

"You going to tell me what's going on with the fires or what?" Nina asked, her voice had the grate of agitation. "I had to read about it on Twitter."

"About a week ago, I watched our buddy Jack—"

"My homeboy!" Bernard interjected.

"I watched Jack fall from the second floor of the east wing of the school."

Nina gasped.

"I ran in, to see if anyone was inside, and found two kids, my students, Lamont and Jamie, almost knocked out from smoke inhalation. I carried Jamie out, after almost killing him by pulling a huge piece of glass from his leg."

"Oh no, Hols."

"He's fine. Traumatized for life, but fine." I blessed myself. "Two days later, our cafeteria caught fire. Sweet Sister T was pushed down the steps. The pathologist said it was an accident, but I don't buy it. Then our school bus caught fire."

"Seems like a fire every day," Bernard added.

"I started my own investigation," I said. "Trusting the cops is as pointless as watering a plastic plant."

"Truth," said Bernard.

"I found a glove in the road, a burnt blouse in my trash can. Must have been onto something because someone opened my mail and locked me in a storage closet."

"I'm sorry, Hols. I didn't know," Nina said.

"How could you know?"

"You've arrived at your destination," Bernard interrupted in an automated voice.

I omitted the tin of matchbooks in the closet—I still needed to discuss it with Bernard.

Bernard kept Nina's bags in his trunk and dropped us off in front of the campus. We stood for a moment, Nina taking in the lush flora. But the sauna of the morning air was already thick, and our history cranked up the heat even higher.

"Feels like we're inside a volcano," Nina said. Cicadas droned in their hypnotic currents, an invisible orchestra. She pulled out her pack of Camels.

"Isn't it too hot to smoke, even for you?" I asked, wanting a cigarette myself.

"First time for everything." Nina lit up, took a drag, and before she could exhale, we heard a voice shouting.

"No smoking! This is a smoke-free zone!" It was Sister Honor rounding the corner with a face of constipation, her short legs moving so fast, as if she was on tracks. She was quicker than I thought.

"Good morning, Sister Honor."

"As you know, Sister Holiday, cigarette smoke is the devil's work," she said, a ridiculous statement made even more outrageous by her mothball halitosis. Her googly eyes sloshed around her head. "Tobacco usage is prohibited on Saint Sebastian's property." She pointed to a NO SMOKING sign, under which was a toppling pile of cigarette butts.

"No worries. We're going to walk away now," I said. "You see this? This is the sight of us walking away."

I noticed that the sidewalk shrine for Sister T and Jack had lost all its flowers but continued to gain new candles.

"Looks like you have a superfan?" Nina asked about Sister Honor.

"She hates me. Hates that I'm gay."

"But you're not gay anymore."

"Of course I am. I'm still attracted to women, just taking a sabbatical from sex and—"

She interrupted tensely. "Didn't they make you sign away your gayness to join the Order?"

I scoffed, but I understood her vexation. This institution— the system I was a part of—was one of the most oppressive on the planet. "Every Sister has a past," I said. "And a present. Believe me. Sister Augustine believes that everyone has a role to play in a brighter future."

She laughed. "But aren't you, like, married to Jesus?"

"It's a fuckless marriage. But really, I'm married to my work."

Nina spun her bracelets around her wrist. School would be starting soon, but standing there with her amid the memorial candles, not sure what to say, or do, time compressed. The moment was dense, a pressure cooker with no release valve. She felt like a memory and a fantasy simultaneously. She punctured the silence. "Scary shit down here. I'm glad you're okay. I've never stopped missing you," she said. "We never talked about that night. The van—"

I couldn't hear any more. "Don't make it harder than it already is."

"That's what she said." She smiled.

I lifted my shoulders. "This isn't a joke. I'm different now."

"Right. I remember. You traded me in to become a nun."

"Shhh." I put my finger over Nina's soft lips to quiet her. We looked at each other for a moment longer than we should have.

With an hour before homeroom was set to begin, I didn't have much time to show Nina the school, my classroom, my new life. I endured the shifty eyes of a police officer as I walked into the reception office where I stole a visitor's pass from Shelly's desk. I brought it to Nina who was sweating and singing to herself on the school steps.

Trudging to my classroom, I was seized by the air. The ambient smell of char and ash made me choke. I couldn't breathe.

"Damn!" Nina smacked me on the back. "You okay?"

My eyes watered as I choked. I stumbled into John Vander Kitt's classroom and grabbed one of the ubiquitous coffee thermoses from his desk, taking big gulps of cold chicory coffee, probably left there the day before. My lungs settled. I took a deep breath.

It hit me quickly, the punch of the buzz. "Shit! Taste this." I handed her the thermos.

Nina took a sip and gagged. "It's mostly vodka." She handed it back to me.

John was blotto on vodka all day, every day.

Dear God, why have you made living so impossible we need to mute the world?

■

I took Nina inside the convent so I could brush my teeth, get that wretched taste out of my mouth. My bedroom door was ajar. The room was empty, save for a tiny lizard who scampered up the wall faster than a thought.

"How cute!" Nina pointed at the brown reptile.

"Get out," I told Nina. I investigated my room and then ducked back into the hallway. "Wait in the hall."

"Why?" she asked.

Panic and indignation flooded me. "Someone's been in my room."

"Weird," said Nina. "You sure?"

"The door's open. I never leave it open. Someone was in there."

Nina shook her head. "Still paranoid, I see."

"I have reason to be. Stay out here."

I walked into my room and looked under my bed. Behind the door. In the closet. Nothing.

"Holiday!" Nina hollered from the hallway and I ran out.

Sister Honor had backed Nina against the opposite wall. With all of her lung power she foghorned, "There are no visitors in the convent!"

Nina scurried behind me in the middle of the hallway, like I could protect her.

"Sorry, Sister Honor, I—"

"Get her out, now!"

"I need to fetch something from my room. Nina can wait here. Okay?"

"Get on with it." Sister Honor's stilted voice knocked the wind out of me.

Back in my room, I scanned the walls and surfaces. I looked under the bed again but saw nothing. I opened my closet. My black blouses and trousers had all been pressed to one side. My four neckerchiefs were unfolded.

"Someone is fucking with me," I whispered to Nina as we walked outside. "Trying to rattle me. If we'd been there one minute sooner, maybe we would have seen them."

From the doorway to the convent, a jarring sight—Sister Honor staring at us.

"That one has been watching me," I said. "She's after me. I know it."

"She's not my biggest fan."

School would be starting in thirty minutes. I had to say goodbye to Nina even though I would have given anything to watch her perform. Almost anything.

"Bye for now," I said mechanically.

Nina's energy was stormy, hovering in the gulf between disappointment and desire.

"Gonna be another year until I see you again?"

"What do you care? You're married."

Nina slid her gold sunglasses to the crown of her head. "Not caring is your specialty. I cared." Her eyes started to tear up. She blinked hard. "I *always* cared about you, about us. And I'm leaving Nicholas."

"What?"

"He's been screwing his therapist for years. Are you surprised?"

"That Nicholas is in therapy? Absolutely. That you have an impossible double standard? Not so much."

Students started ambling toward the main entrance. A black car with the neon Uber sign rolled up. Nina opened the door, tossed her purse onto the floor. She scowled, hopping in the car, and slammed the door with such force I felt it echo in my chest. Hollow, reverberant as a church bell.

I walked a few steps to the courtyard bench. As I sat down, I saw another tormented being. An ambulatory skeleton inching toward me. Riveaux.

"I have dirt for you," I said. I moved over to make room for her.

"What?" She sat down stiffly. She smelled of gardenias.

"John Vander Kitt's a drunk. He's secretly drinking all day on the job. He hides it flawlessly. Maybe he knows more about the fire than he is letting on." Like most of my transgressions, tattling on a friend—doing John dirty—was horrid but necessary. I was the only one smoking out clues, and I had to move the investigation forward, no matter what.

"Very good, Sister." She nodded. "This I can definitely use. Earlier this morning, another Catholic school across town, Saint Anne's, was set ablaze."

"Not again."

"Nine cases of smoke inhalation. Students and a teacher."

"God, have mercy on them." My eyes shut. "Anyone die?"

"No fatalities."

I stood abruptly. Despite everything I had done, the fires kept coming. God couldn't—or wouldn't—stop them. Was it still a test of faith, with so much collateral damage? "I can't handle this right now."

"Sister."

"When did the fire start at Saint Anne's?" I asked. "The exact time."

"6:10 a.m."

"Why was anyone there so early?"

"Play rehearsal."

"Eyewitnesses?"

"Nobody saw anything."

"Anonymous 911 call?"

"Yes," she said, felled. Defeat has a way of making everything smaller.

"Riveaux, what if this didn't start with the first fire? Not that week or even last year? Maybe it is the Diocese. Saint Anne's is under their purview too. The bishop asserting himself as the king."

"The long game play?" Riveaux stared at the lone cloud in the sky.

"It's not checkers," I said. "It's chess."

28

"THE CITY IS ON ALERT," Sister Augustine said in the convent kitchen Thursday night, as we prepared dinner. "Catholics are the clear target." She raised her hands in the air and looked toward heaven. "Forgive those who have done harm in your blessed name, O Lord." She brought her eyes to mine, then Sister Honor's. "Now, we must show united strength and consistency in the face of terror."

"We need to carry on," I said.

Sister Honor gesticulated like she was directing traffic. "No, no, no! We need more police, a longer curfew, and surveillance cameras! The neighbors are scared. Students are traumatized. At least the ones that have been attending. So many parents have kept their children home. We must ask the Diocese to cancel classes until we can ensure safety. Sister Augustine, can you please?"

I was impressed by Sister Honor for once, her worries about our collective safety.

But it was unsettling. Our school and Saint Anne's were two of the four Catholic schools left in the city. With no public funding, student tuition kept us afloat. If well-heeled parents

272 ■ MARGOT DOUAIHY

lost confidence and pulled their kids, we'd be screwed. Dire financial straits.

The Don, the Ghoul, and the Beard were making their play. I had no doubt they planned to sell our sweet sweet New Orleans real estate to the highest bidders and leave us on the curb, spinning a "property sale" as "necessary" to "sustain the mission." Machiavellian maneuvering. Lining their pockets with gold thread. Last I checked, the Vatican's net worth was four billion. Money and lies. Lies and money. Tale as old as time.

"We can't close the school," I interrupted.

"Sisters, please," Sister Augustine replied. "We need solidarity—to stand *together* and share the Gospel. Our Lord is all the protection we need. He will provide."

"We should tend to our students," Sister Honor said calmly. "They need our support. We must put them first."

Again, I agreed with her, but I worried too.

Sister Augustine's white hair peeked out from behind her habit. "Let's work together with the community to show that we are not afraid."

"We *are* afraid," Sister Honor said. "We should halt classes until—"

"But we can't support our students if they are cowering at home," I said, not backing down.

"She is relentless," Sister Honor told Sister Augustine as if I weren't right next to her. "The Diocese decides, anyhow."

"They sure do," I said.

Sister Augustine put her hands on my shoulders, "No fighting, please. It's time to be the catalyst I know you can be," she said.

Sister Honor rolled her eyes. Slobber had collected on her lips during our shouting match.

"Thank you," I said, with a smile meant for Sister Honor. I pulled my black gloves on tighter. The heat and sweat had made them shrink.

"You have been chosen to do the hard work because you are capable. We can handle anything, together, with God."

"Please keep reminding me," I said.

The convent phone rang, and Sister Augustine answered.

Riveaux surprised us with a request to meet in person, and fifteen minutes later, she arrived, looking characteristically dazed. "The police agree with the bishop that all Catholic schools should be closed until we collar the firebug," she said. "We need more patrols."

Sister Honor clamored, "We need a city-wide curfew!"

"The firebug has indeed stepped it up, though a city curfew would be a very tough sell." Riveaux cleared her throat. "It's a pro. That much I'm sure of. These scenes are clean. Neat. Orderly as a chemistry set."

Riveaux babbled but repeated the word *chemistry* more than once, and with emphasis, like she suspected Rosemary Flynn was in on the job. The spree kept spiraling. Maybe it was too big for one person. What if Rosemary Flynn and Sister Honor struck up some bizarre criminal alliance? What if the cops were creating problems only they could fix?

"I just want this to stop." My left eye pulsed.

"Stay and eat with us, Investigator," Sister Augustine pleaded.

"Thank you." Riveaux seemed genuinely surprised by the invitation.

During grace, I prayed for boringness to return to my life. Dinner was agony. Sister Honor's snide remarks about me, the failed sleuth of Saint Sebastian's. For a religious woman, she was a shady bitch. Not all that different from my Brooklyn bandmates, but a touch meaner.

"You overworked the dough again, Sister Holiday." Sister Honor spoke softly. "Let it rest. You poke at it too much."

"We can't all be as perfect as you, Sister Honor." I dipped my toast point into the egg yolk, piercing the membrane. Our dinner that night: white beans and collard greens from our garden, topped with a poached egg from Hennifer Peck, and fresh bread.

"No one is perfect, except our Lord and Savior," replied Sister Honor as she chewed her buttery bread, crumbs tumbling from her smacking lips.

Sister Augustine, looking through the window, said calmly, "Sisters, please stop fighting. Do I need to remind you that we have a Diocese meeting with the bishop on Monday? And anyway, God made us in His image, so we are all perfect."

"Amen," I said.

"Amen?" Riveaux offered.

"Amen," said Sister Augustine with a calm smile. "Thank you for joining us for this humble meal, Investigator Riveaux." Perhaps to counter Sister Honor's barbs, she said, "Sister Holiday has brought new life into our school and convent, and I'm eager to see how she will contribute in even more ways after her permanent vows."

Permanent vows. The words took my breath away. I could hear Nina laughing at me. Nothing is ever truly permanent, except death.

Riveaux said farewell. After clearing the dishes, before my nightly prayers, I sat outside, despite the curfew. I made myself small under the satsuma tree in the convent garden where Voodoo was buried, where Sister T had spent so much time digging, pruning, cultivating, composting, and singing. I pined for Sister T's smile and her gentle way. I'd never forget how she made me feel. Always seen.

I heard tapping on the window overlooking the garden. Sister Augustine waved me inside. In the kitchen, she said, "Curfew must be obeyed, Sister Holiday."

"It's suffocating."

"The police only want to protect us."

"Don't let Grogan fool you. He's a sadist," I said.

"Detective Grogan is a devoted, faithful man who is just doing his job. Please respect his orders. You can do it. I know you can."

Her confidence made me feel lighter. "You're the only one who has faith in me."

She hugged me. "Not the only one. You will be a powerful pillar of the community, Sister Holiday, because you understand *struggle*."

I nodded. She turned and walked away to call the bishop.

The curfew and enhanced police presence had everyone on edge, fumbling in the darkness, but Sister Augustine lit the way. *To share the light in a dark world.*

29

NO CLASSES WOULD BE held on Friday, in accordance with the Diocese's edict. I had to get dirt on the unholy trinity, but that would be harder than raising the dead. Better to concentrate on the leads I could chase immediately. The tick of the clock was ever louder, and I was God's emissary on the case. My mission was as pure as holy water, though my sleuthing could use some refinement.

The morning progressed unceremoniously. I took a quick, cold shower. Trimmed my nails in the sink and watched the clippings disappear down the drain as I ran the water. I changed into my black uniform, wet hair dripping behind my ear, into my blouse collar and scarf.

The first Sister in the convent kitchen always made the coffee, so I placed the heavy kettle on the stove and ground coffee beans in the hand-cranked grinder while the water boiled. I buttered two slices of brown bread and wrapped them in a green cloth napkin to take to school. I would eat them after Mass. It was already so hot in the kitchen, I opened the freezer door and stuck my head in for relief, my face close to the ice tray and our only two store-bought items, bags of Pictsweet green peas and cut corn. When the coffee was ready, I filled my thermos. I wiped crumbs off the counter and walked into the garden for a satsuma.

As usual, Mass was uneventful, except for the ever-increasing attendance, higher that day since students weren't required to be in class. Father Reese was astonishingly unin-spiring, shocking because Sister Augustine had been rousing crowds outside so persuasively. The growing audience needed solace. I watched our parishioners open and close their hym-nals, desperate for comfort, their eyes pulsing. They even smelled of fear. A heady, waxy smell. We all needed direction.

The sky over the Mississippi was layered with three shades of blue. A mild breeze, heavy with jasmine, woke the palm trees. I crossed Prytania Street and nodded to an officer on the way inside the school who regarded me with a slow nod.

The teacher's lounge was empty apart from Bernard who was eating a Snickers and drinking a Coke for breakfast. I slid into the seat next to him. His denim smelled of cut grass and gasoline. The smell made me tremble for a moment.

"Yo. Feels like a ghost town," said Bernard. Faculty were present, but without students, the halls were eerily silent.

"I've been meaning to ask you, but didn't know how"—I put my bread down—"what's the deal with the matchbooks?"

Bernard swallowed his big bite without chewing, and he choked a little. "Huh?" He washed his candy down with a swig of soda.

"I found a tin box of matchbooks when I was locked in the utility closet. Long story. But why so many?"

He lifted his thick eyebrows. "I collect them from every bar I go to hear live music." I could see a small chip on his front tooth as he talked.

"Okay." I felt guilty for asking about it, for not trusting my friend. But I didn't even trust myself.

"My reminder of the places I've been, and the things I've heard." He balled up his candy wrapper and launched it into the trash.

I pressed my forehead into my gloved hands like I do after communion. "I get that. I thought I'd be on tour by thirty. Look at me now."

"Are you kidding?" he said. "You're a star. Always the coolest person in the room." At that moment I noticed Bernard was wearing a black neckerchief similar to mine. He said he'd do anything for me, and I believed it.

John Vander Kitt walked into the lounge. "Greetings, earthlings. Top of the morning to you."

Bernard leapt up to high-five him.

A moment later, a police officer and Riveaux appeared. I had not seen them in our lounge before. It was a bit like seeing your elementary school teacher at the skating rink.

Riveaux said, "Morning, Sister."

"Morning."

"Mr. Vander Kitt," Riveaux said to John, "can we talk?"

"Sure thing, Investigator. Let me put this file in my office first, before I forget. I call this a Milli Vanilli folder." He snorted at his own cheesy joke.

"John, I see you have your coffee there," I said to tip Riveaux off to the location of the booze. The thrill of the investigation superseded my doubts and remorse.

"Vander Kitt?" The officer said in a deep but soft voice. A bead of sweat rolled from his bald head down to his right jawline. "We need to step outside. Can you accompany us?"

"Kathy okay?" John asked anxiously.

"This is about *you*, John." Riveaux lifted her chin and chest. Her body hardened into a shield. What magic words did she recite to turn into armor? Or did the body tell the mind? Fight or flight.

John's usually kind eyes went blank. "What is going on?"

"What's in your mug?" Riveaux pointed. "Drinking on the job?"

"Why, no!"

"It's been confirmed by Sister Holiday." The officer used his thumb to indicate me.

John blinked in surprise. "Confirmed by Sister Holiday?"

I closed one eye, as if that could ease half the pain of the moment. "I'm sorry, but you need help."

He looked at me quizzically.

"Is there anything else you're keeping from us?" I asked.

"No!"

"We are not arresting you," the copper replied. "We need you to leave the premises though. You're drunk."

"Sister Holiday, how—" His legs gave out and he stumbled, his elbows hitting the edge of the table. "You're my friend."

"She'd never—" Bernard stopped himself from completing his sentence when he saw the wetness collect in my eyes.

"John," I said, "I drank from the thermos in your classroom. It—"

"I can explain!" He said and shook his head. "It's not what you think. I'm fine, see. I'm taking care of my family, is all. Big responsibility." John spoke in furious scattered fragments as the cop briskly ushered him out. "A lot on my shoulders. I will get help. Can't lose my job. Kathy's healthcare!"

■

"I make myself sick," I told Riveaux after the scene dissipated.

"You did the right thing. You're looking out for the students."

"I'm looking out for myself," I said. "I betrayed John."

Sure, John and Rosemary's alibi deliveries were suspect, but I wanted to impress Riveaux and Sister Augustine, to prove I was worth keeping around. No one would throw me out again. But Bernard would hate me. I could have ignored John's drinking. He did need help, but there were more humane ways to deliver that message.

The case—I needed it. Obsession kept me going.

What would I have if I stopped?

What else would I lose if I kept going?

I walked out and waited in Sister Augustine's office, eager to tell her how I proved my loyalty to the school. My home. I waited ten minutes. Twelve. Fifteen minutes. I sat in Sister Augustine's office, where students had stewed while they were scolded for some transgression, where they sought spiritual guidance. I felt the weight of a moral position, the need to steel yourself, pay a price for the greater good. We needed movement in the case. To shake something loose.

Sister Augustine never showed up. I looked through her window to the sidewalk. There she was, with Prince Dempsey, their arms lifted in prayer at the shrine.

30

AFTER THE SAD SELLOUT of John on Friday, and my undignified way to address his situation, Riveaux took me and Sister Augustine to the courthouse. We sat in the second row of the stuffy room as Prince's trial commenced. Criminal trials usually took many months to pull together, but when the ADA proposed an extra speedy trial, Sophia Khan happily assented—she was cocky as hell, like her client.

"All rise," the bailiff bellowed. "Today's case is *The People versus Prince Dempsey* on two counts: felony vandalism of the Eau Bénite Cathedral and possession of a firearm without a permit."

I nudged Riveaux. "They dropped resisting arrest?"

"Lucky they still got the firearm charge," Riveaux's words chafed. "He could have said the gun was his 'comfort instrument.'"

Two jurors fanned themselves with paper.

Attorney Khan moved her chair back from the table. Next to her, sitting calmly, was Prince Dempsey, with clean blond hair and a shave. Dressed properly, without BonTon by his side, Prince looked not older but younger, a fresh wholesome lad ready to face the future.

"Ladies and gentlemen of the jury," Attorney Khan started strong, guns cocked, "this is a cut-and-dry case of sabotage against a young man at the margins. Some people might look at Prince Dempsey and think the worst, but I assure you my client is innocent. I urge you to keep an open mind and an open heart throughout this trial. Prince Dempsey is guilty of one thing: being an easy mark for a police department that's regrettably overworked and under-resourced."

She continued with fervor, "This young man has never had an easy life. As a baby, his family was displaced during Katrina, a cruel Act of God"—she looked at me and Sister Augustine—"and he spent years bouncing around the foster care system, finding himself in several abusive situations."

Khan walked behind Prince, each of her footfalls a high-fashion click on the courtroom floor. "Despite all these hardships, Prince Dempsey is striving to build a better future. In fact, he wants to become the first member of his family to graduate high school and attend college. All that is *threatened* now"—she raised both arms, palms to the jury—"because Prince finds himself accused of felony vandalism and firearms possession of which he is absolutely innocent."

Attorney Khan was so close to the jury foreman she practically sat on his lap. "The Defense will show you surveillance footage they say shows my client at the scene of the crime on the night in question. But, technology can be manipulated. There are no safeguards, no one-hundred-percent guarantees that this footage is undoctored. You'll also hear sworn testimony from managers at the animal shelter where Prince

Dempsey was volunteering on the night of the vandalism. As the kids these days say, we've got the receipts."

A younger juror smiled and another chuckled softly.

Attorney Khan shook her head as if exorcising a spirit from the courtroom. "Is Prince Dempsey *perfect*? Are any of us perfect? Of course not." Two jurors nodded. "We are *human*."

"Give me a fucking break." Riveaux elbowed me. "Can you believe this?" Her bones were sharp as pry bars.

■

In the hall during a ten-minute trial recess, Riveaux paced. She was anxious, ready to lift off.

"What's up with you?" I gave her a clean tissue, which she used to mop sweat from her brow.

"I can't remember what I can't remember," she said.

"You're high." I had noted Riveaux's increasingly erratic behavior for some time, first assuming incompetence and at times even suspecting her of being in on the arson. Maybe colluding with the cops. Authority types have it in them. Crafty bastards. Anyone who enforces the rules inherently learns how to break them. But I knew addiction when I saw it. I tried to let the warmth come through my words, but I needed her to know I meant business, that she couldn't screw with me, and I knew she was playing with some kind of fire. "What is it?" I asked. "Vicodin? Oxy? Valium?"

"Finally right about something," she ribbed. "Maybe you're smarter than you look." She tapped her canine tooth. "How did you know?"

"Divine insight," I said. "And your moods. Sleeping in your car. Your nonsense talk. You're on something right now, aren't you?"

"Yes, I mean no." Her cheeks flushed. "I'm always on something. Oxy. Percocet. Valium. All of them. I don't know anymore."

"When did it start?"

"I fell off a ladder six years ago. Investigating a house fire on Annunciation. Cracked a vertebra, ruptured eight discs. Needed three back surgeries."

"Damn."

"Couldn't sleep or sit or *think*. The pain was like nothing else I had ever felt. I couldn't even blink. But Oxy *erased* the pain. Love my Vicodin, too. The float of it." She drifted. "Absolute freedom. But I started forgetting shit. Not logging evidence. Blanking on key details from interviews. Misremembering dates. My mind feels like a different place to me now. This job is different. It's not meant for sentient beings. What we see— you can't imagine. You can't unsee it. You can't take anything from work home."

"Living two lives." I thought of Dad, pistol-hard, a stone heart, so afraid of feeling he turned off every emotion. "How do you even get Oxy? All the lawsuits, doctors cracked down."

She shook her head, wiping away laughter tears or regular tears. I couldn't tell. "Money, honey. Rockwell keeps our scripts filled, hits a new clinic every time he travels. When one doctor says *no more*, he moves on. Smooth operator like Rock gets whatever he wants."

"What does he want?" I thought back to the dirtbag in Riveaux's photo. *A blond devil*, Dashiell Hammett might say. That thin-lipped smirk. I'd love to punch it off his stupid face.

"He wants me like this," Riveaux said, *"dependent* on him, wrong in the head. It's the only thing I need him for."

"Fucker."

"I kicked his ass out yesterday." She retrieved a handkerchief from her back pocket and sopped the sweat from her forehead. "He's off to Houston to stay with his brother. I said I need to get clean. We need a clean break."

No break is clean, I thought. Every fracture buries a ghost inside. "Thanks for telling me all this."

"Well, we're friends," she said.

"We are?"

"Captain fired me this morning. He's been gunning for me for a while. Grogan put a bug in his ear. Good ol' boys hate being on the same level as a Black woman. Terrified of change. And I lost a report and some evidence."

I couldn't believe I ever thought for a moment that Riveaux might be in league with a freak like Grogan, working behind the scenes with that craven fuck.

"What evidence?" I asked, afraid of the answer.

"Your blouse and the glove."

Her words hung heavy for a moment, then landed like swords in my brain. "You lost them?" I asked, incredulous. "They're *gone*?"

"I have a foggy memory of putting the evidence bags in a mailbox uptown."

I almost dropped to my knees. "Dear Lord. Riveaux. They didn't arrest you for that? Tampering with evidence is a crime."

"Losing isn't tampering." She removed her glasses, pressed her eyes with the back of her fingers. "I have no idea what I *think* I am doing versus what I am actually doing."

"What's next?" I asked.

"Rehab in Atlanta, again, and again, until I kill this demon. Or it kills me." Her eyes were milky, like two antique mirrors. "And I gotta quit Rock too."

"I know the feeling."

She pushed her glasses up the bridge of her sweaty nose. "Then I'll go the private investigator route, perfuming on the side. Need to stay busy, put my skills to use. Time to be my own boss."

Jealousy made my palms sweat. "New Orleans has crazy PI rules. You need a thousand hours of training for a license."

"I'll start apprenticing with a PI after rehab."

The plan seemed to calm Riveaux, give her a shred of hope. Just one tiny scrap is all you need.

"You can do it," I said sincerely.

She smiled. "Then you can shadow me and get your PI license."

"What?" I was startled and enchanted. "Don't think the Diocese would sign off on that."

"Who said anything about telling the Diocese?" She smirked. A quick moment of lightness. "Magnolia Riveaux & Sister Holiday, Redemption PI Agency. We'll solve your case and forgive your sins."

"Two for one special." I adjusted my neckerchief, which was soaked obscenely with sweat. "But you have to get us a truck with a working air conditioner."

She whistled. "I got a long list of things that need fixing."

Court resumed its session ten minutes later.

Attorney Khan said, "The defense calls our first witness: Sister Augustine."

Sister Augustine, buoyed by a sense of duty, rose and took her place near the bailiff. Her veil followed her, patient as a feather.

The bailiff moved the leather-bound Bible in front of her lissome body. The room hummed with anticipation. "Please raise your right hand," he said.

As Sister Augustine placed her left hand on the Bible and raised her right arm, her black blouse sleeve slid down. For the first time, with me in the audience and her in the spotlight, I saw her as a person, not my Mother Superior. I studied her face. Her gestures. Her in-between spaces.

The court officer asked Sister Augustine, "Do you swear to tell the truth, the whole truth, so help you God?"

I scanned her face, her calm eyes. The skin on the inside of her right wrist and forearm. Something caught my eye. At the wrist. The place where veins intersect. A dark burgundy mark on the skin. It looked like a tattoo for a split second. No.

I craned my neck, practically toppling over as I looked closer.

"I do," Sister Augustine replied.

It was a burn.

From where I sat, under the play of shadows from the courtroom's fluorescent lights, Sister Augustine's burn had the shape of a cross, the two intersecting lines that saved me. A wound on the inside of her right wrist, exactly where the sleeve on my stolen blouse had been burned.

The missing gauze from the first-aid kit. She had treated it herself.

Instantly I remembered: *You smell like new trees and calendula.* Sister T had said that to Sister Augustine the morning after the first fire.

I looked at Riveaux, spaced out, wriggling in her chair, turning her hands over and over.

"Riveaux," I whispered. "What's calendula used for?"

"Homeopathic remedies. Relaxation. Promotes skin healing. Good for burns."

Burn cream.

31

SISTER AUGUSTINE WAS ON the stand for ten minutes, if that. But it felt like eternity. All the pieces fit, even as they fell apart. I had to hold my hand over my heart, breathe through my mouth, and count the seconds.

Everything was imploding.

In the back of the courtroom, Sergeant Decker and Detective Grogan chatted quietly during Sister Augustine's testimony. She answered each question about Prince, his damaged childhood, his place at Saint Sebastian's, God's love for him. Each syllable felt like a lie.

At the defense table, Prince Dempsey's head bobbed. Attorney Khan said something in his ear and he sat up, attentive. Grogan's eyes met mine. His recent haircut made him look like an army captain.

Before expert witness questioning began for Riveaux, Sister Augustine left the courtroom. I dashed out of my seat but didn't see her. I ran the length of the hallway, but she was gone. I doubled back through the main doors and caught Sister Augustine walking away from the courthouse. Her black veil drifting.

"Sister!"

She turned around.

"I know." I was out of breath.

"You know what?"

"Everything."

"What?" Her face dropped.

"I know what you did. The fires. Jack. Sister T. The school bus. Saint Anne's."

She sighed. "God asks us to do the unthinkable, to carve a new path. This was my duty. God's work."

I put my hands on my knees, tried to catch my breath. "I cannot believe this."

"What God asks of us, we *must* do. The sacrifice." Her eyes were empty. Dead batteries. Nothing flickered. "I am luckier than most women. I . . ." Sister Augustine trailed off. "I will do what God asks."

"No remorse? What the hell *are* you? Are you even human anymore?"

Her face eased into a smile. "Sister Therese and Jack are now infinite in God's Kingdom, like all the people who have been sacrificed since the dawn of time. The impossible is our only true test. You know that better than anyone, Sister Holiday." She held my gloved hands.

I ripped my hands away and raised my voice, didn't care who could hear. "Are you seriously saying this was God's will? This was *your* will."

"God asked Judith to take a life."

Her words were absolutely fucked but delivered so genuinely it was chilling.

She looked down. "Judith felt breath extinguish in her hands. God asked Abraham to sacrifice his own flesh and blood, *his son*, Isaac. My father sacrificed me too. All that pain after the war. He had to put it somewhere. Over and over for years. He couldn't stop himself. My mother pretended not to notice, pretended she didn't hear me scream. Then my belly started to swell."

I gagged. "Your father raped you? Impregnated you?"

"God decreed it—and the pregnancy saved me. At age fourteen, I was sent to the convent—our convent—where the Sisters sheltered me, where I had the child. We brought a bright light, a boy, into the dark world, while thousands of miles away, my father tied a rope. Shame eats you alive."

"I'm sorry."

Shame does destroy you, after it severs you. It almost ended Moose. Might end me at the rate I'm going.

"When the Diocese, those three crafty charlatans, took it all—our power, our autonomy—God *told* me to take it back. Mortal men are weak, that's why they never stop."

Sister Augustine was right about that. Her own father. Moose's attackers.

"You used Bernard's work gloves to start the fire?" I asked, lightheaded, barely able to stand. "You must have dropped them near the ambulance."

"When I lifted my arms in prayer, one slipped," she said. "I burned the other in the school bus."

"Sister T smelled the calendula of your burn cream."

"She urged me to confess, to tell the police," Sister Augustine said in a voice so distant yet close. It didn't sound like her at all, like she was a ventriloquist dummy.

Only the broken want to break others, my mother said.

Sublimation is ruinous. Powerlessness feeds the need for control. Kindling for the fire. Every secret, a seed of poison.

Not a matter of *if* but when secrets strangle you from the inside out.

"You set fire to the school bus, to Saint Anne's, to stir chaos. You put my guitar pick by Sister T's body, stashed my burnt blouse in my classroom's trash bin." Her silence was enraging. "You opened my mail," I said, "went through my things."

"Sister Honor read your mail. She was certain you were involved. You're not the only sleuth at Saint Sebastian's."

"You set me up, played me, from the beginning," I said. "Did *God* ask you to frame me, too?"

I was the easy mark. Sister Augustine, the Holy Ghost. The victim. The arsonist. The devil. Like beauty, evil is in the eye of the beholder.

Sister Augustine smoothed her veil. "I knew you would not question me. I accepted you—utterly lost, hopeless, but oh so ready to follow orders—when no one else would."

"You locked me in the closet."

"You are a wayward soul, needing to be—"

"Free."

"No, quite the opposite. Reliant. Like Prince Dempsey."

"What does that mean? What does this have to do with Prince?"

"You both need me—you and Prince—my two lost children. But sometimes you just needed a small reminder. I underdosed his insulin, only slightly, just as I stoked your anxieties. Only enough to keep you reliant, suspicious. I would never let either of you slip too far." She ticked off her malevolent deeds like items on a grocery list. "What God has asked, I have done. This is His plan, not mine. I would do it all over again." She acted so pious. It was maddening.

"I'm taking you to the bus station. You're leaving New Orleans tonight," I pressed. "After dinner. One last supper."

"This is my home."

"Actually, it's *my* home. You don't deserve it."

■

On the way to the convent that night, I could have told Riveaux everything. That I missed all the clues. It was Sister Augustine who had set the fires, who had killed Jack and Sister T to maintain control, to punish abusive men. To save the church, the school, her story, and her power. She orchestrated the ultimate ruse, and I was a pawn. In Bernard's work gloves, she lit the match. She walked in and out of the cafeteria, on and off the bus before the fires, without being noticed or remembered. People see what they want to see. In the veil and the tunic, nuns are invisible.

Sister Augustine used me. I thought she welcomed me into the Order last year because of the strength of her faith. I could be redeemed, help vivify scripture, she said, stave off attrition, open a new chapter for the church. But she was pulling the strings all along. Wanted to take back what little control she had. Sister Augustine could never be a priest or bishop herself. No woman could. She wasn't going to let the Diocese erase her. Her brain and heart corroded from her own abuse, the institutional rot, decades of festering.

And I deserved it.

All of it.

My penance.

Once Riveaux knew the truth, she'd tell Decker and Grogan. I couldn't talk until I was sure Sister Augustine was gone. Otherwise, she'd be in jail for the rest of her life. Sister Augustine had committed the ultimate sin, but so had I. I already killed one mother. I wasn't going to lose another one.

32

DINNER WAS A STUDY in tense silence. Not even the ceiling fan made a sound. As I ladled Sister Augustine's fish stew, cooked for so long it was falling apart, I was struck by her exceptionally calm demeanor, her stoic resolve. I tried to imagine what script or scripture was playing in that cipher of a mind. At the Last Supper, Jesus told Judas to get on with it. He not only foresaw the betrayal, he didn't stop it. At least in my estimation, he greenlit that shit.

You can't go backward. Only forward. Except for Jack and Sister T, who were in coffins.

And John, who was on unpaid leave, awaiting review by the Diocese. If John's license was revoked, he'd be out of work and Kathy would be screwed. More victims of Sister Augustine. And me.

Thankfully Lamont and Jamie were both on the mend. If they could survive the fire, they'd handle their family's toxic nonsense. Maybe there was one spark of hope. Some healing yet to discover.

■

Bernard lent me his car. I lied, said I needed to help a student with an emergency. Even though I didn't have a license anymore and he had never seen me drive, Bernard didn't flinch. "Whatever you need, Sis."

With the cash he gave me for my Judith tattoo days ago and one hundred dollars I stole from the convent petty cash, Sister Augustine would have enough for a bus ticket to Mexico. I drove her to the bus station, praying we wouldn't be noticed.

The air was septic in Bernard's car. I sweat through my blouse. With the station in sight, I broke the silence: "I thought you loved me."

"This is not about *you*," said Sister Augustine. "This is so much bigger than you."

"You've broken so much. My trust. My heart."

"God will heal your heart, if you submit to Him. The bishop cannot submit—the bishop thinks he is a God, but there is only *one*. My father could neither submit nor repent, and he paid with his life. Mother too, not understanding original sin, or redemption." It was so hot in the car but there was ice in her voice. "Have you learned nothing since joining the Order?"

In the bus parking lot, the door swung open and Sister Augustine stepped out. With the money in her hand, her habit firmly affixed to her white hair, Sister Augustine recited Exodus 15:2. "'The Lord is my strength and my song—he has given me victory.'" She dropped her rosary on the dashboard. "You'll need that."

To any onlookers, we could have been a family. A niece saying bon voyage to a favorite auntie. Or a daughter and mother.

Her bus crawled out of the parking lot without fanfare. It was hazy, silent. No night birds or cicadas. No frogs.

In that disarming quiet, I grabbed the rosary and tried to pray. Tried to talk to God. I wasn't ready to drive back to the church or the convent. The thought was suffocating. My fingers touched each bead, but my brain kept severing the words. I tried a few more times then gave up.

Back in the church parking lot, I shut the door and locked Bernard's car. Walking toward the convent, I felt detached. What had I just done?

The sidewalk shrine blinked like fireflies in the thick night.

That's when I saw it. Parked on the street, a familiar sight came into focus. Riveaux's red pickup was out of the shop.

I ran over to it. The keys, as usual, were still in the ignition. I rapped on the window—"Riveaux?"—but she wasn't there.

From the school's walkway, the interior lights of the church streamed through the stained glass windows.

I stuck my head in. "Hello?"

Riveaux stood in the middle of the church, between the two sections of pews.

"What's up?" I asked. "You need a late-night prayer session or something?"

Talking on her phone, Riveaux raised her hand to signal stop.

As I walked toward the altar, I shook my head.

I couldn't believe what I was seeing.

"Sister Augustine?"

Sister Augustine knelt in front of Riveaux at the altar. Her hands were pressed together, thumb to thumb, in prayer position. Handcuffs locked her thin wrists together.

"What the hell is going on?"

Riveaux, with her hand on Sister Augustine's arm, laughed. "You're too much. You're asking me?"

Sister Augustine didn't move from her position of prayer. Didn't look over or break her concentration.

"You'll never guess who set the fires," Riveaux said flatly and sipped from her water bottle.

I held my heart. "I can explain!"

"You cracked the case." Riveaux never brought her eyes up from the ground, like it was too much to ask. Like I wasn't worth staring square in the face. "Well done, Sister Goldsmobile."

I was speechless.

"I overheard your tête-à-tête after Sister Augustine's testimony." She paused awkwardly, as if she were deciding between empathy or anger. "But it was more than that. I listened to everything you've said in the truck these past two weeks. The answer's always in the evidence. It all pointed to the Order. Y'all had the access, the schedules. I've followed you for weeks. Even watched you wail on Prince Dempsey. Some clichéd nun shit, with that ruler. I trailed you to the station."

"You followed me? Let me tag along this whole time just so you could spy?" I said. "You said we were a team. Friends. You lied!"

"*Me*? You tried to get her out of the country. I'm doing my job."

"Not your job anymore," I corrected.

She ignored me. A stranger suddenly. "After your joyride to the station, I pulled her bus over. I can't officially arrest her, but Grogan and Decker can. I called them. They're on their way."

"No."

"Sister Augustine was relieved I found her. She requested time to pray one last time at the altar, before the handoff to Homicide."

I was shaky. Tried to kneel steadily but fell. My knees hit the hard ground violently, not like the softness of genuflection. "Is Grogan going to arrest me too?" The church spun. The stained glass a wicked kaleidoscope.

"Yep. You were aiding and abetting."

"I'll lie." A strange but familiar instinct found me. Survival. At any cost. "I'll say you were on drugs, high out of your mind, and lost evidence. And I had absolutely no idea Sister Augustine was involved."

"How Christian of you."

A loud bang rang in my ear. The church's main door. Where so many parishioners enter and exit for redemption. Walking toward us were Prince and BonTon.

Sister Augustine stood. Her hands cuffed in front of her.

"Prince, get out."

"Y'all partying hard or hardly partying?"

"Get out!" I repeated. "Now!"

Prince looked at me, then Sister Augustine. "What the fuck?" he yelled. "Why's she in cuffs?"

BonTon gnashed her teeth and lunged at Riveaux.

"Get that damn dog away from me." Riveaux jerked back.

"Or what?" Prince said. "You ain't the police, so you ain't packin'."

"Go outside," I pleaded with him. "Sister Augustine, please make Prince listen."

I turned to see Sister Augustine's reaction, but she was gone. Made a run for it during Prince's theatrics. "Riveaux," I said.

"What now?" Riveaux spun her head in my direction so quickly her glasses almost flung off her face.

"Sister Augustine's gone."

"Damn. Go out front," Riveaux said. "I'll take the side door."

I sprinted past Prince as the dog barked. I ran through the main doors but saw nothing. Riveaux was moving slowly, barely jogging, more wooden than ever. By the time she exited the side door, I had already done two laps around the school.

"Where the hell is she?" I asked.

"She's cuffed." Riveaux was pissed but rational. "And old. She won't get far."

"Sister," I called into the air, "this is not you."

Not that I knew who she was anymore.

Riveaux pointed. "The shed!"

Across the courtyard, the utility shed door was open. Something rattled inside.

I ran to the shed at full clip with Riveaux sweating and trailing behind.

"Sister Augustine."

In the shed I smelled it. That painful, hot, sweet smell. Gasoline.

"Sister, no."

I flipped the light on and saw Sister Augustine kneeling on the wet ground. She had soaked herself in gasoline. The red container that Bernard used to fill the old lawnmower was on its side, empty. Her veil, still on her head, dripped with gas. Her tunic was sopping.

"Sister. What are you doing?"

"It's time." She stood. "The time has come. My rebirth will begin tonight. In God's name we pray." Between her fingers was one of Bernard's matchbooks.

Riveaux was panting behind me. "What's going on here?"

"Back up," I begged. "Give her room."

Sister Augustine walked past me, out of the shed. The vapors of the gas made me see triple. "Sister Augustine. Please."

Outside, in the dim glow of the streetlight, Sister Augustine's smile returned.

I knelt in front of her. "Suicide is a sin."

"So is murder," she said softly. "But it is what the Lord wants."

"But you'll have no time to repent." I cried. "What if it's true? What if it's *all* true? You'll be in hell forever."

At some point, Sister Augustine must have contorted her bony hands in the cuffs to open the red matchbook. She ripped one paper stick from the pack.

"Put down the matches, please," I said. "Remember, 'God created us not to own but to take care of creation.' We're renting these bodies. We belong to God."

Sister Augustine fell to her knees.

I reached out to her.

"You're right, Sister Holiday. My life is not mine to end." She continued the catechism. "'We are stewards, not owners, of the life God has entrusted to us. It is not ours to dispose of.'"

She tried to lift her cuffed, curled hands to the sky, and I snatched the matchbook from her, threw it to Riveaux. The commotion must have alerted Sister Honor. She approached the open door of the shed cautiously.

"I must repent," Sister Augustine said. "Lord, my Savior. All I do, I do for you. I sacrificed our brother Jack and our Sister Therese for your glory."

Sister Honor snarled like an injured animal. "What?"

"Not now," Riveaux urged.

"What did you say?" asked Sister Honor.

"It's all for you, Lord."

"You *sacrificed* Jack and Sister Therese." Sister Honor thundered at Sister Augustine, spit flying.

"Give us space," I said.

Sister Honor grabbed Sister Augustine's arms, lifted her, threw her against the exterior wall of the shed. I tried to pull Sister Honor back, but she pushed me away.

"Stop," Riveaux said. "You're not helping."

"What did you do?" Sister Honor asked venomously.

"I'm not sorry," Sister Augustine said. "I am not sorry."

Sister Augustine moved away from the shed. Sister Honor was as ferocious as thirst. I put my hand on her thick arm again. "What did you do?" Sister Honor asked. "How could you say that? You *betrayed* us all."

Sister Augustine walked backward on the sidewalk, crying. "All I do, all I have done every minute of every day, it is all for God. I would not let us, our work, be erased."

Sister Honor kept yawping in her face as Riveaux held her back. Sister Augustine's tears gushed hard, like Jamie's surge of blood.

"No," shouted Prince. "Stop. Leave her alone." BonTon nipped at Riveaux's leg, making her jump back and lose her grip on Sister Honor.

As Honor wiggled free, her teeth cut the air with endless insults. Sister Augustine cried as she backed up, step by step, until it was too late. We were so focused on stopping Sister Honor's verbal lashing that no one noticed what was happening. Sister Augustine had walked backward into the sidewalk shrine. There were dozens and dozens of candles, but one wick was all it took. Her habit, doused in gasoline, exploded into a wall of flames. Faster than an *Amen*.

"Sister," I screamed. "No!"

"Save her!" Prince circled her flaming body. BonTon squealed.

Sister Augustine was flapping her arms. She roared and fell like a speared beast.

As instinctually as blinking, I reached my hand to her. To save her, or feel the fire myself. Go down in the flames with her. With Mom.

My turn.

A cinder jumped like a flea and ignited my arm. I was too shocked to scream. My arm was on fire. For one evil second, I felt it. The totality of it, the sweet relief of giving up, letting go, letting it all *go*. Not redemption but freedom. The heat was a thrash of serrated knives, cutting through my clothes, burning my skin, scorching the metal cross on my chest.

But then my body was lifted. Riveaux had picked me up and put me down on the dry pavement. I tried to leap up again.

Riveaux held me back. "No."

I howled as Riveaux patted out the lit ember on my arm.

With her veil, Sister Honor was frantically smacking at the constellation of flames eating Sister Augustine, who was on her stomach, screaming. But it was so elaborate, the fire, so furious, as it swallowed our Mother Superior in hot light. Her cries were so high they were almost seraphic.

"Stop it," I begged Riveaux, who leapt like a boxer in the ring, unflinching. She pulled Sister Honor down to the ground.

Prince cursed, hugged BonTon. For all his big talk, the only thing he could do was cry.

I bolted into the shed, walking on the gas-soaked floor, holding my upper arm. *Hail Mary. Mother of mercy, our life, our sweetness, our hope.* The hose was tangled so I threw the bucket into the big sink. Filled it and ran back.

When I returned, Sister Honor was spinning like a Catherine wheel, her entire right arm ablaze. She fell back hard, three feet away from Sister Augustine's firestorm.

"Roll!" Riveaux boomed. "Roll! Cover your mouth!"

I had only one bucket.

Riveaux shouted, "Do it!"

One dose of water for two burning people.

Be it logic, instinct, or God moving through me, I chose Sister Honor, threw the water onto her flaming arm. The eye of fire blinked for a split second as if it were watching me.

It sparked brightly and then died.

"Oh God." Sister Honor was breathless, eyes closed. She held her sizzled arm up, scared to make contact, it seemed.

As the smoke parted, I could see Sister Augustine, a charred carcass on the ground.

"Why did you save me?" Sister Honor propped on her knees. "You should have picked her."

"That's a pathetic way to thank me."

"She's gone." Sister Honor shrank into herself, kneeling on the gritty pavement. "It's over. It's all over."

There were no words except "We'll start again."

"How?"

"Because we have to."

I had lost a mother again, but it wasn't on me this time.

Sister Augustine made her choice.

"I'm sorry!" Sister Honor beat her head, almost tore out her hair. "Forgive me! I'm so sorry."

I looked up and saw Grogan and Decker sprinting from across the street. Decker attended to Sister Honor and Grogan inspected Sister Augustine's body, which was smoldering but perfectly still. Like my addled buddy Jack after his plunge into the unknown. Lights from the approaching fire engines illuminated the street. Prince sobbed, holding on to BonTon's tight loaf of a body.

Kneeling on the searing ground, the burns on my right arm felt radioactive.

Sister Honor moaned, tried not to move her arm as Decker helped her to the ambulance that had parked by the circle of palm trees.

Fire had eaten away most of Sister Augustine's face, like a sea of acid. Fire would always come.

Maybe I was never meant to save my mother, or my Mother Superior. Death isn't just irreversible, it's inevitable. Humans are designed to shoulder loss after loss. *God* is the name we need to hear ourselves say to keep on living. And we need God to test us. Like tempering glass, heat makes us stronger. More sacred and beautiful.

Grogan carried me across the street, a cheap display of valor. "Don't know if you have bad luck or just bring it onto everybody else," he said, his voice like burnt caramel.

Riveaux breathlessly followed. As Grogan jogged back to Sister Augustine's body, she leaned in closer. "I'm not going to rat you out. I won't say that you were helping her skip town."

"How can I believe anything you say?"

She looked me dead in the eyes. "Lie about the bus ticket and lie well. I'll back you up."

"I don't need you."

"You do, actually," she said.

She tapped her canine tooth, turned, and walked away.

▪

Some time later, Rosemary Flynn appeared with a water bottle. Tears streaked her usually perfect mascara.

"The whole city here?" I acted upset to see her, but when Rosemary was near me, lightning simmered in my hands, under my skin, like I was sweating inside my blood.

"Hush and let me fix you up." She steadied my arm, making me scream in pain. "Sorry."

"That's not helping," I grimaced.

"I was on Saint Charles, heard sirens and followed them."

The itch inside my burn was excruciating. Tattoos and scars, maps of where and who I'd been. I wanted to kiss Rosemary as she continued to fumble. To bring my face to hers and hover there. The delicate shock of the first kiss. The voltage that slaps a dead heart back to beating.

Promises. Vows.

I made a promise to my mother, to find meaning. In her death. In this life.

Riveaux and I made a promise to keep each other's secrets.

Sister Honor's eyes were blood red, as if they were dyed like Easter eggs. Her short white hair was exposed. She held my left hand. Drawing a line between this world and whatever's after us, we tearfully recited words that would hopefully rise with the smoke, into the next realm.

"'Ashes to ashes, dust to dust. In the sweat of thy face shalt thou eat bread, till thou return unto the ground. For out of it wast thou taken: for dust thou art, and unto dust shalt thou return.'"

I'm a sinner, but when I touch my burnt arm, the scar form-ing, I feel the heat of something divine, like the Communion wafer melting on my tongue.

I'm supposed to believe that God is a powerful white man with a white beard residing on a marshmallow-white cloud, but I don't. God isn't a person. God is everything, everywhere, in all of this, the details I remember and everything I've for-gotten. The stubbornness of fire. In clues so obvious they blind you. Blood that cleanses and blood that kills. God is perfection, even in devastation. This might be the only thing I'm sure of: God is especially alive in women. The arc of a shoulder, the gray depth of a stare, the hand that is strong enough to reach out and take, the hand that is strong enough to give.

ACKNOWLEDGMENTS

To my agents, Laura Macdougall and Olivia Davies: Everlasting gratitude. Your astute insights, generosity of spirit, and determination kept the fire burning.

To my book angels, Gillian Flynn and Sareena Kamath: Immeasurable thanks for your brilliance and for bringing Sister Holiday to the world. Thanks to the dream team at Zando, and Evan Gaffney and Will Staehle for the iconic, shattering cover.

To the early readers, crime fiction scholars, deep listeners, and magical artists of my life: Puya Abolfathi, Jenn Ashworth, Sienna Baskin, Rebecca Castro, Adam Dunetz, George Green, Summer J. Hart, Tonya C. Hegamin, Hilary Hinds, Lee Horsley, Debra Jo Immergut, Nguyễn Phan Quế Mai, Edie Meidav, Petra McNulty, Anthony Psaila, Michael Ravitch, Liz Ross, Pamela Thompson, and Todd Wonders. Deep appreciation for your incisive minds and neon lightning. Thanks to local firefighters for sharing your expertise (and keeping us safe), and the police officer who kindly let me ride along and learn the ropes.

Support from the Massachusetts Cultural Council, I-Park Foundation of Connecticut, Vermont Studio Center, Sisters in Crime, and Eastern Frontier Foundation Norton Island Residency helped me actualize this work.

Endless thanks to my family for your enduring support. Eternal gratitude to my partner Bri Hermanson, who appreciates the beauty of every day, who never lets me give up.

To the nuns, the mystics, the witches, the stubborn optimists, the Queer healers, the fire breathers: Thank you. To the city of New Orleans, thank you for opening your blazing heart to me.

This book is for you, dear readers, wherever and whenever you are. There is hope for us.

ABOUT THE AUTHOR

MARGOT DOUAIHY is a Lebanese American originally from Scranton, Pennsylvania, now living in Northampton, Massachusetts. She received her PhD in creative writing from the University of Lancaster in the United Kingdom. She is the author of the poetry collections *Bandit/Queen: The Runaway Story of Belle Starr*, *Scranton Lace*, and *Girls Like You*. She is a founding member of the Creative Writing Studies Organization and an active member of Sisters in Crime and the Radius of Arab American Writers. A recipient of the Mass Cultural Council's Artist Fellowship, she was a finalist for a Lambda Literary Award, *Aesthetica Magazine*'s Creative Writing Award, and the Ernest Hemingway Foundation's Hemingway Shorts. Her writing has been featured by *Queer Life, Queer Love*; *Colorado Review*; *Diode Editions*; *Florida Review*; *North American Review*; *PBS NewsHour*; *Pittsburgh Post-Gazette*; *Portland Review*; *Wisconsin Review*; and elsewhere. Margot teaches creative writing at Franklin Pierce University in Rindge, New Hampshire, where she also serves as the editor of the *Northern New England Review*. As a coeditor of the *Elements in Crime Narratives* series with Cambridge University Press, she strives to reshape crime writing scholarship, with a focus on the contemporary, the future, inclusivity, and decoloniality.

（